"I can imagine what you're thinking."

Leigh desperately hoped he couldn't, not when she was thinking how simple it would be to let herself fall in love with a man she barely knew.

Love? Stunned by that unbidden thought, she felt light-headed. Love? No, not with Sam, not with any man who lived in a world of attention and crowds and sounds. A man whose passion in life was music. Not love, anything but love.

His words brought images to her mind that almost took her breath away—to be with Sam, to be held by him, to have him make love to her...

A fire burned deep in his eyes. He took a single step toward her, an action as threatening to her control as any physical contact would be....

Dear Reader,

I'm really excited about the books I'm bringing you this month. I think every one of them is a winner. Marilyn Pappano checks in with *Somebody's Lady,* the sequel to her ultra-popular *Somebody's Baby.* Lawyers Zachary Adams and Beth Gibson met as adversaries in that first book, but this time they're on the same side of a difficult case, one that tests all their professional skills as they work side by side. Of course, emotions have a habit of coming to the surface in such situations, and this one is no exception. Can "city" and "country" meet and make a match? If you know Marilyn's talents, you'll know this book is a must read.

Paula Detmer Riggs will also put you through an emotional wringer in another must read: *Paroled!* When Tyler McClane got out of prison, all he wanted was to forget his ex-wife's unjust charges, charges that had destroyed his career and torn his daughter from him. But Caitlin Fielding wasn't about to leave the past alone, not when she knew her sister had wrongly sent a man to prison—with her own unwitting help! Not when a little girl's future happiness depended on setting things straight with her daddy. I don't want to tell you any more, because you should experience this wonderful book for yourself.

To complete the month, we have Mary Anne Wilson's *Echoes of Roses,* a beautifully wrought story of a man who's the idol of millions, but wants only one woman, a woman with a secret she's sure he'll never understand. And welcome new author Sally Tyler Hayes. In *Whose Child Is This?* she has written a stunning debut book filled with characters who will touch your heart.

Next month, we have a very special book from Joyce McGill, but that's all I'm going to say for now. I hope you'll join me then to hear all about it.

Yours,

Leslie Wainger
Senior Editor and Editorial Coordinator

MARY ANNE WILSON

Echoes of Roses

SILHOUETTE·INTIMATE·MOMENTS®

Published by Silhouette Books New York

America's Publisher of Contemporary Romance

SILHOUETTE BOOKS
300 East 42nd St., New York, N.Y. 10017

ECHOES OF ROSES

ISBN: 0-373-07438-7

First Silhouette Books printing July 1992

Printed in the U.S.A.

Books by Mary Anne Wilson

Silhouette Intimate Moments

Hot-Blooded #230
Home Fires #267
Liar's Moon #292
Straight from the Heart #304
Dream Chasers #336
Brady's Law #350
Child of Mine #374
Nowhere To Run #410
Echoes of Roses #438

MARY ANNE WILSON

fell in love with reading at ten years of age when she discovered *Pride and Prejudice*. A year later, she knew she had to be a writer when she found herself writing a new ending for *A Tale of Two Cities*. A true romantic, she had Sydney Carton rescued, and he lived happily ever after.

Though she's a native of Canada, she now lives in California with her husband and three children, a six-toed black cat who believes he's Hungarian and five timid Dobermans, who welcome any and all strangers. And she's writing happy endings for her own books.

For Leslie Wainger,
whose passion for "Country" was my inspiration.

And Sarah Temple
(Cheryl Arguile)
a fellow writer and friend,
who understands the true meaning of networking,
and on one crazy afternoon,
helped me discover
an ancient sleeping waiter
in a restaurant from the Twilight Zone.

Prologue

Sleep had become her enemy.

Leigh Buchanan avoided it as much as possible, and when she was exhausted and had to rest, she took two small white pills and drifted into nothingness.

The pills left her with a dry, cottony mouth, fuzzy thinking, and the sense that she hadn't really rested, but they kept the nightmare at bay. Then they stopped working.

Now Leigh lay in the bed, alone in the darkness of the bedroom in her loft, waiting, knowing that the moment she drifted into sleep, the nightmare would come again. The same nightmare that had plagued her for more than a year.

She felt her eyes grow heavy, her lids fluttered shut, and as sleep crept on her, she hoped that tonight would be one of those nights when she didn't dream. She just wanted to rest and not remember.

She let herself go, falling into the grayness, and for a heartbeat, she knew a peacefulness that almost made her cry.

Then it was gone and the nightmare came at her in a rush.

It was always the same and always horrifying.

One minute Leigh was in the bed in the loft, the next she was standing in the middle of Satch's art gallery. But instead of the black and white marble floor, the dead white walls that set off her canvases, the gallery was overlaid by a red haze. The long central corridor and the side rooms were empty and the air swirled the red haze into drifting haloes.

Leigh stood in the middle of the main room, knowing she should leave, but knowing she couldn't. She was trapped until this ran its course. Then it started. Satch was there, coming out of the haze, lean and elegant in a black tuxedo. Coming toward her, his hand out. Then people were everywhere, blurred, distorted figures that seemed to float above the floor.

They swirled around her, staring at her, not looking at her paintings. They pointed at her, their mouths moving, but no matter how hard she tried, she couldn't make out what they were saying. A dull roar surrounded her, and it grew to a thunderous crash that splintered into sharp, jagged sounds that pummelled Leigh, battering her from all sides.

Dizziness robbed her of her balance, and she reached out. She knew she was holding on to Satch even before she looked up. "Please, I have to leave," she said.

Satch, with his blond good looks, stared down at her. And no matter how many times she'd had this nightmare, she never was prepared for the look in his blue eyes—the pity and revulsion.

"You can't quit." She knew what he was saying, but she couldn't hear him. "I gave you this show. You owe me."

She looked around, praying for an escape and saw her parents. "You'll be perfect again," her father, a large man with sad eyes, was saying. But his voice was only in Leigh's mind. "Perfect," her mother echoed deep inside Leigh, the slender woman pressing a delicate hand to her chest.

Leigh wanted to hide from their words, but pressing her hands to her ears wouldn't stop them. Closing her eyes to shut them out wouldn't kill the echoes. The nightmare robbed her of all control.

The red haze deepened, swirling faster and faster around her, the faces of those close to her distorted and frightening as they swept past her.

Rage and fear mingled in her, until she was screaming at the people in front of her. "Stop it! Stop it!"

Her mother was crying. Her father was shaking his head. And Satch was staring at her with pity.

"Stop it! Go away! Leave me alone!" she screamed at them. "Just leave me alone!"

With gut-wrenching suddenness, Leigh broke free of the nightmare. She lurched into wakefulness, her face wet with tears, her legs tangled in the sheets and her hands clenched in fists at her sides.

In that split second, everything was gone—Satch, her parents, the party, and she was plunged back into reality—a world of complete silence. She couldn't hear a thing, could only feel the remnants of her own screams vibrating in her soul.

She was exhausted, her breathing was ragged and she had to force herself to relax her hands and spread her fingers on the coolness of the bed linen. She bit her lip hard, willing herself to calm down. She wasn't sure she could survive many more nights like this.

If only things had been different, if she'd never been sick, if she and Satch could have had the life she'd dreamed of having, if she didn't live in a world of silence… She pushed away those thoughts. She couldn't change any of the past, but she knew what she could do. She could make her own future.

And that meant leaving. This city, this loft, the people she saw every day only reminded her of the person she'd once been and of what she would never be again.

She'd make her escape and start over away from the pity, the suffocating protectiveness and the irrational belief of others that she could be the person she was two years ago. *That* Leigh Buchanan was gone forever.

She sat up, raked her fingers through the tangle of strawberry blond curls that tumbled around her face and shoulders, then got out of bed. In her short nightgown and bare feet, she made her way into the main room of the loft that was divided into her studio, a conversation area, a tiny kitchen and a side nook she used as an office.

She didn't turn on any lights until she'd crossed the bare hardwood floor to her desk. Then she snapped on a lamp and reached for the atlas she'd taken out the last time she had the nightmare. She flipped the book open where she'd marked the pages with a bright pink strip of paper and stared down at the map labeled "The West Indies."

Her gaze flicked over the line of islands in the Leeward chain on the Caribbean, then with her forefinger, she touched a tiny dot northeast of Martinique.

Serenity Island.

Serenity? She stared at the tiny dot on the blue paper. Maybe that was too much to hope for. What she'd take was a place she could live and not have to deal with her parents or well-meaning friends, a place she could paint and have some peace, a place where there wouldn't be any nightmares.

She'd first heard of Serenity Island from Kathy Swan, a girl she'd gone to college with. Kathy had spent vacations on the island in a house her family had owned for years. And she'd told Leigh, "It's all green and unspoiled with the most beautiful beaches you've ever seen. Water so clear you can count the rocks on the bottom. There's one main village, Sainte Margarite, a handful of locals who keep to themselves and so much peace and quiet you won't know what to do with it.

"Our house is on the cliffs on the southern end of the island. It's private, and you can be there weeks and never see another human being. It's empty a lot of the time, and my folks like people to be there. So if you ever want to just get away and vegetate, all you have to do is ask. It's yours."

That offer had come five years ago, just after they'd graduated, and it had been repeated over the years in the letters that Leigh and Kathy had used to keep in touch. She just hoped the offer was still good.

She sank down in the chair by the desk, pulled notepaper and a pen out of a side drawer and quickly wrote a letter to Kathy. She told Kathy partial truths, that she was nearing burnout, that she needed to get away for a while and rest, that she wanted some of that peace and quiet and she wanted to know if the offer for use of the house on the island still stood.

Leigh had never written to Kathy about her illness. It had made her feel less changed to keep in contact with a friend who wasn't uncomfortable with her, who didn't see her as different. And she didn't want or need more sympathy and pity.

She finished by asking Kathy to write back as quickly as she could with her answer. Then she put the letter in an envelope, addressed it, snapped off the light and went back into the bedroom.

After placing the letter on the nightstand, Leigh smoothed the mussed sheets, then lay back down and stared into the shadows above her.

"You're quitting and running away," her mother would say when she heard about Leigh leaving. But Leigh knew there was nothing to quit. There was no miracle cure, no chance that she'd ever have her hearing again. But she was running—for her life, or for what was left of it.

If she couldn't stay at the Swan house for a while, she wouldn't give up. She'd just find some other place where she could be alone. She'd sublet the loft and walk away.

She closed her eyes and felt a degree of easing in her now that she'd made her decision. Tugging the sheets with her, she rolled onto her side and pulled her knees up to her chest. Maybe it was because she felt she had some control again, but something in Leigh told her the nightmare wouldn't be back tonight.

For the first time in a long while, she let herself relax, and when she drifted into sleep, only the sound of silence surrounded her.

Chapter 1

Leigh's first glimpse of Serenity Island came two weeks later through the tiny window in a twelve-passenger commuter plane she'd taken from the airport in San Juan.

She knew they were getting ready to land when she felt the vibration of the engines change and sensed the slight tipping of the plane toward the west. When she looked out the window, she saw the island, a chunk of land the color of emeralds surrounded by the deep turquoise of the Caribbean.

Serenity Island. Her new home.

Kathy's answering letter had arrived four days ago, and it had been even better than Leigh had hoped for.

"The house is yours, literally, if you want it," Kathy had written.

My parents can't get down there much anymore, and the kids have their own lives. My father has been considering selling for almost a year. He says you're welcome to go down there and spend some time at the house, and maybe you'll want to stay and buy it. Enclosed is a key and a map to the property. Go and see it, find out if the isolation will drive you crazy, then let us know what you decide.

It had only taken Leigh two days to pack, arrange to have some things shipped later and book a flight out of New York to the island.

As the plane began its descent, Leigh held the armrests and didn't take her eyes off the island. It came closer and closer, expanding into a vast greenness all around. She felt the plane touch down on the narrow runway. Its tires bounced sharply on the blacktop, then the plane steadied and taxied past a series of flat-roofed buildings to come to a stop by a metal hangar.

The flight attendant opened the door, and someone on the outside pushed metal steps up to the plane's side. The four other passengers got up, and Leigh grabbed her overnight bag and purse and headed for the door. She was the last to leave and step out into warmth, pure greenness and air so clear that it almost shimmered in the afternoon sunlight.

She gripped the handrail on the stairs to steady herself, then looked down and saw a spindly-legged man in baggy shorts and an explosively loud floral shirt, standing about ten feet away from the stairs. With grizzled features, a leathery tan and shaggy gray hair peeking out from under a broad-brimmed straw hat, he could have been anywhere from fifty to seventy years old. And he held a sign in front of him that read, "Taxi to Paradise."

The moment Leigh read the sign, she knew this man was her answer to how she was going to get to the Swan house. She went down the stairs carefully, and before she could cross the blacktop to the man, he came to her. Thankful that he looked directly at her while speaking, she was able to read his lips.

"I'm Johngood, miss—all one name," he said and doffed his hat. "My mother's idea of a joke. She thought if she put the word 'good' in my name, I'd have to be good." He shook his head, then flashed her a grin. "And I am, at lots of things. I drive a taxi, I fix anything that's broken, I build things, I rent out a boat by the hour, I cook great meals and I know all the history of this island."

"I'm impressed," she said, "but all I need, at least for now, is a taxi ride to a house on the southern end of the island."

"What house?" he asked.

She put down her overnight bag and fumbled in her purse for the map Kathy had sent with the letter. "This shows where it is."

He took the map, studied it, then handed it back to her. "No problem." He motioned to a beaten-up old sedan that looked as if it had been purple at one time. It sat by a gate near the hangar. "My taxi. She'll get you where you want to go on the island," he said. "For a fair price."

"What would a fair price be to drive me to the house?"

"It's a ways out of town, but for you, ten dollars, flat rate."

She had a gut feeling she should dicker to get a cheaper price, but she didn't have the heart to do it. "That's fine," she said.

"All right. You've got a ride." He looked at Leigh's overnight case. "How much more luggage do you have?"

"Three suitcases," she said.

"I'll get them for you," he said, reaching for her overnight case. "But first, let's get you in the taxi and out of the sun."

He turned and headed across the blacktop toward the taxi, and Leigh followed him. He tossed her overnight bag onto the front seat along with his sign, then opened the back door for Leigh. After she got inside, he closed the door, then hopped in the front and started the engine.

"My luggage," Leigh said.

Johngood turned to look at her over his shoulder. "I'm not about to carry it all this way," he said, and the next thing Leigh knew, he was driving through the gate and out onto the runway to the plane.

He stopped by the side near the open cargo door, got out, and ignoring the annoyed looks the ground crew gave him, he found her luggage and put it in the trunk of the taxi. Then he got back in and turned to Leigh. "Now, we're going to your home."

She barely had time to enjoy the phrase "your home" before he took off in a screech of tires, out through the gate and past the airport buildings. To say Johngood drove like a madman would be to give madmen a bad name, she decided as he headed down the middle of a two-lane road that led away from the airport. Thank goodness no other cars came in the opposite direction, because Leigh had a feeling Johngood wouldn't give up any of the road for another car.

He roared straight ahead, the gas pedal to the floor, past lush greenery that hugged the sides of the road, catching glimpses of the ocean beyond the occasional open areas carpeted with wind flattened sea grass. She watched him, and the only good thing about his driving was the fact he didn't try to talk. With a clenched jaw, he just drove.

And he didn't slow until he came to a pair of stone pillars. Then he swung right and onto a gravel drive. Ahead of them was a cleared area, with a rough lawn of sea grass, and at the end of the drive was the Swan house. As soon as Leigh glimpsed it, she knew she was really home.

The house was two-storied, made of rich natural wood, with a peaked roof and a porch that appeared to wrap completely around the house. The house looked comfortable and safe.

While Johngood drove the taxi onto a circular area that swept past steps that led up to the porch, Leigh took the key out of her purse. When the car stopped by the steps, she got out, noticing the way the late-afternoon sun touched the windows with gold and reflected the beauty of the backdrop of a cloudless sky.

Then she went up the stairs, put the key in the lock and pushed the door back. She stepped inside, into a great room that seemed to be filled with space and light. High beamed ceilings were whitewashed, with several huge fans hanging from them. Bare wood floors had been bleached to a pale oak, and the furniture was natural wicker, accented with blue, pink, turquoise and yellow.

She moved slowly across the room to the floor-to-ceiling windows that formed the back wall. She touched the coolness of the glass and gazed outside, all the way down to the silver ribbon of beach below. The way the house had been built on the very edge of the bluffs made her feel as if she were standing in the air, that if she went out onto the decking, she could surely fly.

She smiled at that whimsy, not even remembering the last time she had thought something so foolish and so lovely. Surely she had made the right decision in coming here. The house had been waiting for her, ready to welcome her, and she knew already that she was going to buy it from the Swans.

She was suddenly aware of the vibrations of footsteps on the floor under her feet, and it startled her. She'd completely forgotten she wasn't alone, and when she turned, Johngood had put her bags just inside the door, but he was right behind her, studying her intently. "Is something wrong?" he asked.

"No, why?" She bluffed, hoping against hope that she could pull it off.

"I was talking to you, but you didn't hear me."

Just when she was beginning to feel safe, she was reminded that she wasn't, that she'd never be. "No, I didn't hear you," she admitted and tried another bluff. "I wasn't paying attention, and—"

He stopped her with a shake of his head. "No need to explain. I understand."

He knew, but that didn't mean he understood. And she waited for the pity to show in his eyes, for him to say how sorry he was, how unbelievable it was, but none of that happened.

Johngood simply shrugged, then matter-of-factly asked, "Will you be needing help around here?"

She knew he knew she was deaf, but he wasn't going to say anything else about it. Relief almost made her lightheaded. "Yes, I think I will. Are you available?"

"For a reasonable sum, I'm very available," he said with a sudden grin. "I'm at your service. Just tell me what you need done."

She looked around, then saw the phone by the couch and looked back at Johngood. And she found herself asking him to do something she could never do for herself. "Would you be willing to make a few phone calls for me, maybe once a week?"

"I would be willing," he said, still smiling. "For a reasonable sum."

She found herself smiling back at him, and all the original positive feelings about the house were starting to return. Yes, this was going to be a good place to live.

Los Angeles, California, July 4

The man at center stage in the huge amphitheater that overlooked the Pacific held the complete attention of the capacity crowd. In tight blue jeans and a red suede jacket cut short at the waist and worn over a collarless white silk shirt, Sam Patton looked whipcord lean and as comfortable with the spotlight as most people are with breathing.

A white Stetson partially hiding his shoulder-length dark hair and pulled low in front gave him a dangerous look. The spotlight etched the strength of a strong jaw and high cheekbones, but didn't touch his shadowed eyes, and he was leaning so close to the standing microphone that he was almost kissing it.

As his hands caressed the strings of his guitar, blending its sound with his backup band that was lost in the deep shadows outside the spotlight, his deep voice eased over the words of a song that had brought Sam into country music stardom seven years ago—"Echoes of Roses." His deep, rough voice sang the words with the intimacy of a lover who knew all the secrets of his love.

As he neared the end of the second verse, Sam heard the audience's appreciative murmurs as the graphics screen behind him came to life. He didn't turn, but he knew the screen had lit up like the night sky with a wash of twinkling stars. Then his stage name, Boone Patton, swept from left to right, the letters formed from long-stemmed red roses.

As the display shifted to a single rose against a blue background, Sam heard something over the music that caught his attention. Someone was calling out to him, the sound low, but intense. It wasn't from the audience. This person was calling, "Sam," and it came from offstage to his left.

As casually as he could while he kept singing, he glanced in that direction and saw his manager, Ted Bigelow, just out of sight from the audience in the side curtains. Ted, a heavyset man with gray hair caught back in a ponytail, was in his shirt sleeves, his tie gone, and his face was unnaturally flushed. When he made eye contact with Sam, Ted gave him the wrap-up sign. And he mouthed the word "Stop!"

Sam glanced back at the audience and kept singing, never missing a note or a word. But his mind was racing. Why would Ted stop a show before they could do the last big number? There was a lot of money invested in the finale, an all-out patriotic salute to the Fourth.

As he finished "Echoes," there was a moment of pure silence, then the audience burst into thunderous applause. This was the last set of shows on a long road tour that had begun four months ago in Nashville, and Sam had to admit that for the past two weeks he'd kept going by shifting to "automatic pilot." But he knew this show had been good, that everything had clicked with the audience.

He bowed low, straightened and as he turned and handed his guitar to Leo Sellers, his bass player, he got close enough to say "That's it—finish up without me" to Leo. Then he turned back to the audience who was on their feet.

He thrust a clenched fist in the air, then with the chant of "Boone, Boone, Boone" following him, he strode offstage to where Ted was standing. When Sam was barely out of sight of the audience, Ted stepped toward him, grabbed him by his arm and pulled him clear of the stage.

"Why in the hell did you have to take a bow?" Ted demanded, yelling to be heard over the audience's cheering and clapping.

Sam glared at Ted. "Why in the hell did you stop the show like that?" he demanded as he jerked free of the man's hold on his arm.

Ted moved closer and shouted, "We've got big trouble!"

That's when Sam saw the police coming toward Ted and him, five or six uniformed officers who looked grim and determined. "What sort of trouble?" he asked Ted.

"I'll explain as soon as we get out of here," Ted said, leading the way out of the backstage area. Sam followed and immediately the police all but surrounded him, heading down the side corridor with him.

As the finale music of the backup band began, Sam was rushed down the corridor, into an area that was normally filled with activity during a show. Now it was eerily empty of everything except more police near the door of Sam's dressing room halfway down the corridor.

Sam hurried through the air-conditioned area, the chill air making his damp hair stick to his temples and neck. He saw Ted ahead of the police, moving faster than he'd ever seen the man move. Dampness showed in patches on Ted's shirt, and his skin had an unhealthy flush.

Sam had thought they were going to his dressing room where the police seemed to be congregating, that that was where they'd explain what was going on. But as they neared the room, Ted kept going right past the open door. And the police around Sam didn't even slow. When Sam got to the door, he glanced inside and stopped dead.

Someone bumped into him as he stopped, a hand nudged him in the small of his back, but he didn't budge. He stared into the fifteen-by-twenty-foot space and saw the full-length mirrors that lined part of the space had been shattered. The shards that still hung on the walls reflected a crazy jigsaw of more destruction.

The costume changes Sam had left in the room had been cut to shreds, reduced to rags of sequins, suede and denim and scattered all over. Bottles of toiletries and makeup had been smashed, spraying their contents everywhere. Stunned by the sight, Sam took a step closer and that's when he saw someone lying on the floor in the middle of the destroyed clothes, shattered mirror and spilled cosmetics.

Paramedics were bent over the man who was wearing a guard uniform, working furiously with I.V.'s and oxygen, and two other men were setting up a stretcher. At first Sam thought the man must have had a heart attack or a seizure, but as one of the paramedics moved, Sam saw the blood. Bright red, it seeped through thick pads and bandages that were pressed against the man's back and around his chest.

Before Sam could do or say anything, he was being forced away from the room. The cop nearest him grabbed him by his arm and said, "Come on, Mr. Patton," as he hurried Sam away from the dressing room and down the corridor.

He ushered Sam into the manager's office at the end of the hallway and finally let go of him and stepped back. Sam couldn't get the image of what he'd just seen out of his mind, and he wanted answers. Ted was standing by a bar set into the wall to his left, a drink in his hand, his florid face tight. One other person was in the room, a slender man who stood in front of the windows behind the desk. He had dark hair combed back from a gaunt face, intense eyes under heavy brows and he wore an immaculate gray suit with a subdued tie. He looked past Sam and spoke to one of the police by the door.

"Check on what's going on down the hall, Beckman, and get back to me as soon as you know anything."

Sam heard the door behind him close, then he looked back to Ted, who was fixing himself another drink. "What's going on, Ted?" he demanded, his voice ragged and slightly hoarse. "You stop the damn show. A man's lying in my dressing room bleeding all over, and the room's completely destroyed."

When Ted turned, it unnerved Sam to see the hand that held his glass was shaking. "It's a nightmare." He tossed the drink to the back of his throat, grimaced, then took a shaky breath. "Detective Lopez can explain everything to you. I need another drink."

When Ted turned back to the bar, Sam looked at the other man who was still by the windows. The firework display was just beginning behind him, with explosions, whistles and brilliant showers of color shooting into the night sky. But Sam only saw the dark-haired man. "Detective Lopez?"

The man nodded, and as he came around the desk, Sam realized that Lopez was at least five inches shorter than his own six feet. "Yes," the man said in a low voice. "Detective with the Los Angeles Police Department. And you are Boone Patton."

"Sam."

The man frowned at Sam. "I thought your name..."

"My name's Samuel Boone Patton. I use my middle name professionally," he said as he took off his hat and tossed it onto the desk, then tunneled his fingers through his damp hair. "But I answer to Sam in my real life." While he took off his oppressively heavy jacket and laid it on one of the two leather chairs by the desk, he added, "You can call me anything you like, as long as you tell me what's going on."

"Someone got into your dressing room and ransacked it. We think a security guard heard something and went in to investigate. He was stabbed three times in the back."

Sam stared at the man, waiting for the punchline. This had to be some horrible joke. But there wasn't a trace of humor in the detective's face. A man had been stabbed. Sam moved to the closest chair, and without taking his eyes off Lopez, he sank down into the leather. "Is he...alive?"

"Barely. The paramedics are working on him right now."

Sam felt the blood draining from his head, and he sat forward, burying his face in his hands. He exhaled in a rush, then dropped his hands to his thighs and looked up at the detective. "When did it happen?"

"Probably an hour or so ago. They didn't find him until one of your people went in to get something. And they found a note. That's when I sent them to get you off stage."

"What note?"

"This one," Lopez said and pointed to a single sheet of lavender paper on the desk not more than three inches from where he'd put his hat. A wilted rosebud was beside it. When Sam would have reached for it, the detective stopped him. "Don't touch it. It has to be processed at the lab. Just read it."

Sam leaned forward and saw childlike writing on the paper, the *i*'s in the words dotted with hearts, writing he'd seen before.

My dearest Boone: I tried to be patient and to give you time, but I can't take much more. I know you love me, but they're making you pretend you don't. They won't let you sing our song, or even smile at me.

I can't live like this without you, and I won't let you live without me. We are meant to be together forever.

Love.

Below the last word, someone had left a bright red impression of lips.

"You've had other notes like this, haven't you?" Lopez asked.

Sam stared at the words until they began to blur, at the blood red lipstick, then he moved back, sinking against the support of the chair. "A couple, but they were just letters, fan letters that were a bit off base and they had rose petals in them." He shook his head sharply, then ran a hand over his face before he looked back at Detective Lopez. "The person who wrote this was the same one who did that in the dressing room?"

"Looks that way. We found this note and the rose stuck behind a piece of the mirror on the wall."

"Oh, God." He swallowed hard. "The notes have been weird, but I never would have dreamed..." His voice trailed off when he ran out of words to describe his shock and horror.

Lopez glanced at the note, then back at Sam. "People like the woman who wrote this note and the others live in a fantasy world. She obviously imagines that you're being forced to keep away from her. She probably thinks that you would love her if she just had a chance. And no one's going to get in her way. She probably saw the guard as one of 'those' people, and she thought nothing of trying to kill him. Or maybe he just surprised her and she wanted to get rid of him. She obviously came prepared. We didn't find a knife anywhere and the M.E. says it had to be at least a five-inch serrated blade. We're dealing with an unstable, angry person."

Words that this man spoke in a calm, even voice were out of a nightmare. "Angry?" Sam ground out. "God, she's stabbed a man. That's not angry or unstable, that's insane."

"You're right," Lopez said with that annoyingly calm voice. "She's insane, and she's obsessed with you."

Sam stared at Lopez as the words sank in, and he realized something that made his chest feel as if a two-ton weight were pressing on it. "She thought the guard was me, didn't she?"

Chapter 2

Sam watched Lopez casually take a seat on the corner of the desk "No, I don't think so." But there was no reassurance from his next words. "I think we're dealing with a woman who thinks she can't have you in this world, so she'll go into the next world with you."

Sam took a breath into his tight chest and avoided looking at the piece of purple paper on the desk. "A murder suicide?"

"I think that's a worst-case scenario."

He looked away from Lopez and at fireworks outside that were almost over. Sam almost laughed at the man's impersonal choice of words. "I'd say that's the worst case, all right."

"Mr. Patton, things aren't going to go that far. That's why I'm here. What I need to know from you is when you started getting those notes and what they said."

He glanced back at Lopez. "I don't know. Maybe the first one came a month or so ago. Ted told me the office got two or three a day sometimes, rambling letters that didn't make a lot of sense. Ted read a few of them over the phone to me and showed me a couple. They were all on that paper with the lipstick."

Lopez looked toward the bar area. "Did you keep them, Mr. Bigelow?"

"Sure. They're filed away at the office." As Sam turned to him, Ted held up the glass. "Do you want a drink, Sam? You look like you could use one."

He needed something. "Yeah, anything," he said and looked back at the sheet of purple paper.

When Ted brought him the drink, Sam closed his hand around the coolness of the glass, then sipped the amber liquid. As the fire of whiskey trailed down his throat, he heard Lopez speaking to Ted. "I'll need to see those other notes."

"No problem," Ted said, as he crossed back to the bar.

"Were there any threats in the other letters?"

Sam sipped more of the alcohol, welcoming the spreading heat in his middle, then rested the glass on his thigh. "Not really," Ted said.

A sudden sharp knock on the door made Sam's hand jerk and the whiskey almost sloshed out of the glass onto the denim of his pants. Sam twisted to look at the door as Lopez called, "Come in," and the uniformed cop who had escorted Sam to the manager's office looked inside.

"Thought you'd like to know that they're taking the guard to the hospital. He's alive, but he's still unconscious. The paramedics said not to expect him to wake up anytime soon . . . if he ever does."

"Thanks," Lopez said. "Stay on it." As the officer left and shut the door again, Lopez looked at Sam. "You understand that she's saying she's willing to kill you and herself to fulfill her fantasy, don't you?"

Sam downed the rest of his drink in one gulp and almost asked Ted for another, but decided against it. The haze of alcohol wasn't what he needed now, no matter how appealing it was to think of hiding from this horror and the overwhelming feelings of being totally exposed and vulnerable.

That feeling was eerily like those he'd experienced almost ten years ago when he'd just started in this business. He'd stood in the wings at a Nashville club waiting to go on as a warm-up act to one of the big names in country music. The emcee had boomed over the loudspeaker, "And now, a new star shooting into the Nashville skies, Boone Patton. Give him a down-home Nashville welcome!" Then someone had pushed Sam in the small of his back, nudging him onto the stage into the heat, into the blinding lights and into the roar of the crowd.

For an instant, he'd felt exposed and vulnerable, then he'd pulled the brim of his hat a bit lower, clutched his guitar in a death grip and strode to the microphone. As soon as he'd heard the first bars of the lead-in from the backup band, he'd felt good about where he was right then. He'd felt jitters sometimes, even nervousness over the years, but never that feeling of being totally vulnerable and exposed—not until now.

"You accept as a fact that she sees the only solution as death, don't you?" Lopez persisted.

"Yeah, I accept that," Sam muttered as he leaned forward to put his empty glass on the desk by the sheet of purple paper. "You hear about things like this, but..." Anger was surfacing to mingle with the horror, and he struck his thigh with the flat of his hand. "Damn it all. I've got everything I ever dreamed about. A kid from Connecticut hits it big in Nashville, gets to live out his dream, then some lunatic crawls out from under a rock."

"They're all around," Detective Lopez interjected in that maddeningly even tone, then changed directions. "What song did she want you to sing?"

"She wanted Sam to use 'Echoes of Roses' as his lead song every night," Ted said. "She gets upset when he mixes it in the lineup and that sometimes he doesn't do it at all."

Lopez looked questioningly at Sam. "Why that song?"

Sam shrugged. "I don't know, except it was my first big hit, sort of a trademark."

"But why would that song mean something to her? I assume you've had other hits?"

"Some," Sam murmured.

"A lot," Ted broke in.

"Then why that song?"

"I don't know," Sam said sarcastically. "How in the hell would I?"

Lopez ignored Sam's tone and asked, "Can I get a copy of the lyrics?"

Sam saw Ted come to the desk and stand by the chair that held Sam's jacket. "I'll get you a copy when I get the other notes for you."

"Good," Lopez said, then motioned to the purple paper. "It's perfumed. Do you recognize it?"

Sam moved just close enough to catch a hint of a sweet and heavy perfume that made him vaguely nauseated. "'Dreaming,' I think."

Lopez looked impressed. "I can't tell the difference between perfumes."

"Neither can I, but I was asked once by a fan magazine what my favorite perfume was. I didn't have a clue, so the reporter gave me a list. I liked the name. I had no idea what it smelled like or I never would have chosen it."

"But a fan would think you loved it?"

"I suppose so. What do we do now?" Sam asked as he sat back far enough so he couldn't catch the perfume's scent.

Lopez took a notebook and pen out of an inside pocket of his jacket. "We have to start at square one. That means starting with the logical suspects." He flipped open the notebook and rested it on his thigh. "How about ex-wives, lovers, mistresses?"

"There are no ex-wives, and as far as any lovers go, you can rule them out."

"I wouldn't exclude past loves that quickly. You know what they say about a woman scorned."

Women in Sam's past hadn't been scorned, they'd simply slipped out of his life. No one he'd met had ever become more important to him than a few good times and some pleasant memories. "Scorned or not, the woman who wrote the note calls me Boone. I told you, I go by Boone Patton in public, but in my private life, I'm Sam. No one who's been close to me would call me Boone."

Lopez rocked slowly back and forth, but didn't write anything in the notebook. "Good point. The problem is that that eliminates a handful of people and leaves us with one of your fans. I think that leaves a hell of a lot of potential suspects."

"Ten years' worth," Ted said.

Lopez didn't look terribly impressed. "You've probably got—what do they call them—groupies?"

"I guess every performer has them," Sam conceded, uneasy with the whole concept of women wanting to be close to Boone Patton. They didn't even know him, yet they had turned up naked in his hotel rooms, and they'd chased him from theaters to waiting limousines while his entourage tried to fight them off. Once he'd had his shirt literally torn off, his back and arms crisscrossed with scratches and clumps of his hair yanked out, before he could get into the safety of the car.

But that sort of craziness was a far cry from someone wanting to kill him. "Fans can get pretty intense."

Lopez raised one eyebrow. "I've heard about girls that follow bands and performers, who would do anything to get into the star's bed." He gave Sam an assessing look. "Any disappointed ladies you walked over or dumped after a wild night in some hotel room in some long forgotten city?"

Sam knew his expression was tightening. He wouldn't deny that he'd had his share of wild times at the first, long-legged blondes who felt it was their duty to be with Boone Patton, but it hadn't taken long for him to figure out that his purpose in life wasn't partying. It was being the best he could in the business, and he couldn't do what he wanted to do professionally and burn the candle at both ends.

"I've never claimed to be a saint," Sam said. "But on the road I'm either in my bus traveling to the next show, or rehearsing, or performing."

"And no women to make things easier?"

Right then Sam had a thought so foreign to him that it stunned him. In that moment he wished there had been someone, a woman who had taken some of the loneliness out of his time on the road, who had wanted him for who he really was, not what she thought he was. A woman soft and yielding in the shadows of the long nights, who warmed his bed and filled his thoughts.

Then he caught himself and pushed that thought aside. He'd known a long time ago that choices in life were everything, and timing came next. He'd made the choice to concentrate on his career, and the timing had never been right with any of the women he'd known.

"No one important," he said with real truth. "No wild nights, no drugs, no booze, no orgies and no unsuspecting women left in my wake." Nerves were making the whiskey in his stomach churn. "What now?"

"The bottom line is protecting you and getting whoever wrote that note. Right now, you have to get out of sight. I'll get as much protection as possible, and they can work with whatever security sctup you have at your home."

"I don't have any," Sam said as he stood. "I just bought a home out here, in the Malibu hills, and it's being renovated. They're putting in a security system, fences and gates, but it won't be done for a month."

"Then, if I were you, I'd take my family and start looking for a place that can be made secure," Lopez said. "Maybe a hotel suite or the house of a good friend."

"My family's out of state, back in Connecticut."

"Wife and kids?"

"No, just me and my peoplc," he said. "My band, my backup singers, the road crew, drivers, and—"

"I get the idea. And that makes it simpler to stash you away somewhere."

Sam knew this man had to deal with this sort of thing all the time, but he certainly didn't, and the idea of being "stashed away somewhere" was repulsive to him. "Why don't you just put me in jail?" he muttered.

"We will if we have to. But for now, no jail, just a safe place where you can keep out of sight and be protected. You'll need to cancel any public appearances for the next week or so, if it's at all possible."

"That's covered," Ted said from the bar area. "Sam's at the end of his road tour, and there's nothing but a few charity events until the middle of August when he does some major dates."

"Good," Lopez said. He tucked the notebook back in his pocket without writing in it at all and he stood straight. "We need to get moving on this. Figure out where you're going to stay, and we'll escort you there, then I'll arrange for protective surveillance."

Sam was at a loss. The idea of being locked up in a hotel suite was abhorrent. He'd suffocate. But he had no other place to go. He couldn't go back home, not if it meant possibly drawing this lunatic toward his family. And he couldn't involve anyone in the band or any of his crew in this. And Ted— He glanced at his manager where he stood behind the chair. No, he couldn't pull him in any further. The man had a wife and two children. "I don't know where I'm going to stay."

Ted spoke directly to Lopez. "You can't keep this out of the press, can you?"

"Not a chance."

"In a few hours Sam's going to have his face on every newscast and every newspaper front page, and the press is going to be coming after him. It's sensational news, a love-crazy fan who's going to kill him."

"Ted, that's enough," Sam said quickly, sickened by the images his words conjured up.

"Does he have to stay in Los Angeles?" Ted asked Lopez.

The detective shrugged. "We can't give him police protection outside this jurisdiction, but there's no reason he can't leave, as long as he's available if we need him."

"I'm not going back to Connecticut, Ted," Sam said quickly.

Ted crossed over to Sam. "Hear me out on this. You need to get away from here, and not back to Nashville or Connecticut. The press knows your background and could find you in a matter of hours. So could this lunatic, if she's kept up at all with your bios." He looked at Lopez. "I've got a vacation home in the Caribbean. It's on a small island, and Sam could go there and just disappear. It's quiet, remote and the house is pretty isolated. He wouldn't have to see or speak to anyone for as long as he's there."

"An island?" Lopez said.

"Serenity Island."

"It sounds good."

"Well, it doesn't to me," Sam said quickly, before these two had him shuffled off to the ends of the earth. "I think I should stay right here. Maybe whoever's doing this will make it easy on all of us and come after me. Then the police can get her."

"Don't even think that way," Lopez said quickly, showing the first sign of emotion. "That only works in bad movies, Mr. Patton. I want you out of the picture completely, and Mr. Bigelow has offered a viable solution."

"You could use a break from this business," Ted said to Sam. "You'll burn yourself out if you don't get away. You've seen it happen to others. This way you get to rest, and you can disappear without being locked up."

The phrase "locked up" made Sam's blood run cold. But he was honest enough to admit that he had never been good at being alone. He'd hated it when he was small, and he hadn't outgrown it when he became an adult. He liked people. He liked performing and being involved in the business. Being surrounded by sound and music and people was the climate that he thrived in.

He'd heard people say that "music was their life," and he'd thought how phony that sounded. But it was the truth with him. Every phase of this business fascinated him, and he seldom took time off. Now he was either going to be locked up or sent to an island where he'd be totally alone, and where his only conversations would be with his own face in the mirror when he shaved.

"There's a phone to keep contact," Ted was saying, "and a television, even though there's only one station. There's a full sound system installed. Sam, think of this as a working vacation, if the idea of a vacation is too scary for you to deal with. Take your guitar, do some writing and keep out of sight."

"I'd recommend it," Lopez said.

Sam looked from Ted to Lopez, then gave up. "I don't have much of a choice," he muttered.

Ted went around behind the desk and reached for the phone. "I'll call and arrange for a private charter. Sam can go directly to the airport from here and stay on board until they take off."

Lopez started for the door and tossed over his shoulder, "You take care of that, and I'll get some security to give you an escort to the airport." He stopped at the door and spoke directly to Sam. "I'd rather you didn't go back to your place for anything. I'll send a car over to get whatever you need. Just make a list."

Sam felt as if all his control had been snatched out of his grasp, and he hated it almost as much as he hated this person who was tearing up his life. "One of my people can do that. Maybe Leo or Steve. They'll know what I need and where everything is."

"All right," Lopez said, then left, closing the door behind him.

When the door shut, Sam sat forward to bury his face in his hands. He heard Ted telephoning for the plane, and while he made the arrangements, Sam had a flashing memory of the guard on the floor in the dressing room.

What if he'd gone into the room and surprised the woman? What if all that anger had been centered on him while she had a knife in her hands? He could be lying in his own blood on cold tile. He looked up at Ted, who was just hanging up the phone.

"It's all set," Ted said. "It's chartered in my name. You're just a nameless passenger."

Sam raked his fingers through his hair. "Ted, the man who was stabbed. Do whatever you can for him. See that he gets whatever help he needs no matter what it costs."

"I'll take care of it."

"And his family—"

"I'll take care of them, too," Ted said as he crossed back to the bar. "Another drink while we wait?"

"No, thanks." Sam stared out at the night sky through the windows, the fireworks long gone. "I should be staying here, not running away."

Ted uttered a jarring profanity, then said, "If I were you, I'd run as fast and as far as I could." He came back to Sam and looked down at him. "Just get the hell out of here and save yourself."

Sam stared at his hands clenched on his thighs. "Ironic, isn't it?"

"Ironic?"

"I'm going to go through hell on Serenity Island."

In the six months since Leigh had come to the island, she'd only driven into Saint Margarite with Johngood three times—once to have the papers for the house sale notarized, once to start an account at the local bank and today.

She'd been nervous about coming in again, but as she stepped out of the general store where the post office was located into the midday heat, she felt as if everything had gone well. She'd made her deadline with Satch, sent off the promised paintings to his New York gallery and would have to wait for his reaction. Maybe he'd been wrong when he'd said she'd lost control of herself and her talent after her illness.

She slipped her sunglasses on for protection against the brilliance of the late-morning sun, and even though she was dressed minimally in white shorts, a pale blue tank top and sandals, she'd forgotten to pin her hair up. She could feel the curls beginning to cling to her neck and shoulders.

She stepped aside to let Johngood pass with a box of supplies he was loading in the taxi, and she moved into the shade of the roof overhang. Running her hand around the back of her neck, she lifted the weight of her hair and felt the suggestion of a breeze on her damp skin.

Johngood headed back into the store but stopped in front of her. That was his way now. He either stood right in front of her, or he touched her to get her attention. He never talked about her deafness, he simply adjusted when he was around her. And Leigh didn't feel the pressures she'd become so used to when people found out about her deafness. The man accepted her as different, but equal.

"Do you need anything else while we're here?" he asked.

"No, I got everything I need."

"One more load, then we're ready to head home," he said then ducked into the store.

Leigh leaned against the rough wooden wall of the store and narrowed her eyes to the almost deserted street in front of her. She really did have everything she needed. She had control of her life, the nightmares were gone and she hoped she finally had control of her talent again.

What she'd just sent off was very different from what she'd been producing. She'd used the natural shades all around her to create sweeping scenes of the island in the mists of morning, in the clear sun and at night. It was the island she saw from her own home.

She'd forgone the raw primary colors and the intense subjects she'd painted after her illness. With hindsight she recognized the fact she had probably echoed her own tension and pain. And now the pain and tension were almost nonexistent.

As Johngood came back outside and headed for the taxi with the last box, Leigh inhaled deeply, taking in the sweetness all around her. She almost didn't remember what tension and pain felt like. She watched Johngood close the trunk and signal her he was ready to leave. With a nod, she walked out of the shade into the sun and toward the taxi. But before she could get to the open front door on the passenger side, Leigh felt a vibration in the air, the kind she felt when a heavy engine was running close by.

At the same moment, she caught a flash of movement near the taxi on the street. Reaching out to lay her hand flat on the warm metal of the taxi roof, she looked up as a large red Jeep swung into the parking space in front of the taxi. Then the vibrations from the engine stopped skimming across her bare skin, and the driver stepped out into the street.

Her instant impression of the man was of lights and darks, of a lean, sinewy build defined by tight black jeans and a plain white T-shirt worn with scuffed running shoes. Dark hair, cut short at the sides, yet long enough in the back to fall to his shoulders, framed a face that seemed to be all planes and angles. His features looked as if they had been hewn by a careless hand, from a slightly crooked nose to a strong jaw shadowed by the beginnings of a beard.

He was hardly what she would call handsome. Certainly not the classical handsomeness of Satch, but the sum total was fascinating to her. As an artist, she knew a desire to see those features done in oil. But her response wasn't entirely artistic. No, the sum total of this man added up to something that made Leigh feel her breathing quicken and her skin flush.

When the stranger turned and she found herself pinned by the intense gaze of shadowed eyes under dark brows, she was very glad she had the protection of her sunglasses. Then he was moving toward her, around the Jeep, stepping up onto the wooden board sidewalk. With a slanted glance at her that skimmed over her in less than a heartbeat and a slight smile that lifted the corner of his wide mouth, he moved past and headed for the store.

Leigh jumped when Johngood reached through the door of the taxi and touched her leg. She looked down, seeing him stretched across the seat, crooking his neck to look out at her. "Are you ready?" he asked.

"Yes," she said, and when he drew back, she scrambled into the taxi and pulled the door shut, not looking at the store.

"No, I don't know who he is," Johngood said as he started the taxi and put it in gear. "But I bet he's the one the private plane brought in a while ago."

"I didn't ask who he was," Leigh countered.

He smiled at her, then pressed the gas and took off, barely missing direct contact with the Jeep in the process. "But you would have."

"No, I wouldn't have," she said quickly.

His smile only grew. "Sure," he said and increased the speed of the taxi.

Leigh sat back, wishing she could smile about what had just happened, but she couldn't. Not after what the man in the Jeep had done to her. No, not done to her. What he'd made her feel and remember. She closed her eyes. Things she didn't want to feel or remember, not with any man.

Maybe if she hadn't gotten sick, if she hadn't had her life rearranged on the most basic levels. Maybe if she was a different person. She clenched her hands in her lap. There was no way she wanted a man like that to ever look at her with pity or, worse yet, revulsion. No, a man like that had no place in her world.

She opened her eyes and looked out at the road ahead, then the water to the right and inhaled the freshness in the air that rushed in the open windows. This was her world. It was what she wanted. No, it was what she needed to survive.

As Sam entered the general store, he wondered if it was the long flight, or the tension, or the craziness of his banishment to this place, but he thought that he had never seen a more beautiful woman in his life. The delicately sculpted face partially hidden by oversize sunglasses had been framed by reddish-blond curls that fell freely around her slender shoulders. He had noticed high cheekbones, the sleek sweep of her graceful neck and a small, straight nose.

And as he'd walked around the back of the Jeep to head for the store, he'd come within four feet of her and had a full view of a figure that more than matched the rest of her beauty. Not tall, probably no more than five and a half feet, she'd looked provocatively leggy in skimpy white shorts. A tank top had clung to high breasts, and full lips that didn't need lipstick to enhance them had been slightly parted. He'd caught a hint of flowers and freshness before he reached the door to the store.

He found himself smiling, something he hadn't done for what seemed an eternity. Then he heard a car door close, and as he turned to look back outside, he saw the taxi pulling away from the curb in a squeal of tires. The old car came within inches of striking Ted's Jeep before it took off to the south and disappeared from sight. The woman was gone, and he didn't even know who she was.

And his smile was gone with her. He was down here to hide, and that meant staying away from everyone, even gorgeous women. Regret and anger mingled. He hated being forced into isolation like this, and he hated not being free to make contact with a woman who stirred him in a way no woman had for a very long time.

"Help ya?" someone called out, and Sam turned to his left and saw a heavy woman dressed in a brilliant pink smock sitting behind a counter along the wall that held a plaque that read Postal Service. Gray hair was pulled straight back from a full, flushed face, and worked into a single braid that fell over her shoulder. Three large, flat crates were propped against the front of the counter, and stacks of various-sized parcels took up a good half of the counter area.

Sam crossed the creaky wooden floor, passing sagging shelves that held a bit of everything anyone could want. He smiled at the woman. "Yes, ma'am. I need to stock up on groceries."

"You came to the right place to do that, but don't call me ma'am. My name's Gertrude." She eyed him. "I remember people real good," she said, and for a second Sam thought she'd recognized him. "But I don't remember ever seeing you on the island before."

You've got a big ego, he chided himself. This island wasn't exactly a hotbed of country music fans. "It's my first visit," he said with an easy, relieved smile.

"Then look around." She made a sweeping motion to the store behind Sam. "Help yourself. I have anything you could want or need. I don't give credit to anyone but those I know, and I don't take credit cards." She reached behind the counter and pulled out a plastic shopping basket. "Use this for your things."

Sam took the basket, then moved around the store, picking out anything that looked simple and easy to make. When he had the basket full, he went back to the counter and saw Gertrude struggling to get one of the three flat crates onto a floor dolly. Sam put the basket on the counter, then helped her.

"Thanks," the woman said as she straightened, her round face flushed from all the effort. "Didn't know they'd be so heavy, and Harvey, my husband, he takes off fishing, leaving me here, knowing we have to make the late plane with the mail." She shook her head. "I think he does it on purpose so he doesn't have to do the hard work."

Sam looked down at the top crate and saw the delivery address—The Gray Gallery in New York. He'd heard of that gallery. Ted had mentioned it a while ago along with others when he'd been trying to convince Sam to invest some of his money in art. It was an influential gallery in a trendy neighborhood, and it specialized in unique and expensive works. "Are these paintings?"

"Most likely. The lady who brought them in is a painter."

Sam knew he shouldn't ask any more, but something in him wouldn't let go of the image of the woman outside. "The woman who was just in here, the blonde—are these hers?"

Gertrude moved back behind the counter and didn't answer until she was sitting on a stool swiping at her face with a hanky. "Yeah, that's the one."

"She's a local?"

Gertrude smiled at that. "No. She's only been here a few months. First time I ever saw her up close was today." She leaned her elbows on the counter. "Real pretty lady, but a bit strange."

"How so?"

"She has a way of looking at you."

"How?"

She shrugged that off. "I don't really know, just sort of intense." Then she laughed. "And she's good friends with Johngood. That's enough to qualify her for being strange."

Sam should have known a woman like that wouldn't be alone, at least not for long. "They're close?"

"Yeah. The old codger goes up there two, three times a week. Says he's working for her, driving her around and fixing things." She leaned closer and rolled her eyes expressively. "Johngood works like I'm skinny."

"He's the old guy that drives the taxi?"

"That's the one. Up to no good, if you ask me," she said.

Sam smiled as he absorbed a real sense of relief that Johngood was a guy in his sixties who drove a taxi. As the storekeeper rang up his order, Sam glanced down at the crates nearby and read the return address, "Leigh Buchanan, Serenity Island."

At least he knew her name, but that was it. He knew instinctively that if he did any more than this, if he tried to see her again, it wouldn't be a question of *if* he'd get to know her, it would be *how deeply* he got involved.

"Will this be all you need?" Gertrude asked.

Sam looked at her and knew that she didn't have what he needed. Worse yet, the person who did was a stranger he'd never see again.

Chapter 3

A half an hour later when Sam walked into Ted's home and the door closed behind him, he was surrounded by dimness and a silence that was almost tangible. The house, a sprawling bungalow on the bluffs above the beach, was built around one huge central room. Through open doors on either side, he could see a bedroom to the right, a small kitchen to the left of the door, and a den of sorts next to it.

Heavy drapes blocked the sunlight and the air inside was stale, giving the house a closed, suffocating feeling. Sam put down his luggage, then started flipping switches by the door until he succeeded in turning on two huge ceiling fans. As they began to rotate and the air stirred, he crossed the wood plank floor, went past the furniture shrouded in dust covers and at the windows, he reached for the curtain pull and tugged on it. The drapes slid back and exposed a wall of French doors and beyond them a view that looked like a framed painting.

For a moment he wished he'd been able to see the paintings Leigh Buchanan sent to New York, wondering if they had captured this beauty on canvas. As thoughts of the woman came back to him, he opened the doors, pushing them back to let fresh air inside. Then he turned to the empty room with its shrouded furnishings and the only sound the soft whirring of the fans and the ocean in the distance.

Being totally alone was something he hadn't experienced since he was a child. Although he had known he wouldn't like it, he hadn't thought he'd hate it the way he did right now. And he wondered if isolation had ever killed anyone.

He scanned the room, saw the sound system Ted had spoken of, built into the wall to his right, and he crossed to it. He flipped the power switch, heard the low hum, then pushed the button for the radio. He spun the dial, found some rock music and he turned the volume up until he could literally feel the sound bouncing off the walls.

Sam never remembered his dreams.

He was sure he dreamed. He'd heard that it was impossible for a person to go a single night without dreaming, but beyond an occasional nightmare when he was little, he forgot his dreams as soon as he opened his eyes. Until the second night he was on the island.

Sam didn't even go into the bedroom that overlooked the beach far below until well after midnight. With the French doors open to the night and with the music on the living room system turned almost all the way up, he fell into the huge poster bed. Lying on his back, his arms spread at his sides, he stared at the shadows above him.

He wasn't tired. There was nothing here to tire him, and he felt restless and oddly edgy. Closing his eyes, he inhaled and exhaled in time to the music, letting the heavy beat of a familiar rock tune flow through him, the words drifting through his mind. And somewhere he lost track of the words to the music, then the music itself and he slipped into a restless sleep.

He didn't really know when the dream began, because he eased into it so gradually. When he finally realized he was center stage at the amphitheater, he wasn't surprised. There was no backup band, no singers, just him alone in the single spotlight sitting on a stool with his acoustic guitar resting on his thigh. No sequins or leather, just denim and cotton, and his old running shoes.

Then he realized it was Sam Patton on the stage, not Boone, and he accepted that. He looked out at the audience, and saw nothing but darkness at first. He could feel himself being watched, but when the spotlight began to spread and expand, it exposed empty seats. As it inched farther back, Sam saw a single person in the middle of the theater, and he knew instantly it was Leigh Buchanan.

She sat very still, her hair loose and wild around her face, and her shoulders exposed by a strapless gown of deep blue and fashioned in sequins. As she stood, Sam stopped singing and slipped off the stool looking out at Leigh.

"Why are you here?" he heard himself ask, his voice echoing in the emptiness all around.

She came toward him down the center aisle, and she moved in total silence. He never took his eyes off her, and when she neared the stage and looked up at Sam, exposing the sweep of her neck as she lifted her chin, he saw her eyes for the first time. He couldn't tell the color, but he felt the impact of the gaze.

"Why are you here?" he asked again.

She touched the edge of the stage with the tips of her fingers. "So you wouldn't be alone." She glanced at the empty auditorium, then turned the full intensity of her gaze on him again. "Do you want me to stay?"

Sam wanted to shout that he never wanted her to leave, that the idea of her walking away could kill him, but he couldn't say a word.

"I'll go," she said, then turned and started down the aisle.

Sam dropped his guitar and ran to the edge of the stage. In one leap he was on the ground, but it wasn't the floor of the auditorium. There was sand under his feet and the auditorium was replaced by a clear night sky, water and fresh air.

And Leigh was moving away from him, the sequin gown glittering in the moonlight. He ran after her, and as he got close, he reached out and knew he was going to touch her, to feel her under his hands. In a single heartbeat, she was turning to him, her hair floating around her shoulders, and in that instant the isolation he'd felt for the past two days began to dissolve. It was as if someone had thrown him a lifeline in the form of a woman with spun-gold hair and haunting eyes.

Then he realized that he couldn't feel her. No matter how tightly he tried to hold her, there was no sensation of skin, of softness, of heat, or substance. He knew she was going to drift away into the night if he couldn't hold on to her. And if she left, he'd be well and truly alone.

"No!" he screamed, "no!" But she became more and more insubstantial until she was completely gone.

"No!" he screamed again, and the sound of his own voice jarred him awake.

He bolted up in bed, his hands pressed palms down on the mussed sheets and his breathing rapid and shallow. A breeze came through the open doors, skimmed over his bare skin and caught at the dampness there, chilling him. Exhaling harshly, Sam shook his head to clear it of the images that persisted. He realized the room was filled with the pale light of dawn, and the bed linens were tangled around his legs.

He sank back against the headboard and glanced at the phone on the side table. For a moment, he thought of calling Ted in Los Angeles just to hear another person talk, and damn the time difference. Then he thought better of it. He didn't need to hear a man talking right now.

With a harsh laugh, he got out of bed. What he needed was fresh air, something to take the lingering images of the dream out of his mind.

Stepping into a pair of jeans, he padded barefoot out onto the deck off the bedroom and gripped the waist-high wooden rail with both hands. Inhaling deeply, he looked down at the beach and for a moment he wondered if he was really awake or still dreaming.

Running along the edge of the water was a lone figure, and even from this distance, Sam recognized Leigh. Had the dream become reality, or was reality a dream, after all?

Sam watched Leigh. In hot pink shorts and a white top, she seemed to glide along the water's edge, her face lifted toward the rising sun, her hair confined in a low ponytail, glinting with gold. This image of her was a thousand times more potent than the dream image had been moments before. And he didn't want this to dissolve the way the dream had. He didn't want her to disappear. So he lifted his hand and called out.

"Miss Buchanan! Leigh!"

But she kept going.

"Leigh!" he yelled at the top of his lungs, but she didn't hear him.

Acting on impulse, Sam hurried back through the house, not bothering to do more than grab a T-shirt before he ran outside. As he pulled the shirt on, he went to the bluffs and saw wooden steps that led to the beach. He hurried down and saw Leigh jogging toward an outcropping of rocks.

"Leigh! Leigh!" he called as he ran after her, but she didn't stop.

As the space between them narrowed, he could see her more clearly, the lines and curves of her body under indecently skimpy running shorts, her slender arms, the muscles flexing in her lithe legs. As he realized how desperate he looked running after her, he faltered, then stopped by the shoreline. He watched her getting nearer to the outcropping of rocks that looked as if they defined the boundaries of the cove Ted's house occupied.

What kind of fool was he to let loneliness drive him to do something this foolish? He didn't need or want any involvement right now, especially not under these circumstances. Reason told him it was all wrong, that he had to keep to himself, but his body wasn't listening to reason. And Sam was almost relieved when Leigh took any decision out of his hands by jogging around the rocks and disappearing from sight.

Leigh had a game she played when she jogged, and as dawn came, spreading the pale beauty of pastel colors over the water, she pretended. She had memories of sounds, and as she jogged along the shore, her feet striking the damp sands and splashing the swirling water, she pulled up sounds locked in her mind, and put them with the scene all around her.

Water lapping the shore, seabirds crying, the sound of the breeze rushing past her. She could imagine all of it, carry it in her mind and experience it. With her face lifted to the sun, she jogged down the beach, happy in the world she made for herself.

But when she cleared the outcropping at the edge of the cove and went around it to get to the beach that led down to her house, the pretending stopped. She knew she wasn't alone on the beach.

When she'd lost her hearing, she'd been told that her other senses would sharpen, that they would become more keen, and they had. Right now she knew with a certainty that there was someone with her on the beach.

She stopped, the water swirling around her bare feet and she looked around, expecting to see Johngood on the bluffs waving to her, or coming toward her down the beach. But she couldn't see anyone. She turned a full three hundred and sixty degrees, then looked at the outcropping and re-traced her steps to it.

She touched the granite roughness as she looked around the rocks and back the way she'd come. She shouldn't have been shocked when she saw, not more than twenty feet away from her, a man looking right at her. Not just any man, but the one she'd seen at the general store in the village. And the sight of him stunned her.

He stood absolutely still, staring back at her, his feet bare, his rangy frame in snug jeans and white T shirt. The early-morning sun touched his long dark hair that looked mussed by more than the gentle breeze coming off the water, and the shadow of a new beard darkened his jaw.

His eyes were dark, and she couldn't quite see the color, but when his gaze met hers, she saw an unmistakable surprise, followed rapidly by the definite fire of appreciation touched by desire.

The look almost took her breath away, and the contact made it impossible for her to turn and leave.

Sam had been ready to consider himself lucky he hadn't made a fool out of himself and to head back to the house.

He hadn't been prepared for making eye contact with Leigh Buchanan.

The sunglasses she'd worn in town had hidden incredible blue eyes, the sort of blue that the poet and songwriter in him might have called "pools of midnight," the deepest blue he'd ever seen.

For a moment, all he could do was stare, then he threw all rational action out the window and went closer. "I'm sorry," he said. "I didn't mean to startle you. But I saw you from the house, and I . . ." He felt like a tongue-tied teenager, and found himself blurting out, "I thought this was a private beach."

As he spoke, she moved slowly from behind the rock and stood in front of him, the morning breeze teasing the curls that were loose now and caressing her bare shoulders. And she stared at him—hard. Not an impertinent stare, but an unblinking gaze of such intensity that he felt his stomach knot. She recognized him. She had the same way of staring that fans had the first time they saw him up close. That look that made him feel as if they were trying to memorize every part of him, as if all they had to do was draw in their breath and they could inhale him.

He almost turned right then and took off, but he realized something wasn't right. She wasn't coming toward him to touch him, to make the contact that some fans felt was their due. No, she quite simply just looked at him with those incredible eyes. And his uneasiness shifted to something more basic.

"I was told this beach was private, that I'd have it all to myself," he said, trying to fill the silence with some logic so he wouldn't be wondering what it would be like to skim those rebellious curls away from her shoulders, or what it would be like to wake to her beside him in the early morning.

She kept watching him, her gaze lingering on his lips, and he felt a heat begin to rise in him. No, this look wasn't one of recognition and he didn't understand it. He remembered what Gertrude at the store had said. "She has this way of looking at you."

All Sam knew was the way she was looking at him was making him tense, and he felt as if he had lost control of this confrontation somewhere between the first glimpse of her from the deck and meeting her gaze around the rock. And he wanted that control back. "You're trespassing," he said bluntly when she stayed silent.

Leigh stared at the man, unable to get past the way just this sight of him disturbed her and made her think and feel things she'd been certain were gone for good. Then she realized his mouth was moving, that he was saying something, and she concentrated on his lips.

"You're trespassing," he was saying as he slowly came toward her.

Her first instinct was to turn and run, to keep going and leave this all behind. But she didn't move. She felt riveted to the spot. "Trespassing?" she finally said.

He stopped about ten feet from her and hooked his thumbs in the belt loops of his jeans. He cocked his head and narrowed his eyes as he studied her. "I was told that the beach that went with the house was private, that no one else used it."

She glanced past him at the house on the bluffs. No one had been in that house since she'd been here. She looked back at him, disturbed that he was even closer now, so close that she could see fine lines fanned at the corners of his eyes, eyes that were a deep, true brown. "This is your beach?"

"For the next few weeks. I saw you from the house and came down to see what was going on."

She shook her head. "I had no idea someone was living here. I was just out jogging."

"So I see," he said as his eyes skimmed over her, then came back to meet her gaze. The fire that look was coaxing to life in her was echoed in the brown depths.

She didn't want it to shift the way it had with most of the men she encountered. Once they knew she was deaf, there was the backing up, either figuratively or literally, the "I don't believe it," then the pity. That was something she'd never want to see in this man's eyes.

Then she knew she never had to. All she had to do was turn and leave, to get away from him before he knew, before there was any reason for him to know. He'd said he was here for a few weeks. She'd keep her distance. All she had to do was walk away and never look back.

"You're right," she said. "It's private. I'm trespassing, and I won't do it again. Sorry." With that she turned and headed toward her house at a slow jog. Her heart raced, and each time her feet struck the damp sand, she fought the need to look back, to see what he was doing.

Sam stared after Leigh, not at all sure what had just happened. He certainly hadn't meant to scare her off, or force her to leave. He'd just been talking, trying to fill spaces until he could figure out what to say to her. And now she was jogging slowly down the beach away from him.

As she left, he remembered his loneliness over the past few days and instinctively knew that once she was out of sight, he'd be more lonely than he'd ever been in this place. Rationally, he knew he should let her go, but instinctively, he knew he couldn't. Besides, she obviously had no idea who he was. And what would it hurt to talk for a while and hear another voice?

Impulsively, he started after her and called out, "Miss Buchanan, wait a minute."

But she didn't hesitate. She kept going, her hair lifting in the breeze, her shapely legs moving with a fluid ease that was both seductive and annoying as it built distance between them. He just wanted her to stop. He ran as fast as he could and called out, "Just a minute," but she kept going. Then he reached out, just as in the dream, but when he caught her by her upper arm, that's where the similarities to the dream stopped.

He felt warmth and silky smoothness under his hand, and he felt her start so violently that it shocked him. She spun around, her hair suddenly free, and she jerked her arm free. He was facing her, so close that he could hear her ragged breathing, see the paleness to her skin and the shock in the depths of her blue eyes. "Wh-what are you doing?" he stammered.

He held up his hands palms out. "I didn't mean to startle you. I called out, but you must not have heard me."

She moved back half a pace, and her paleness was dotted by high color at her cheeks. She hugged her arms around herself. "What do you want?" she asked in a voice that held a seductive huskiness.

He felt on the defensive and that wasn't what he'd intended, not with this woman. "I just wanted to tell you, you can use the beach anytime you like. I didn't mean to run you off." He wished that she'd do something besides stare at him like that, then as if she'd read his mind, she moved. But it wasn't what he wanted. She took another step back, putting more distance between them. "Please, I'm only here for a few weeks. Don't interrupt your schedule for me. Use this beach anytime you want to."

"Thanks, but I don't need to. There's plenty of beaches around here," she said.

He shrugged and took a feeble stab at humor. "I guess an island is never undersupplied with beaches, is it?"

That nervous attempt to lighten the atmosphere brought the shadow of a smile to her full lips, a hint at the brilliance Sam was sure would be there if she let herself go. But even that hint brightened his day immeasurably.

"You're right, and I'll use one of them."

Sam regrouped. He'd never had to beg a woman to be in his immediate vicinity, and he wasn't going to start now. But on the other hand, he wished he could wake up every morning of his stay here and see her there, down on the beach, the sun glinting off her curls, her long legs gliding over the sand.

"This isn't going right," he admitted. "Let's start over. Hello. I'm Sam Patton."

Sam couldn't see any recognition in her eyes, just a wariness that he didn't understand. But she didn't run or ignore him. Instead, she said in a low voice, "I'm Leigh Buchanan."

"Leigh Buchanan," he echoed. "Nice to meet you." He pushed his hands in the pockets of his jeans and rocked forward on the balls of his feet. "And where do you live?"

She motioned with her head behind her. "Farther down the beach."

"Ah, so we're neighbors," Sam said.

"No, just in the vicinity."

He wished that she'd smile again, but she didn't. Instead, she seemed more nervous with each passing moment. She dug at the sand with her toes and crossed her arms on her breasts. It was obvious she wanted to leave, and it was just as obvious to him that he didn't want her to. "Have you been on the island long?" he asked, as those blue eyes watched him intently.

"Six months," she said, as he looked toward the water.

"Then you're not here on a visit?" he asked, his eyes skimming over the horizon.

She didn't say anything, but he sensed her moving, then she was almost in front of him, looking at him questioningly. "Pardon me?"

"You're living here permanently?"

She nodded and her expression eased just a bit. "Yes. Are you living here now?"

He grimaced at that. "Here? No."

She frowned up at him, drawing a fine line between her huge blue eyes. "Vacationing?"

"Marking time is more like it," he murmured.

She shook her head, her golden hair tumbling seductively around her shoulders. "It sounds as if you don't even like it here."

"Like it?" He glanced up and down the beach, then back to Leigh. "It's fine, I suppose. I'm just not used to all this . . . this emptiness."

"Emptiness?" she asked with a touch of surprise.

"Maybe that's the wrong word. Maybe I meant . . ." He searched for the right word. "I guess I meant space."

She cocked her head, her eyes narrowed on him. "Where are you from?"

"Civilization."

Her expression turned rueful. "Oh, sure. Crowds, crime, congestion, traffic and smog."

"Not your sort of thing, eh?"

Her expression tightened a bit, and he thought he saw wariness in her eyes again. "No, not my sort of thing."

He motioned up and down the beach. "And this isn't my sort of thing."

Leigh knew how expensive it was to rent a place on the island, and she couldn't conceive of anyone being here unless they really loved it or had money to throw around. She remembered what Johngood had said about the private plane. But this man didn't look wealthy. He didn't make sense on any level. She brushed out her loose hair, annoyed it had come out of the clip. "Then why are you here?" she asked bluntly.

"I told you, marking time."

"Until what?" she asked, really interested.

"Until I can get on with my life."

"And how long will that take?"

He lifted one eyebrow. "A few days, a week, maybe longer."

"So you're in isolation here?"

"I thought I was, until I found out I have a neighbor."

She was not about to think of this man as a neighbor. "I'm over a mile down the beach. That isn't exactly next door."

"You jogged that far?"

"Farther," she admitted.

"How far?"

"About four miles a day." She felt a smile tug at her lips, an expression that seemed very near the surface when this man was around. "It's a great tension reliever. Maybe you should think about it."

A slow, easy smile spread over his face, and Leigh felt her chest tighten. "Is that an invitation to go jogging with you?"

Leigh felt flustered, and she knew it was time to leave, to forget that this man was on the island. "No, just a suggestion," she said quickly and added, "and I need to get going. Nice meeting you, Sam Patton, and try to enjoy yourself while you're here."

Sam was about to ask her if she wanted to join him and show him how to enjoy the island, but before he could think of what to say or do, Leigh had turned and was heading down the beach.

Sam stood staring after her for a long moment. Finally, he turned and started to walk back toward Ted's, but stopped when he saw the sun glinting off something shiny in the sand. He stooped down, brushed at the sand and exposed a silver clip with pearls clustered on it. He glanced back in the direction Leigh had disappeared, then scooped up the clip. It had to be Leigh's.

He looked down at the clip, then pushed it into his pocket and started back to the house. The sun felt warm as it rose in the sky, the air held a sweetness from blossoms that he couldn't see and he felt so alone that it was almost a physical ache in his middle.

The woman stared at the item on the front page of the Los Angeles paper.

Theodore Bigelow, the manager of Boone Patton, country-western singer and three-time Grammy award winner, called a press conference today and denied that there is any connection between the assault on a security guard at the Ocean Air Amphitheater on the Fourth of July and his client's performance there the same evening.

Along with Bigelow was Detective Richard Lopez of the Los Angeles Police Department. Lopez stated they are going on the assumption that the attack stemmed from an attempted burglary in the dressing room that the guard tried to foil. They are following all leads and have asked for any help the public can give them.

Patton, who bought a permanent home in Malibu just two months ago, issued a statement through Bigelow that he was shocked by the incident, and will offer to help the injured man and his family in this time of distress.

She stared at the paper, then dropped it on her desk and sat forward. Closing her eyes so tightly that she could see colors explode behind her lids, she controlled a need to scream. No connection with Boone? That was called damage control. She understood that, but she wondered if they understood what was happening? That they were making her do this. They were forcing her to get to Boone any way she could, to be alone with him and make him understand why they had to be together forever.

But she didn't even know where he was. No one was talking.

Then she opened her eyes and realized how stupid some people were. She picked up the paper again. "Patton, who brought a permanent home in Malibu just two months ago..." She dropped the paper and reached for the phone. If he bought property, there had to be something on file from the deed or the escrow. And it made sense that he'd be at the new home.

Hitting the buttons for information, she waited through five rings before the information operator answered. "Thanks for using Pacific Bell."

"I need the number for the hall of records."

While she waited for the number, she reached to touch the single red rose she had on her desk in a small crystal vase. She caressed the silky petals, then slowly closed her fingers around the flower and crushed it in her hand.

Chapter 4

Sam stepped into Ted's house and stood very still just inside the door. There was nothing here. He'd meant it when he'd told Leigh that there was nothing but emptiness all around, but he hadn't told her that he felt it even inside himself. Without his road crew and entourage around, the people he lived with twenty-four hours a day, seven days a week, fifty-two weeks a year, he felt singularly empty.

He took the clip out of his pocket and looked down at the silver-and-pearl fastener. Just holding it made him even more aware of being alone. With a low oath, he closed his hand around it, then crossed to the stereo to turn on music to ward off the silence. But before he was halfway across the polished wood floor, the phone rang.

Sam hurried across to grab the cordless receiver on the table by the couch, thankful to have someone to talk to. "Hello?" he said.

"Hello there."

Sam sank down on the loose-cushioned couch and almost sighed with relief. "Good to hear from you, Ted," he admitted.

"How's it going down there?"

He looked out the windows at the unending blue sky and ocean blending at the horizon. "It's quiet enough here to make a person a basket case."

"Not any person. Just you."

"All right, just me, but it's unnerving to be so isolated and cut off from everything."

"Some think that Serenity Island is as close to paradise as you can get on earth," Ted countered.

Sam had a sudden image of Leigh running along the beach, and he knew she was the sort of woman who would make a man think of paradise, not some out-of-the-way island in the Caribbean. He held up the clip and stared at it. "That's their opinion."

"Obviously not yours," Ted said.

Sam got up and crossed to the stereo, laid the clip on the shelf above the unit, then turned on the tape deck, keeping the sound low. As the soft rhythms of a guitar instrumental filtered through the room, Sam tapped the clip with the tip of his finger. "Are you going to tell me what's happening back there?"

"Actually, nothing much. There's more going on in the press than in reality. Reporters have been all over the place looking for you. One of them even found your parents' place."

"What?" Sam asked as he drew his hand back from the pearls and silver.

"It's all right. Your father convinced them that he doesn't know where you are."

"He doesn't, does he?"

"No, just me and my wife and the detective. Did any of this make the news down there?"

"I haven't noticed. But I'm sure it will, sooner or later."

"I gave a press conference today and denied that you were connected to the incident in the dressing room and told them you would do anything you could for the guard's family."

"Did they buy that?"

"I guess so. We went with the theory that it was a burglary that got out of control. Detective Lopez went along with me."

"How long will it take to get the security system installed at the Malibu property?"

"I put everyone on overtime, and it should be ready in two weeks at the most. Sooner, if everything goes the way it's supposed to."

"The sooner the better," Sam muttered.

"At least you're in a safe place until it's ready."

"Yeah, I'm safe," Sam said, and looked around the very empty room, then leaned back against the shelves. "At least no one's recognized me."

"I didn't think anyone down there would know you, or if they did, I doubt that they'd even care. They're pretty friendly but easygoing and not easily impressed."

"You didn't tell me that you had neighbors in residence."

"Where?"

"The next house down the beach."

"Oh, the Swans' house. I heard it sold a while back."

"Do you know who bought it?"

"I've got no idea. Why? Is there a problem?"

"No, no problem." Sam turned and looked back at the clip. "Do me a favor, Ted?"

"Sure, what?"

"Remember when you were after me to look into art as a tax shelter and an investment?"

"I remember that you weren't interested."

"I've been considering it, and I think you might have an idea there. You mentioned a gallery in New York, the Gray Gallery, and I'd like you to check out an artist shown there, Leigh Buchanan."

"What's going on with you?"

"I'm asking you to check—"

"Since when do you give a thought to your investments?"

Sam closed his eyes. "Since now. Just check on Leigh Buchanan's work and get back to me."

"Why that artist?"

"Ted, just do it," he said, his answer more abrupt than he intended. "Oh, hell, I'm sorry. I'm beginning to feel as edgy as a long-tailed cat in a roomful of rocking chairs." He opened his eyes and looked out at the distant water. "Tell me, Ted, just what do you do when you're down here day in and day out?"

"I relax," Ted said with a faint chuckle. "I suggest that you start learning how to do that very thing and enjoy being there. Put this mess out of your mind and go swimming or go for long walks on the beach, sit in the sun, sleep all day, rest, recharge your batteries."

"That sounds like a lot of work to me," he countered with tight humor.

"I think you're the only person I know who would have to ask how to enjoy paradise."

"Thanks, Ted, and goodbye. I think I'm hanging up now."

"Good. Go and *relax,*" he said, then the line clicked.

Sam flipped off the phone, then reached for the stereo and turned the volume up until he could feel the base vibrating all around him. He stood in the middle of the throbbing sound, letting it beat on him, but all it did was aggravate him. He didn't need to relax, and he didn't need someone else's music rumbling around and through him. What he needed was to make some music of his own and get something positive out of these days of exile.

He turned off the stereo, picked up his guitar and went out on the deck and dropped down into one of the canvas chairs that faced the ocean. As he leaned back, he rested his guitar on his thigh, propped his bare feet on the railing and closed his eyes. With the warmth of the sun on his face, he let thoughts drift in and out of his mind, but there weren't any new ideas for songs there. No snatches of lyrics or pieces of tunes. He felt as if the emptiness of the land all around was echoing inside him.

When Leigh got back to her house, Johngood was waiting for her on the top step of the porch. Dressed in frayed, cutoff jeans and a tie-dyed T-shirt in hot pinks, lime greens and oranges, he watched her come up the stairs toward him. He stood when she stopped on the step below him.

"I was beginning to think you forgot," he said looking down at her, his dark eyes narrowed with a disapproval that she didn't understand.

She swiped at her flushed face, pushing the damp tendrils of hair off her cheeks and temples. She had no idea what he was talking about. He certainly didn't need her here for him to work on reinforcing the stairs down to the beach, and he had his own key. "Did you forget your key?"

He shook his head emphatically. "I've told you, you don't have to lock your door, and..." He pushed his hand in the pocket of his cutoffs and pulled out a key tied to a thin strip of leather. "I have my key. I'm talking about your weekly call. It's this morning."

The call. Maybe she'd forgotten just because she hated doing it, but she knew the alternative was even worse. If she didn't call, her mother would probably be down here on the next flight out of New York to check on her. "I'm sorry. I got sidetracked," she said.

"Now you're here, so let's do it."

She watched him turn and cross to the door, unlock it and hold it open for her. She hesitated, then hurried across the veranda and into the coolness of the house, and she went directly to the phone by the wicker-and-fabric couch that was turned to face the view.

"Let's get this over with," she muttered as she reached for the phone. She turned as Johngood came up behind her and held it out to him.

"How can you do that?" he asked, studying her.

She didn't need this right now. "I told you, I got distracted on the beach," she said, knowing that calling those moments with Sam Patton a distraction was like calling breathing a hobby. "There's a man near the far end of the cove," she said quickly. "And we talked for a while."

"I wasn't asking about some tryst you had on the beach," he said with a lift of one eyebrow. "Although that could be interesting."

"I wasn't talking about a tryst," she countered, hating the blush she knew was staining her cheeks. "It was a simple meeting of two strangers."

"Too bad," he said with a shake of his head, then added, "What I was asking you was how you always know when I'm coming up behind you in the house?"

This was the closest Johngood had ever come to asking her about her deafness, but there was genuine curiosity replacing the teasing in his expression. And that made it easy for her answer. "The floor," she said, pointing to the thick planks. "I can feel the vibrations when someone's walking on it.'' She sniffed and wrinkled her nose. ''You've been working on the taxi again, and you smell of oil and grease.''

''The compensations in this life,'' he said philosophically, then took the phone from her and dropped down on the couch. ''Are you ready?''

She exhaled and sat down beside him. ''As ready as I'll ever be.''

While Johngood put in the long-distance call to New York, Leigh rested her head back on the high cushions of the couch. Only she and Johngood had been in the area before, and knowing Sam Patton was near unsettled her. Certainly not the way she'd felt when her parents had shown up on her doorstep two months ago. But his presence wasn't welcome, either. Not when he could scramble her thoughts just by looking at her.

She rubbed her bare arms with the palms of her hands. No more involvements, no emotional complications. She had her life, and a man didn't fit in it at all.

She was jolted out of her thoughts when Johngood touched her arm to get her attention. Sitting up straight, she opened her eyes and looked at him. ''She's on the line,'' he said.

Leigh massaged the nape of her neck with her fingertips, trying to ease the tension that was collecting there. But she wasn't sure if the tension came from having to take this contact, or if it was from the contact she'd experienced earlier on the beach. ''Tell her everything is fine here. That there aren't any problems. I'm doing well.''

Johngood spoke into the receiver and repeated her words, then listened intently. Finally, he looked at Leigh. ''Do you need anything, money, supplies or...'' He hesitated and she knew he was listening to her mother again. ''Or the friendly faces of your family?'' he finally finished.

The tension increased as Leigh shook her head. "No, nothing," she said. "I have enough friendly faces right here."

Johngood smiled at that, and spoke into the phone again. "She says there is nothing she needs right now, but thank you, anyway."

Leigh smiled at his attempt at diplomacy by paraphrasing her statement. He hadn't been here when her parents had surprised her by showing up, but he'd lived through the fallout, her anger and frustration after she'd managed to talk them into leaving.

Johngood was looking at her, tapping her hand to get her attention again. "She says that she really wants you to think about getting that special phone that has the keyboard and printout. That you're too shut off down here, and that she's worried about you and that something could happen and she wouldn't know about it until it was too late."

When Leigh held out her hand for the receiver, Johngood just stared at her. But when she grabbed it, he let go and watched her as she spoke quickly into the mouthpiece. "Mother, I don't want that phone. I can write a letter if there's anything I need to tell you that I can't do this way, and I'm not too shut off. If anything happens to me, you'll be the first to know. Johngood will call you himself, and in the meantime, I'm doing just fine here on my own."

She quickly handed the receiver back to Johngood, and for the first time she could remember, she was almost thankful that she didn't have the ability to hear the hysterics she knew would come over that line. Johngood listened carefully for a very long time, rolled his eyes heavenward, then looked at Leigh as he held the receiver away from his ear.

"She's sorry she upset you, but she thinks you're emotional because you're alone too much, and she wishes that you would come home for a while, and while you're there, you could see a doctor she heard about." She knew he must be seeing her rising anger and embarrassment on her face, but he gave no clue as he kept talking. "She says that a person named Satch is asking for you, that he wishes you would come back to New York, and be there for the next showing. If you did, it would make it easier all around, and—"

Leigh reached for the receiver again, but this time she put her hand over the mouthpiece and leaned closer to Johngood. "Enough of this. Tell her I'm healthy and fine, that this is my home and I don't need a doctor. I just need to be left alone. And tell her to tell Satch that I won't be there for the next show or any other showing he has."

She realized she was holding the receiver so tightly that she could have snapped the plastic. Very carefully, she relaxed her fingers, but kept the mouthpiece covered. "Just get her off the phone, Johngood. This call is over."

Johngood didn't look away from Leigh as he took the phone and put it to his ear. "I'm sorry, I had trouble with the connection for a minute," he lied. "She says that she's feeling good, that the island agrees with her. She can't make the next show, but she'll call you at the regular time in a week." He listened for a very long moment, his face giving away nothing, then he said, "Of course I will Mrs. Buchanan." He listened again, nodded, and said, "All right, Mrs. Buchanan, good day," and hung up.

"I never asked you to lie to her, Johngood. That wasn't in the deal."

"Did you really want me to say those things to her?"

She closed her eyes for a moment, then looked back at Johngood's impassive face. "No, of course not."

"I knew that."

"What did she say?" she asked. "And don't lie to me."

"I wouldn't think of it," he said without hesitating. "She said that you are very stubborn, that you don't know what's good for you, and that you don't belong here. She and your father are sick about it, but don't seem to have any way to make you come back to New York where you belong."

Leigh knew she was getting more and more tense with each passing word. "What else?"

"And she said that she wants me to check on you every day, make sure you're all right and need for nothing. But I am to do it unobtrusively because you wouldn't like it if you knew about it."

"So you're telling me."

"I said I wouldn't lie. I keep my word." He spread both hands palms up. "Besides, she says she'll pay me a reasonable sum of money for doing it."

Leigh uttered a very unladylike oath. "And you aren't going to do it, are you?"

"Of course I am. She asked me nicely. She's worried, and she's willing to pay good money." He tapped her hand where it was clenched in a fist on her thigh. "Relax. I'm no baby-sitter. You do what you want to do. I'll be around, put your mother's mind at rest and keep her from coming down here. That's the most important thing, isn't it?"

She should have known he understood, after all. "And meanwhile you'll get paid a reasonable sum?"

"You pay me for working, and she pays me for doing what I've been doing anyway." His grin deepened. "I'm making out all right."

"And you think this is all a joke?"

"Of course. Life is a joke," he said as he stood, then looked down at her. "Laugh at it. If you can't, you're lost."

He was right. There were good jokes and bad jokes, and she'd had her share of the bad. Amazingly, she found that she could actually smile at this whole situation. "You're quite a philosopher and you're getting paid for it."

She could see him laughing, then he said, "I guess this means you can stay here for a while longer."

"That's the plan."

"Good. Now, I'm supposed to be working on your safety rail on the stairs." He started to go out, but stopped and looked back at her. "You said there was a man on the beach who distracted you earlier."

She stood and pushed her loose curls back from her face. "Yes. He said he's staying in that house on the bluffs."

Johngood frowned at her. "Have you seen him on the beach before?"

She felt her face warm a bit, and turned to head for the studio. "He's the man we saw at the store in town a couple of days ago, the one with the red Jeep," she tossed over her shoulder, and didn't look back to see what Johngood had to say about her meeting with Sam Patton.

When she got into the studio, she inhaled the mingled scent of ocean air drifting in through the open windows and the pungency of oil and turpentine. The fragrance closed around her like an old friend, and as she crossed to her work in progress, a seascape of the view from a small cove on the far side of the island, she forgot everything except the vision she had of this work.

The sun was beginning to slide toward the west, spreading the richness of reds and pinks in the sky, before Leigh stood back from her painting and studied it. She had the essence, the mists that hung over the shores at morning, the sense of vast openness and the touch of eternity that she felt here. It was what she'd been hoping for, but for the past hour, she'd been fighting the urge to put a person in it, a lone man by the water's edge. Without putting a brush to the canvas, she knew that man would have long hair, a lean body and dark eyes.

As she began to clean her brushes, she felt the steps of Johngood on the hardwood and looked up as he came around the large canvas. He stopped, looked at the painting, then glanced at Leigh. "You've got that right."

"You know where that is?"

"Sure, Solomon's Cove." He pointed to a rock formation that cut into the water, shutting off access to the cove on the north end. "It's the only place on the island that has a rock formation like that besides the one between here and the next cove."

Her hands stilled on the brushes she was working to clean the paint from. She could almost feel the roughness under her fingertips when she'd touched the rocks and looked around them to see Sam Patton watching her. "You sure know this island," she conceded as she went back to cleaning. "Are you finished work for today?"

"Almost, I just need to go down below and pick up the tools before I leave. There're two flights coming in tomorrow morning, so I won't be back here until after lunch."

"You don't have to come tomorrow if you're busy."

"But I gave my word to your mother." He didn't blink. "I keep my word."

Leigh met his direct gaze. "Just how much did my mother offer to pay you?"

"I told you, a reasonable sum. Enough to make her feel better," he said. "Now, is there anything else you need before I head home?"

She slipped her brushes into their holders to dry. He wouldn't lie to her, but he wasn't going to tell her a direct truth, either. "No, I'm fine. I'll finish up here, then maybe go for a swim before dinner."

* * *

Sam sat on the deck for most of the day, the guitar resting forgotten by his chair, and he let his mind roam. His thoughts kept returning to his encounter on the beach, to how the emptiness was pushed back for a short time by a woman with dark blue eyes. "Pools of midnight," he whispered. "Pools of midnight."

The words nudged at him, bringing brilliant images of Leigh into his mind. The idea of losing emptiness and having a person's essence fill him began to weave together. And he knew there was a song there, but it was just out of reach.

He settled lower in the sling-back chair and narrowed his eyes to the clear sunlight. Maybe Ted was right that he'd been close to burnout. Maybe that was why the song wasn't coming to him. Or maybe he was trying too hard because he was so desperate for a diversion that would take his mind off the rest of his life.

He stood and went back into the house to turn on the stereo. But his hand never touched the power switch. Instead, Sam reached for the clip sitting on the higher shelf.

He closed his fingers around it, then switched on the tape of classical music and headed into the bedroom to change. It wouldn't hurt to get out of the house, to take a walk on the beach, and in the process, he could return the clip to its owner.

A damned good diversion.

Sam knew he'd walked for at least a mile past the outcropping where he'd met Leigh that morning, and he still hadn't seen another house. There were seabirds in the air, the gentle rippling of a warm breeze and twenty- to thirty-foot bluffs topped with rich greenness, but no house, and no blue-eyed woman.

He closed his hand over the clip in his pocket as he came to a sweep in the bluffs that almost touched the tide line, and he stopped. Maybe Leigh's house wasn't visible from the beach, and maybe he'd passed it long ago without knowing it. He almost turned back. But knowing he'd be heading back to the empty house and long hours this evening kept him going.

He walked along the narrow strip of beach between the jutting bluffs and the foam of the incoming tide and looked up to find himself on a broader beach. That's when he saw the house.

What Ted's had in character, this house had in spades. It looked like a giant eagle nesting on the edge of the bluffs, smug and secure while being supported by massive pilings that had been forced into the granite walls of the bluffs. The low sun set the windows on fire with reflected gold, and a deck that wrapped around the ocean side of the house was empty.

This had to be the Swan house, but he couldn't see any access to it from the beach. He went farther along the beach until he was almost under the house, then saw wooden pilings that had been laid on their sides to fit into steps cut in the bluffs. It looked as if someone had been working on a hand railing that was being set into the rock on one side.

He started toward the stairs to go up to the top, but before he could reach them, he heard someone call out.

"Hey, you. What're you doing here?"

He turned to see a small man in a neon-colored tie-dyed T-shirt and cutoff shorts that revealed bow legs. Scraggly gray hair stuck out from under a straw hat, and his heavily lined face was pulled into a deep frown.

"I asked you what you're doing here?" the man repeated.

This had to be Johngood, the man who had been driving Leigh in the taxi in town. "I was looking for Miss Buchanan," he said.

"And what would you be wanting with her?" Johngood asked.

"And why would you be asking?" Sam countered.

The man squared up, his feet spread, his hands on his hips. "I'm her friend. How about you?"

"I'm her neighbor."

He hesitated, then surprisingly he smiled, a toothy grin. "Oh, so you're the man staying at the Bigelow place."

"That's me." For a minute, Sam thought the man had recognized him, then that thought fled when the man spoke again.

"And you'd be the one Miss Buchanan met on the beach this morning?"

"Right again."

His face sobered. "And what would you be wanting with her now?"

The man went from friendly to looking remarkably like a guard dog in the matter of a moment, and Sam didn't know if he was annoyed or amused. "I'd be wanting to talk to her... if that's all right with you."

"Ain't up to me to approve or disapprove, it's just that Miss Buchanan likes her privacy, and she wasn't expecting no one."

"I know. I was out for a walk, saw the house and thought I'd be neighborly and drop in." He decided that there was no point in continuing to spar with this man, so he took a step toward him and held out his hand. "I'm Sam Patton."

The man took Sam's hand in a surprisingly strong grip. "Johngood, all one word. I work for Miss Buchanan."

"That's what the lady who has the store told me."

He laughed at that. "Ah, Gertrude sees all, knows all and tells all."

"Johngood? You're still here?"

Sam turned at the sound of the familiar softly husky voice. Leigh was at the foot of the stairs, one hand on the side rail. And before he had time to think, he felt a reaction in him that took him by surprise. It went beyond the basic physical response he felt at the sight of her. It went beyond appreciation for a stunning body in a skimpy bikini worn under a lace cover-up and beyond tanned legs that seemed to go on forever. It even went beyond huge blue eyes in a beautiful face.

When Sam turned and saw Leigh, he felt genuine pleasure to be near her again. He felt a deep, intense joy that she was here and he was here. And he knew right then that Leigh Buchanan would never be a simple diversion for him. There was nothing simple about what was happening to him.

Chapter 5

"I decided to do a bit more work before taking the tools up to the house." Johngood looked at Sam. "Then I saw him heading for the stairs."

The dark blue eyes turned on Sam and he felt every nerve in his body come alive. Disturbed by his thoughts, he took the clip out of his pocket and held it out to Leigh. "I found this on the beach and thought it might be yours."

She looked at it, then came closer and skimmed the clip off his open palm, barely making contact with his skin. "Thank you," she said. "I thought I'd lost it."

"Why didn't you tell me why you were here?" Johngood asked Sam.

"I didn't get a chance," Sam said, then looked at Leigh. "You came down to go for a swim?"

"Yes, I did."

"Would you mind if I join you? I hate swimming alone."

She hesitated, and he could see her clearly weighing his offer before she shrugged. "The beach is free to enjoy." She looked at Johngood. "How about you? Do you want to go for a swim?"

He shook his head and looked vaguely embarrassed. "No, I don't think so. I can't swim."

Sam saw Leigh's eyes widen. "You live on an island surrounded by water and you can't swim?"

He shrugged. "I don't plan on having to swim if I go to Martinique, so what's the problem?"

Leigh laughed at that, a brilliant burst of pleasure at the absurdity of the situation, and Sam found himself watching her and wishing he could keep that joy in her face forever.

"Johngood, you're truly a world-class philosopher," she said, the laughter still gentling her voice.

"Exactly," the little man said. "Now, I need to get the tools up to the house. I'll be seeing you tomorrow." He touched his hand to his forehead, and with a slanted look at Sam that was totally unreadable, he moved past them and crossed to pick up a metal tool chest. Then he started up the stairs.

Leigh watched Johngood go upward, and when he ducked out of sight at the top, she turned back to Sam. When she'd seen him at the bottom of the stairs talking to Johngood, she'd almost gone back up to the house before he saw her. But she'd made herself go down, telling herself that he was just a man and she wouldn't let him stop her from going swimming.

Then she'd faced him on the sand, and found herself wondering how she could have ever thought he was "just a man." He was achingly male, radiating sexuality, and she'd been thankful that Johngood was there as a buffer. But now Johngood was gone, and as she turned back to Sam, she knew how wrong she had been not to retreat to the house the minute she'd seen him down here.

He was no more than five feet from her, calmly taking off his clothes. He tugged his T-shirt over his head, exposing a strong chest with a pattern of dark hair that formed a suggestive *T* over tanned skin and rippling muscles. Then he tossed the shirt onto the sand at the foot of the stairs, and she almost stopped breathing when he undid the button of his jeans and slid down the zipper. For one instant, she thought he was going to swim nude.

But as he stripped off his pants, she saw he was wearing an indecently brief pair of bright red swim trunks. With a flick of his hand, he tossed his pants onto his shirt and looked at Leigh. Just the sight of him standing in front of her, his muscular legs dusted with dark hair, his hands on his hips and that broad expanse of bare skin made her mouth go dry.

"Do you swim every night at this time?" he was asking.

She nodded, afraid to look away from him in case he asked her something else, but almost as afraid to keep staring at him. "Most of the time."

"How's the swimming around here?"

"It's great," she said, and dropped her towel to the ground at her feet. She tried to be casual taking off her cover-up, but as soon as it fell around her ankles, she headed for the water. "The water's warm," she tossed over her shoulder. "And there aren't any real currents in the cove."

Then she was in the water, the warmth swirling around her bare legs, moving up to her waist. She dived into the low waves, and stroking away from the shore, she didn't look back. She didn't stop until her arms began to tire. Treading water, she turned and saw Sam surface about five feet from her, water flattening his hair and dripping off his spiked lashes.

"I thought you were training for a marathon," she saw him say, noticing his rapid breathing before he shook his head sharply to clear his face of water and clinging tendrils of hair. "I think I need to do some workouts."

"Do you jog?"

"No. I've never had the time to."

"Too bad, it's good for the cardiovascular system," she said.

"I'll remember that," he said, a slight smile tugging at his lips. "I could use some cardiovascular help right about now."

She could see he was still breathing a bit hard. "Let me know when you're rested enough to head back," she said.

He raised an eyebrow in her direction. "I'm not ready to die, just a bit winded. And I'm ready to head back anytime you are."

"I'm ready now," she said.

"All right, let's go."

"Sure," she said, then dived sideways and began to stroke back toward the beach, but at a slower pace. She glanced to her right, saw Sam stroking through the water, staying right beside her. He looked at Leigh at that moment, their gazes locked, then he smiled, winked and broke into a faster, stronger stroke. Within seconds, he was two lengths ahead of her, and she swam harder to keep up, but she was a full length behind when they neared the shore and Leigh felt the bottom with her toes.

As she stood, Sam straightened in front of her and turned to look at her.

"You lied to me," she sputtered as she pushed clinging hair back from her face and flicked it behind her shoulders.

"No, I was just covering myself. I really don't jog and I'm not in very good shape."

Leigh looked at the man defined by the glow of the setting sun, at the flat, muscle-hard stomach, the broad shoulders and strong arms, and she wanted to laugh at him. He was in *very* good shape. Ducking her head, she moved through the water past him, and spoke without looking at him. "A lie by implication is still a lie," she muttered and kept going to the beach.

She didn't stop until she was at her towel, then she picked up her lace cover-up and slipped it on over her wet suit. When she finally turned, she saw Sam behind her, pushing his legs into his pants. The water immediately darkened the denim in the pattern of his suit, and as Sam snapped the button at his waist, he looked up at her.

"Do I get the silent treatment just because I was kidding with you? I told you I'm sorry. I won't do it again."

He must have been talking to her all the time she was walking onto the beach and to her things. She hadn't even thought about that, and it made her flustered and embarrassed that she'd totally forgotten. "You don't need to apologize. I overreacted."

"One thing you have to know about me," he said. "I have this really perverted streak in me when it comes to competition. I hate to lose." He swiped at an errant trickle of water that started down his temple. "I think it's because I come from a large family, all boys, and it's a fact of life in my family that if you lose, you never live it down. I've never quite gotten over that."

She picked up her towel and began to blot her hair. "And you used to swim a lot when you were a child?"

"Not really. I just competed a lot with my brothers." He narrowed his eyes. "Do you always swim that fast when you're alone down here?"

She wouldn't tell him how she'd stroke out, then float, letting her mind supply the sounds of the water, the cries of birds, the sigh of the breeze. And how she felt complete. "Sometimes."

"Good cardiovascular exercise," he said with a smile.

The sun was below the horizon and dusk was rapidly coming, making it harder for Leigh to see Sam's lips clearly. And that brought back the old panicky feelings. She could feel them surfacing. "I need to get back to the house," she said quickly and held the damp towel to her breasts.

Sam studied her in the soft light, then he spoke impulsively, yet from a real need to keep her there. "You wouldn't want to come back to my place for dinner, would you? I'm no gourmet, but I can whip together something edible."

"Thanks, but I've got work to do."

He tried to hide his disappointment. "Some other time," he said.

"Good night," she said softly, then turned and headed toward the stairs in the bluff.

Sam watched her climb the stairs until the failing light blurred her image, smearing it into the coming dusk, then he turned to pick up his shirt and leave. But he saw something on the sand where Leigh's towel had been—the pearl clip. He scooped it up.

"Leigh," he started to call, but as he looked at the stairs, Leigh was already on top and disappearing from view. Closing his hand around the clip, he turned and headed back to Ted's house.

When dawn came, Sam had been up for almost an hour and was sitting on the deck, watching the colors of the rising sun creep over the house to splash the sky with pinks, yellows and pale lavenders. A gentle breeze stirred the sea grass and the low-growing trees that rimmed the far expanse of the open area, and a subtle sweetness tinged the clean air.

He sat very still, the air warm on his bare skin, and his eyes never leaving the beach. Just when he was about to give up, he saw her. She was jogging smoothly and rhythmically, her hair loose, shorts and a skimpy top exposing a lot of tanned skin. He watched Leigh until she went out of sight to the west, then he stood and went into the house.

Taking his time, he dressed in cutoffs and a yellow tank top, caught his hair at the nape of his neck with an elastic band, then went outside. He wandered barefoot across the grass and down the stairs in the bluff. When he stepped onto the beach, he headed to the water's edge and looked in the direction she'd gone, but couldn't see anything.

He had no idea how long it would take Leigh to jog the distance down the beach, but he found that he wasn't in a hurry. He could wait until she came back this way. He slipped his hand into his pocket and closed it around her clip.

Leigh lost herself in her running, letting sensations flow around her, and she could almost block out Sam's visit last night. She could almost block out her reaction to him when they swam together, and she could almost block out her error of keeping her back to him as they came out of the water.

It was so much simpler when she knew no one down here but Johngood and Gertrude at the store. So much less complicated. And she wished it could be that way again. With Sam close by, her nerves were kept on edge.

She got to the end of the main cove and turned to head back, running at an easy pace, letting the breeze lift her hair and brush across her skin. He was from a large family. She remembered he'd told her that last night. And he was disrupting her world. She wanted to be left alone.

As if to underline her lack of control since Sam had appeared on the scene, she looked ahead and saw him standing on the beach at the tide line, watching her. She almost stopped and ran the other way, then reason prevailed and she made herself keep going, her stride eating up any protective distance there might have been between herself and Sam.

He raised his hand to her as she got closer and she could see him speaking to her. She caught the words "beautiful morning," and she improvised when she got closer.

"It's lovely, isn't it?"

"Absolutely," he said.

He stood in the water, the lapping waves swirling around his ankles, and try as she might not to notice things about this man, she saw his bare legs, the way his hair was pulled back from his face and fine lines fanned at his eyes as he squinted in the fresh light of a new day.

"You're up early," she said for lack of anything else to say.

"I've been up for hours." He half grimaced, half smiled, as if what he was about to say was both annoying and amusing. "I've always been a night person, but since I've been here, I'm awake before the sun's up."

"And you don't miss all of this glory," she said, motioning to the sun that was rising higher in the sky, glinting off the soft swells of the Caribbean.

"You're a morning person, aren't you?"

"I am now," she said. "I didn't think I was until I got down here, but I love this time of day."

"You never did tell me where you came from before you decided to live here."

"New York."

"The big city. No wonder you weren't up early there. All the excitement happens after the sun goes down."

"It sounds as if you know New York."

"I've been there a few times." He glanced at the ocean that ran as far as the eye could see, then back to Leigh. "Did you jog there?"

"No, I never even thought about it. I didn't start jogging until I came here."

"Would you mind if I jogged a little way with you now?"

She hadn't expected that question from him. "I didn't think you did that sort of thing."

"It's good for—"

"Your cardiovascular system," she finished for him. "I know."

"I just found that out, and I want to have a better cardiovascular system. I also know that I need stress management. I think jogging might come under that heading."

He wasn't smiling, but she could have sworn she saw laughter lingering deep in his eyes. He had no idea how much jogging helped her stress management . . . until now. "All right. If you want to," she said, and made very sure he wouldn't be saying things she couldn't see him say while they ran. "But you can't talk while you run. It's against the rules."

"What rules?"

"My rules."

"Good enough," he said.

"And this isn't a race."

"Understood," he said. "We'll stay neck and neck . . . so to speak."

She started off and he fell in step to her left, his legs keeping pace with hers. When they got to the stairs that led up to Leigh's house, she stopped and turned to look at Sam. She almost laughed.

Sam was breathing hard, bending over, his head hanging down, his hands braced on his knees. Perspiration gleamed on his bare skin, and his hair in the ponytail was sticking to his neck and back where it touched his skin.

"Are you all right?" she asked, hoping there wasn't any hint of laughter in her voice.

He looked up at her, his mouth open as he sucked in air. "You did that on purpose to get even with me for the swimming thing yesterday, didn't you?"

"I did what on purpose?" she asked.

"You tried to kill me."

She did laugh at that, and got a hard frown from him in payment. "Kill you? I was jogging slower than usual today."

"Oh, sure," he said as he straightened up, his hands resting on his lean hips. "And you're not out of breath, either, are you?"

"Not particularly."

"You used to run all the time with your brothers and sisters, didn't you?"

"No, I'm an only child. The only person I ever ran with was my dog."

His lips began to arch upward. "And you always beat him, didn't you?"

"Well, he was old and had arthritis."

"I'm only thirty-five, not particularly old, and I don't have arthritis yet, so I don't have any excuse."

"Except that you're out of shape."

"Touché," he said as he came closer. "But I'm not hopeless, am I?"

He was far from hopeless, and being this close to him made Leigh feel distinctly breathless. It was time to leave. "No, of course not. I have to get to work."

"Work?"

"You're here for a break, but I live here, and that means I work here, too."

"What sort of work?"

"I'm an artist, and by now I'm usually working. I like the morning light."

"Oh, a creature of habit?"

"I guess so. It makes life easier and simpler." Something he certainly didn't do. "And I have to get going."

"Have a good day at work."

"And you have a good day relaxing," she said, waiting for him to turn and leave so he couldn't say anything to her that she didn't hear.

With a lift of one eyebrow, Sam nodded to her, then turned and started off down the beach, walking slowly. Only when he was near the outcropping of rocks did Leigh start for the stairs to go up to her house. Work was what she needed right now. Something to involve her to the point that she wouldn't think about Sam.

Sam went home with vaguely sore muscles and a day looming ahead of him filled with nothing but time and emptiness. But after he showered, he stretched out on the bed, letting the breeze drifting in the open French doors skim over his bare skin, and the next thing he knew he was waking from a deep, dreamless sleep.

He opened his eyes to sunlight, felt muzzy and disoriented, then he turned and focused on the bedside clock. At first he thought it read twenty minutes after ten, then he sat upright as his eyes focused. It was really ten minutes to four.

With a sigh, he sank back on the bed and stared at the ceiling. Sleeping in the middle of the day was something he never did. Then he smiled as he realized that he didn't usually jog in the morning, either. And, in an hour or so, he'd head out to swim again with Leigh. The idea intrigued him.

The phone by the bed rang, and Sam rolled on his side, then reached for the receiver. "Hello?" he said as he settled on his back.

"You're stuck inside that house, aren't you?" Ted asked over the line. "I thought I told you to get out in the sun and relax."

"I am relaxing," he said, and was a bit surprised that he really meant it. "I'm unwinding, enjoying the island. I've gone swimming and jogging."

A bark of laughter exploded over the line. "Saints preserve us, will wonders never cease to happen?"

Sam rested his forearm across his eyes. "Ted, jogging and swimming are good for the cardiovascular system."

"Excuse me, is this Sam Patton, the same Sam Patton who sat at that place and didn't have the vaguest idea of what to do with the water and the beach and the clean air?"

He grinned. "I'm a fast learner."

"Good for you."

"Ted, what's this call for?"

All the teasing drained out of his voice. "You got a letter today."

"Oh, God," he groaned, shocked that for a brief spot in time he'd totally forgotten why he was hiding down here. "Read it to me."

"Lopez has it, but I can give you the gist of it. She said that she's sorry about the guard, but he got in her way. And she knows that the only way out of the suffering is for you both to die."

"Who in the hell is she?" Sam muttered. "And what did I ever do to make her hate me so much?"

"She doesn't hate you. She loves you, in some convoluted, psychopathic, sick way."

"Yeah, really sick. What's Lopez doing about it?"

"He's on top of it. He's running down a few ideas, and I'm pushing the work crew at the Malibu house. Once that's in, you'll be safe as if you were in a sealed fortress."

He thought about his first glimpse of the place in Malibu, the old oaks along the drive, the chaparral on the hills, the wild mustard and buckwheat. The house sat on the highest rise on the acreage, a sprawling adobe that had been built in the 1920s. He'd fallen in love with it instantly. It would give him space to do what he wanted to, and it was close enough to Los Angeles to take care of business.

"That's not exactly the way I envisioned that property."

"Maybe not, but it's a good idea to secure it."

"Sure." He let his arm fall on the pillow behind his head and realized that the sun was slanting more sharply into the room. "Ted, I've got to go. I'm ..." He hedged. "I have things to take care of."

"Sure. I'll be in touch when I know anything else."

"See you," he said, then put the receiver back and climbed out of bed. Quickly, he dressed in his swim trunks, pulled jeans on over them, tugged on a plain T-shirt, and headed out of the house.

When Leigh went down for her afternoon swim, she stopped at the bottom of the stairs and looked up and down the empty beach. Sam wasn't there. She'd expected him to be waiting, dressed in those skimpy trunks, telling her he was here for her scheduled swim. And she hated the feeling of disappointment that nudged at her because he wasn't here.

Then she grabbed at a single, rational thought, that she should be relieved. She didn't have to deal with the way the sight of him could make her feel. She could swim without worrying about his being close by, about his accidentally touching her, his skin brushing hers, and she didn't have to worry about his saying something that she couldn't catch because of dim light or because she wasn't facing him.

She laid out her towel on the sand, slipped off her cover-up, then headed toward the water. When the warmth was up to her waist, she dived into the low waves. After she swam beyond the surf, she flipped onto her back and just floated, letting the swells lift her, then gently lower her, letting the peace that was around her envelop her.

She watched the sky over her deepen with the colors of coming twilight, and saw sea birds fly over in a V-formation toward the south. And for a moment she could remember the sound of water lapping around her ears and the cry of the sea gull.

She could forget about having to make another call to her mother soon, forget about Satch wanting her back for the next show, about her mother's constantly insisting that she see any new doctor that claimed to have a miracle cure. She could even pretend that she hadn't been looking for Sam when she came down to the beach and that she wasn't just a bit disappointed he hadn't shown up.

She stroked her hands lazily at her sides and moved her feet just enough to stay afloat as she drifted parallel to the shoreline. When she realized the sun was setting, that the sky was ablaze with rich colors that came just before dusk, she knew she'd been out here long enough. Reluctantly, she righted herself and turned, surprised to see she was well over three hundred yards from the shore. Her house looked beautiful, the colors of sunset reflecting off the glass, and she started to head for the shore.

But she took no more than two or three strokes when sudden, excruciating pain exploded in her. It was as if her leg had been caught in a vise, and the agony centered halfway between her foot and her knee. It came so quickly, making her gasp, and she knew total panic when she began to slip under the water. She flailed with her arms, trying to get her head above the surface, then she gasped for air, managing to take more than a little water into her mouth.

Acting on pure instinct, she tried to grab for her leg and the focal point of her agony, but that action snatched any remnant of control from her. The world lost the reality of up and down, and her body cartwheeled in the water, her feet changing places with her head. She churned at the water, pushed as hard as she could with her hands, but she couldn't find the surface. And she couldn't stop the saltwater that was being forced into her mouth and nose.

Sam got to the beach under Leigh's house as the sun touched the horizon, but Leigh wasn't anywhere to be seen. Then he spotted something bright on the beach near the foot of the stairs that led to the top of the bluffs, and he crossed to it. Her towel and the robe she'd worn yesterday were laid out on the sand. She was here or she'd left without her things.

Sam turned to scan the beach again, then he looked out in the water to try to spot her. At first he didn't see anything, just the rise and fall of the incoming surf. As he scanned the horizon, he thought he saw movement beyond the low breakers. Then it was gone. He jogged toward the water, then as it swirled around his bare feet, he looked to the area where he thought he'd seen something move.

Then he saw it again and knew it was Leigh, but something was horribly wrong. Her arms flailed wildly in the air, the water churning around her, then she was gone. Nothing moved.

All-encompassing fear gripped him. "Leigh!" he screamed as he stripped off his T-shirt and jeans. He tossed them behind him as he ran into the surf, then dived into the waves. He pushed through the water with as much speed as he could manage, the sound of his heart hammering in his chest keeping time to his strokes. Then he stopped and screamed her name over and over again, but he couldn't see anything but the rise and fall of the gentle swells.

"Leigh!" he screamed, his own voice echoing back to him from the walls of the cove, then he turned away from the beach area, and he saw her, not more than forty feet from him.

But a raw fear choked him. She was facedown in the water, all movement gone. He lunged in her direction, stroking fiercely toward her. "Leigh, for God's sake, don't drown," he gasped, his voice almost gone from screaming.

He got within ten feet of her, close enough to see her long hair drifting on the water, her body bobbing facedown, her arms out to her sides.

"Leigh, hold on," he called, then he was within feet of her, inches, and he reached out for her.

Chapter 6

A sudden, overwhelming calm descended on Leigh the second time she went under, and her mind became clear. All the panic was gone, and she knew all she had to do was relax, stop tensing and float until the pain began to ease. Then she could make it to the shore using just her arms to stroke through the water.

As she came up for the second time, she pulled air deeply in lungs, then, trying to ignore the pain, she let herself go. "Relax, relax," she told herself as her body naturally turned facedown in the water. With her eyes closed, she concentrated on what she would have been hearing right now—the beating of her own heart, and the rush of water all around her.

And it worked. The pain began to gradually diminish, the knot in her calf slowly easing. Cautiously, she flexed her toes on her right foot, and the action only brought a bearable tugging at the back of her leg.

She knew that in a few more seconds, she could start to go back. As she turned her face to the right to take another breath, someone was there, grabbing her by her arm. The next instant she was being jerked around, and when she screamed, her mouth filled with water. She was going under, her body tangling with another body, legs with legs, arms with arms, then she was being pulled upward. An arm crooked under her chin, jerking her to the surface, and she had no idea what was happening.

She only knew she was out of control and it terrified her. She was being dragged backward, and with her calf pain completely forgotten, she gasped in air, closed her eyes and with all her might twisted sharply to her right. She felt the hold on her falter, and taking what advantage she had, she lunged forward, away from the contact, going headfirst underwater again.

She stroked twice before she broke the surface, swiped at the water that ran over her face and into her eyes, then she blinked to clear her eyes and found herself looking right at Sam Patton.

His long hair was dark and flattened to his head, and water dripped off his lashes. Shock and confusion were clearly etched on his face. "My God, I thought you were drowning," she saw him say before he shook his head sharply and sent a spray of water from his hair everywhere.

Leigh felt the coolness mist over, and she trembled as she swirled her arms at her side to stay afloat. He'd been trying to save her life and she'd thought... She didn't even know what she'd thought. "I—I had a cramp."

"You were floating facedown," he said, and she could tell his words were touched with anger just by the way his mouth moved.

"I was trying to relax before I started to swim back to shore."

"I was screaming at you, and you didn't move."

She had been making believe she could hear rushing water and all the while this man was calling out to her. As she faced him in the water, she found herself wishing she knew what her name would sound like on his tongue. That thought only deepened her embarrassment. "I really appreciate what you did," she said quickly.

He looked from her to the shore, then back again, his eyes narrowed. "Are you swimming alone?"

"I always do." She wasn't about to explain that her evening swims were as important to her as the early-morning jogging, a time for pretending and feeling free.

"Did you ever get a cramp before?"

The cramp. She'd all but forgotten about it, and she let herself feel for a minute, testing her calf muscle by flexing her foot. There was no pain left, just tenderness and monumental embarrassment. "No, I never have."

"Can you make it back to shore on your own or do you want me to help?"

The idea of him touching her again was so disturbing that she spoke quickly. "The cramp's almost gone. I'm sure I can make it back."

He ran a hand over his face, then looked at her. "I'll swim with you to make sure there aren't any more problems."

She didn't know what else to do or say, so she turned toward the shore and set off. Using just her arms as much as possible, she went as quickly as she could, all the time watching the beach come closer and closer. Yet every atom of her being was centered on the man behind her.

And with each thought, she was reminded of the way he'd felt against her in the water, his hands on her, his legs and arms tangling with hers, and she forced herself to swim faster and faster. The sooner she put distance between herself and Sam, the better off she'd be.

Sam watched Leigh in front of him, stroking a bit awkwardly through the water, but keeping up a pace that was far from slow. And he knew how little she'd been in danger out there. And he could admit to himself how much he'd overreacted.

Overreacted? God, he could still feel the way his heart had hammered against his ribs when he'd first seen her struggling. And he could still taste the acrid fear that had been in his mouth when he'd seen her facedown, her hair a swirling halo on the blue water.

He dropped back a bit, putting about ten feet between himself and Leigh, too aware of his reactions to her and the splashes of the bright pink patches of her bikini dotting the blueness of the water.

Finally, he felt his feet brush the sandy bottom, then dug his toes in and straightened in waist-deep water. He looked ahead and saw Leigh struggling to her feet and he barely got out the words "Take it slowly," before she doubled over and tumbled headfirst into the low waves that washed onto the shore.

Sam lunged toward her, grabbing for her flailing hand, then he had a hold on her and pulled her up out of the water. Without thinking, he scooped her up. For a second he was only aware of how light she felt in his arms, of the body heat that came immediately when her skin touched his, how skimpy her bathing suit was, and the tension he could feel in her body.

"That must hurt like hell," he said as he looked down to find her eyes closed and her teeth biting so hard on her bottom lip that he was surprised she hadn't drawn blood.

Pain etched a fine line between her eyes and started a trembling in her that unnerved him. "Hold on," he said as he moved as quickly as he could to get out of the water. He strode across the warm sand to where she'd left her things, and carefully lowered her onto the towel.

Sitting on the pink terry cloth, she pulled her leg to her breasts and held tightly to her calf. Sam moved around in front of her and dropped to his haunches. "Let me help," he said, speaking to center his thoughts and take his mind off that moment when he covered her hand with his and eased it off. "Just relax. Don't tense. It only makes the muscles tighter."

He didn't look up, not about to meet the blueness of her gaze while his hands massaged her calf. He might be a good Samaritan who risked his life when she would have done just fine without his rescue attempt. But he was a man. And being this close to her, touching her and hearing her soft whimperings and keeping his touch as impersonal as possible was just about the hardest thing he'd ever had to do.

Leigh stared at Sam as his fingers closed around her calf. When he began to knead and probe the knotted muscle, she leaned back, bracing herself with her hands flat on the towel and she closed her eyes. She had wanted to get away, to put distance between the two of them, and because she'd tried to rush, he was still here, every bit as close as he'd been in the water.

His fingers gently worked her muscles, and gradually his ministrations banished the horrible pain. She exhaled, then finally opened her eyes. A mistake, she thought when she found him watching her from less than two feet away. His long hair clung to his neck and shoulders, with water trickling from it and down his bare skin, but it was his eyes that demanded all of her attention. In those dark depths framed by lashes spiked from the water, she saw such raw desire that it stunned her.

Was it an echo of her own reactions? Was he able to read what she'd been feeling at his touch? This stranger with sleek skin and a sensual curve to his lips, was robbing her of all rational thought and filling her head with fantasies that heated her skin and started a fire so deep in her soul that it threatened to consume her.

What would happen if she reached out and touched his jaw, felt the suggestion of a new beard, or brushed back the clinging strands of damp hair at his temples? Then she realized his mouth was moving, that he'd been talking to her and she had no idea what he was saying. And that answered all her questions.

Desire was transitory, and giving in to passion was a thing of the past for her. She knew that. Satch had proven that to her. And the one thing she never wanted to experience again was having the passion of a man being replaced by pity.

She made herself stay very still and covered her inability to hear with "I'm sorry. What were you saying?"

"I asked if that feels better?" he said, his fingers still on her leg but not moving.

"Much better, thank you," she managed to say.

He sank back on his heels, his eyes unfathomable now, and his hands drew away from her to rest on his thighs. Her sense of loss as the contact broke was almost overwhelmed by her sense of real relief. If he wasn't touching her, if she wasn't feeling every stroke as if it encompassed all her reality, she could think straight.

She touched her calf with the tips of her fingers and looked away from Sam. "Thanks," she said. "I appreciate your help, but I should be getting back to the house."

Before she could try to stand, Sam touched her on her knee. She jerked slightly at the new contact, then made herself look at him. "What?"

"I said, don't get up. Let your muscle relax for a few minutes before you try to walk."

She looked away from his face, to his muscular legs. Then she looked up, saw his bare chest with the clinging T of dark hair that disappeared into the low waistband, and she quickly looked upward to his face.

For a moment she could have sworn he knew just where her thoughts had tried to travel, but with the setting sun at his back, his eyes were shadowed. At least she could still see his mouth. "You moved too fast getting out of the water, so take it easy this time, all right?"

She nodded, knowing that when she walked away, she had to make it on her own. She didn't want to have to lean on him, to touch him or have him touch her again. That path would only lead to pain and hurt.

She looked away, reaching for the extra towel by her side and quickly began to dry her hair. Then she dropped the damp towel on her legs and pushed her hair back off her face. When she looked at Sam, he moved abruptly, as if he was going to touch her, but instead he reached past her and picked up her lace cover-up and shook it out.

Then he leaned forward and put it around her, his fingers skimming over her throat as he tugged the thin material over her shoulders. And this time she stared at his mouth, at the full bottom lip and the slight upward curve at the corners. When he said, "Thank heavens it's like taking a bath in that water," she saw it.

"It's always warm," she said and offered him the towel she'd used on her hair. "It's a bit damp, but you're welcome to use it."

Without taking his eyes away from hers, he reached for the terry, then roughly ran it over his head. "Thanks," he said, then tossed it back to where it had been originally. He tunneled his fingers through his damp hair, vaguely spiking the shorter strands on top, then smoothing the longer strands back.

As he sat there on his heels watching her, she tried to think of something to say, anything that could break the tension that was growing in her. "You said you're just down here for a vacation?"

"A break." He watched her intently. "Why are you down here?"

That question took her aback and she found herself hedging on the answer. "I needed a change of pace and some peace and quiet."

"Well, you certainly got that here, didn't you?"

Until you came, she wanted to say, but simply nodded.

"And you came from New York," he said.

"Yes."

"Wasn't this a shock to the system?"

She almost smiled at that. "No, a balm for the nerves."

"You're an isolationist, aren't you?" he asked with a curve to his lips.

"No, a person who's perfectly happy alone."

That sobered him. "Really?"

"Don't look so surprised. I get to do what I want, when I want and how I want."

"I've heard about people like you, but I don't know if I've actually ever met one."

"I take it you're not one of us?"

"Hell, no," he said, and she could tell he almost laughed at that. "I like people. I like being around people."

"And you don't like your own company?" she asked.

"Sure, of course I do. I'm no self-hater, but I also like the company of others." He smiled, an expression that was getting vaguely blurred by the failing light, but lost none of its impact on Leigh. "Especially pretty ladies in pink bikinis who add excitement to my life."

She knew she had to leave, if not because of his words, because the light was getting worse and soon she wouldn't be able to see what he was saying to her. "I'm feeling better. I should head back to the house."

As she moved to get up, he reached out and took her hand, standing at the same time, pulling her up with him until she was facing him on the sand. "Thanks again for your help," she said quickly, drawing her hand free of his.

But there was no escape, at least not an easy one.

Sam didn't move at first. He simply looked down at her, then ever so slowly raised both hands and gently framed her face with his heat and strength.

Leigh had heard the fantasies about the world stopping in its orbit when something incredible happened between two people, but she'd never believed it until now. Her world had ground to a stop the moment Sam touched her. And she couldn't move. She couldn't breathe.

After what seemed to be an eternity, Sam lowered his head and his lips touched hers. Leigh closed her eyes as the taste of the salt of the ocean mingled with the essence of the man. The contact was staggering to her, fierce and dazzling, drawing a cord of passion through her that started deep in her soul and spread to every atom of her body.

And it rendered her incapable of doing anything but absorbing the bombarding sensation. Heat was everywhere, his hands branding her skin, his hips against hers. Then slowly he drew back, his face no more than inches from her, his breath fanning her face with seductive warmth and the world began to move again.

And along with the resumption of reality came the need in Leigh to fall into this man's embrace and the fear that if he knew she was deaf, he'd turn and walk away. That terrified her. She knew instinctively that once she'd let herself experience what she could find with Sam, the pain of his rejection would totally devastate her. The tumultuous day she broke her engagement to Satch would seem like a walk in the park by comparison.

Out of self-preservation, she finally moved, turning away from Sam, reaching blindly for her things. Then she had them clutched to her chest and chanced one look back at him. The shadows of night were coming, but she clearly read "I'm sorry" on his lips. So was she, more than he'd ever know.

"I have to go," she said, her lips feeling vaguely swollen from the kiss. Then she turned her back on him and headed for the stairs.

Sam could taste Leigh on his lips even as she walked away from him toward the stairs that led up to her house. He could taste her and he could feel the basic response in his body to the foolish action of kissing her. If she hadn't looked up at him like that, if her lips hadn't parted, if she hadn't been wearing that bikini, and if he wasn't more lonely than he'd ever been in his life, he never would have kissed her, he reasoned.

Before he even finished that thought, he knew the magnitude of that lie. He would have wanted to kiss her if they had been in the middle of New York at noon on a Friday and she'd been dressed from head to toe in khaki.

And if she'd responded to him at all, he would have taken her right here on the sand. And that thought stunned him. Even in his worst days, he'd never been free and easy with sex. He'd never had a woman just to have a woman. Before it became fashionable to be concerned about your partner, he'd been cautious. Physical love had become synonymous with commitment to him around the time he'd gotten over being a "star," but his need to commit to one person had never fully materialized. That's what stunned him so much. The idea of commitment with a woman like Leigh wasn't unfathomable to him at all.

And she was walking away, offended by his actions, or scared or angry. He didn't know and he had to. "Leigh," he called as she neared the stairs. But she didn't stop. "Leigh," he called again as she touched the handrail.

She hesitated, then turned back to him. "We need to talk," he called. "Tomorrow. I'll come by around nine. All right?"

Leigh saw Sam in the gathering dusk, the colors of twilight smearing the sky behind him. Regret ate at her. Yet she knew that stopping this now was the right thing to do. She didn't want to offend him, or make an enemy, but she couldn't risk seeing him again. With a lift of her hand, she waved goodbye to him, then turned and headed up the stairs.

Sam saw her wave, letting relief wash over him. They'd talk. He'd tell her who he was, why he was down here, and how much her being close by meant to him. He'd only met her a few days ago, yet she seemed a part of his world. The woman with eyes that looked like "pools of midnight."

The moment the woman went through the double glass doors into the reception area of the firm, she knew something was wrong. No one was at the main desk and she could hear voices coming from down the hall that led to the conference room. There were no meetings planned for today—at least she hadn't been told about any. But then again, no one knew she'd left two hours ago to go to the hall of records.

She hurried past the desk and went back toward her office that was just two doors away from the conference room. As she went down the wide corridor, she saw the door to the conference room ajar and she could see several people sitting around the polished table. Ted Bigelow was directly opposite the door, leaning forward talking, and a slender man in a well-tailored brown suit stood behind him, his back to the door.

She stopped with her hand on the knob of her office door, but she didn't go inside. Instead she stood there, watching, listening. Then two men hurried out of the room, heading toward her, but they passed without even looking at her.

She was used to being ignored. People in general didn't usually notice her. Men never did. Not until Boone.

She hugged her arms around herself, narrowing her eyes as she focused on Ted Bigelow in the other room. And she remembered being in that very room the first time she'd ever seen Boone. He'd walked through the door, dressed all in black leather and wearing his white hat, looking for all the world like a hero in a fairy tale. She'd just been leaving to go to the fax room, and she'd run right into him.

She could still remember every small detail of that day. The smell of leather, the way he caught her by her arms, keeping her from falling backward, the smile on his face when he'd looked down at her, and the fact that in that moment, he'd rescued her from a life of muddy grays and off-whites, and taken her into a world of color and emotion.

And he'd held her by both arms to steady her. "Are you all right?" he'd asked, that gravel-edged voice low and seductive in her ears. Oh, he'd said the right things, polite things, but she'd seen the desire in his eyes, the parting of his lips. If the men in the room hadn't all gathered around, more worried about damaging a big client than her being damaged, she knew he would have kissed her right then.

She held tightly to herself, watching Ted Bigelow waving his hand as he spoke to someone out of her sight. How she hated all of them for coming between herself and Boone. They'd filled his head with lies. That's why he hadn't done what she asked. She hated them almost as much as she loved Boone. Almost as much as she had loved Ray when she worked for him.

No, that wasn't right. Ray was part of the dreams. He hadn't been real, but Boone was very real. And she loved him, really loved him. And she wanted to be with him forever. Death was permanent, something no one could ever alter. And Boone would be with her forever.

Her thoughts ground to a halt when the slender man behind Ted Bigelow turned and looked out the door at her. She'd seen that look before. Assessing and cutting. She held her breath and looked away before there was eye contact, deciding against going into her office.

She clutched her purse to her middle and hurried back the way she came. The man in the brown suit was a cop. Probably the detective they'd written about in the paper. And there would be more cops coming around. She didn't want any contact with them, ever again. She'd had her fill of them.

Smug men who took her away and put her in that hospital in Atlanta, put her in a room where she couldn't see the sky or breathe fresh air. Where the drugs made her calm and mindless. She'd never let them put her back in one of those places again.

She went through the doors into the hall and hurried to the elevators. She never should have come back here. She had the copies of the paperwork she'd found at the Hall of

Records that had Boone's address in Malibu, and she had everything else she needed.

She pushed the Down button and stared at the dull beige doors. It would take her an hour to drive to Malibu in the afternoon traffic. And in less than two hours, this could all be over. She held her purse tightly, feeling the hard shapes of the pill bottle and the small gun she'd managed to buy yesterday. Two hours. It seemed like an eternity.

Sam never expected to be able to sleep that night, not with all the images of Leigh bombarding him, the memories of the feel of her, the taste of her. But he'd barely lain down in the large bed when he slipped into slumber. He slept for hours, not stirring until clear sunlight was pouring into the room.

He lay very still, absorbing a sense of anticipation that was filling him. Then he sat up, stretched his arms over his head, and as he leaned back against the headboard, he had to admit that coming here hadn't been as bad an idea as he'd thought at first. Not when a woman like Leigh was close by. A woman who excited him, fascinated him, confused him and tasted like honey in seawater.

"Damned poetic," he muttered as he got out of bed and walked naked to the open French doors. He looked outside, down at the beach, half hoping that Leigh would be running along the sand. A glimpse of her first thing in the morning was almost a physical longing in him now. And that brought other ideas of waking up next to her, turning to face her, touching her.

With an expletive, he turned and headed for the bathroom and a shower. He was acting like some teenager with his hormones running rampant. As he stepped under the cool water, it controlled the outward signs of how thoughts of Leigh affected him, but it didn't stop the images that burned in his mind.

Leigh had the nightmare that night for the first time since she'd been on the island. But this time it altered, shifting from the gallery to a busy street, and from Satch to Sam. It was Sam coming toward her, his eyes filled with pity and sadness. And it broke her heart.

She awoke with a raging headache, a stomach that felt as if it had been tied into knots and the knowledge that if she tried to jog, her head would fall off. She took a couple of aspirins, stayed in a warm bath for a long while, and by the time she got dressed in white shorts, a blue halter top and slipped on thong sandals, she felt marginally human.

She didn't have to look too far for the reason the nightmare had come back—Sam Patton and the way he'd kissed her on the beach. He'd left her feeling frustrated, restless, on edge and vulnerable. And she knew she had to forget all about it. She had to stay out of his way until he left the island, and then she could get back her sanity and the life she'd chosen for herself. And nights filled with peace and sleep.

She walked through the house, unlocked the front door so Johngood could get in when he came later, then went into the studio area. As soon as she inhaled the scent of oil paint and turpentine, she felt centered and focused. Everything else fell by the wayside, and she took the canvas she'd been working on off the easel. With a newly primed canvas in its place, she reached for the wooden box that held her oil paints.

When Sam got to the top of the stairs and saw Leigh's house up close, he was even more impressed by it. It seemed to be hanging out into space, a natural extension of the land it was built on. The deck was empty and he couldn't see any signs of life.

Slowly he walked across the high sea grass, along the side of the house and out onto a wide graveled parking area. He saw steps that led up to the full-length porch and the entry. He crossed the gravel to the steps, then went up to the door. When he rapped on the wood, the door silently swung back.

"Leigh?" he called, hesitating by the partially opened door. "Leigh, it's Sam. Are you there?"

When he didn't get an answer, he pushed the door farther open. As it softly thudded against a wall, he saw into Leigh's home. And, oddly, it reminded him of her. It seemed to be all light and airiness, with delicate color, clean wicker furnishings and slowly moving ceiling fans.

"Leigh?" he called again as he stepped into the cool silence of the house. "It's me, Sam."

As he inhaled, he caught a hint of the scent that he knew now had clung to Leigh, a light flowery scent of fresh air and sunlight touched by summer blossoms. He took another step inside, but he couldn't see anyone.

Then he heard a sound, something dropping, a faint tinny clink, and he went farther into the huge room. He saw double doors across the room to his left, doors that stood open. As he started toward them, he could see a couple of paintings propped against the far wall, soft, evocative seascapes with light flooded over them. He caught the pungency of paint and thinner as he went closer, then heard another noise.

"Leigh?" he called.

When he got to the door, he reached out to touch the cool wood of the frame, and saw Leigh.

She had her back to him, and she stood in front of a huge easel that held a canvas washed with a multitude of shades of blue. A floor-to-ceiling bank of windows that overlooked the ocean let sun stream in to streak her loose hair with gold and make the sleek smoothness of her skin exposed by very short shorts and a skimpy halter top almost glow. And she had no idea he was here.

Sam felt like a voyeur, knowing he should back out and call again to warn her. But he couldn't take his eyes off her. She was very still, then abruptly made a sweeping stroke across the canvas with the brush in her hand. A vein of deeper blue streaked across the canvas, like lightning in a summer's sky.

"That's beautiful," he finally said, and as he took a step into the room, his foot kicked a small can that lay on the floor, sending it flying. It clattered against the window, then ricocheted sideways, coming to rest just behind Leigh's bare feet.

Sam expected her to jump, to scream, shocked by the sharp clattering noise that was fading into nothingness, but she didn't react at all. She kept studying the canvas in front of her, totally absorbed in her work, as if she hadn't heard a thing.

Sam stared at Leigh. She was beautiful. She was a woman who had touched him in some strong and wonderful way right from the very first time he'd seen her. She was bright and funny and she turned his world on end.

She very carefully reached down, swirled her brush on the palette snapped to a side table by the easel, then straightened to touch the brush to the canvas and sweep a streak of pale yellow under the blue.

"Leigh?" he said.

Again, she didn't react, and the truth came to him so suddenly and so clearly that it hit him like a fist in the stomach. He pushed his hand in his pocket, felt the pearl clip and closed his hand so tightly around it that it bit into his palm.

He had to try twice to say "Leigh, can you hear me?"

Nothing.

Shock made his stomach churn, and Sam closed his eyes to block out her image as a single word formed inside him, a word that seemed as obscene as any four-letter curse.

Deaf.

Leigh Buchanan, the woman with eyes like "pools of midnight," who made him dream dreams and indulge in fantasies, was deaf. And it all made horrible sense to him now.

She ran away from him on the beach because she never heard him. She had watched him intently not out of intense interest, but so she could read his lips. She'd floated in the water and never heard him calling to her. She didn't even know he was less than five feet from her now, because she had never heard him say he'd come to see her today at nine, and she never heard the sound of the metal can hitting the window.

Leigh Buchanan was deaf.

Chapter 7

Sam inhaled, then slowly opened his eyes. And when he saw Leigh still by the easel, his shock began to change into a deep rage that he'd never experienced before. God, life wasn't fair. Not to her, and not to him. And in that moment he realized the magnitude of the dreams and fantasies that she'd brought into his life. Dreams and fantasies that were as empty as he felt right now.

All he could think of was getting outside without her ever knowing he'd come inside. He didn't want to look into those deep blue eyes, to know that the woman he'd been enthralled by couldn't hear his voice, that she couldn't hear anything. She didn't know who he was because she couldn't hear music . . . she couldn't hear *his* music.

He spun away from her to leave, to put as much distance as he could between himself and this nightmare.

As Leigh put her brush back in the holder, she felt the vibration of footsteps on the floor. She glanced at the small clock on the table by the easel—nine-fifteen. Why was

Johngood back here now? She turned as she called out, "Johngood? What are you . . . ?"

But her voice died when she saw Sam just beyond the studio door in the great room. Dressed in cutoff jeans, a red tank top and scuffed running shoes, he was turning slowly to look at her. Every feature of the man seemed imprinted in her mind at that moment. She could see the dampness in his hair from a recent shower or swim, the way his eyes narrowed as he frowned slightly, and the strength of his shoulders and arms. And she wasn't at all prepared for the pleasure at seeing him that almost immediately pushed aside the surprise to find him in her home.

"I thought you were . . ." She touched her tongue in her lips. "I'm sorry. I didn't hear you come in. I left the door open for Johngood. He was coming back later, and I didn't want him to give me a lecture about how unnecessary it was to keep the doors locked on the island." When Sam didn't say anything, she blurted out, "Why are you here?"

He moved toward her as he took something out of his pocket and held it out to her. "I found this . . . again," he said.

She went forward, meeting Sam at the doors to the studio, and when she got within a few feet of him, she could smell the fresh air, the soapiness and that subtle maleness that clung to him. Then she looked down at his hand and saw her pearl clip held between his thumb and forefinger.

"Where did you find it this time?" she asked as she looked back up at him.

"On the beach. You must have dropped it again," he said, his enunciation slow and careful.

Leigh stared at him and hoped that she was imagining things, that he wasn't speaking carefully and clearly because he was afraid she couldn't read his lips. Then she looked into his eyes, and her heart lurched sickeningly in her chest.

God help her, but he was looking at her with pity. She felt stunned and had to literally make herself take the clip out of his hand, being very careful not to make any skin-to-skin contact. She pulled her hand back, pushing it behind her and closed her hand around the metal and pearls. The gripping ridges cut into the palm of her hand, but she didn't care. "Thank you," she managed.

This was worse than she'd even imagined it would be. Her pain was sharp and focused, and anything she'd ever felt before paled in its wake. There was no desire in his eyes, no teasing and no flirting. And she felt a grief welling up in her for what had briefly flashed through her life, then had disappeared so completely. The same look in Satch's eyes had hurt her badly, but the look in Sam's brown eyes almost killed her.

"You . . . you didn't have to make a special trip to bring back the clip," she managed to say.

He pushed both hands into the pockets of his cutoffs. "I actually came to make sure you were all right after what happened yesterday afternoon. I told you I was coming around nine to check on you, to talk."

She felt cold all over, her stomach tightening horribly with each word Sam spoke to her, each word pronounced slowly and with great care. She supposed that he was talking louder, too, in some vain hope he could make her hear him if he yelled. "I'm sorry. I didn't . . ." She touched her tongue to her cold lips. Just say it, she told herself. Say that all you saw in the twilight was him looking at you across the beach, his hand lifted. "I didn't hear you."

"I know," he said, and the simplicity of the statement killed any lingering hope that she'd been wrong.

"You don't have to do that," she said.

He lifted one eyebrow. "Do what?"

"Speak like that. I don't have any trouble reading lips." She couldn't help the tension she knew must edge her voice. "I can understand what you're saying if you just speak normally."

He looked as uncomfortable as she felt, rocking forward and back on the balls of his feet. "I'm sorry. I never . . . I won't do that again."

There's a lot you won't do again, she thought with regret, having to make herself keep eye contact with him. "I appreciate you bringing the clip back, and I'm fine. The cramp's gone, and I'm none the worse for wear."

His eyes flicked over her, their dark depths neutral now, guarded and unreadable. The life was gone. "Good. Now, I should be going so you can get back to work."

She could feel the urgency in him to leave as clearly as she felt the clip she still held in a death grip behind her back. "Thanks for coming," she said, brushing past him to go to the door. For that instant, she felt overwhelmed by the presence of the man, then she had distance and was reaching out to grip the doorknob with her free hand.

As she turned, Sam was right behind her, so close that she could see a pulse beating in the hollow of his throat. The urge to press her finger to that frantic beat, to feel it echo her own rapid pulse, flooded over her, playing havoc with her breathing, then Sam slipped past her without making any contact.

She watched him go onto the porch, hesitate, then without looking back, he walked away. It shouldn't have felt as if she was losing part of her own soul to see him go. Not when she barely knew him, but that didn't stop her from feeling as if she was being swallowed up in an aloneness that settled somewhere behind her heart.

Quickly she closed the door, leaned back against it and closed her eyes. Slowly she slipped down until she was sitting on the cool wooden floor, then she pulled her legs to her chest, wrapped her arms tightly around them and hit her knees with her fist that held the clip.

"Damn it," she muttered, "Damn it, damn it, damn it!" She lifted her hand and threw the clip as hard as she could across the room, watched it hit the wicker back of the couch, bounce in the air and plummet to the floor.

As she stared blindly at the piece of metal with inlaid pearls, it began to blur and her eyes burned and ached. She swiped at her eyes, shocked and angered by the moisture clinging to her lashes and cheeks.

When she'd first found out she was deaf she hadn't cried. When she'd realized it was permanent, she hadn't cried. When she'd broken up with Satch, when she knew she had to leave everyone and be alone, she hadn't cried.

Yet now, because a man she hardly knew had stopped looking at her like a woman and regarded her as something to be pitied, she was crying. She pressed her forehead to her knees and the tears turned to sobs. And once she started, she couldn't stop.

Six hours later, Sam still didn't understand completely why he'd walked away from Leigh. As the sun began to sweep toward the west, he sat on the deck, his chair tipped back, his bare feet resting on the safety rail, and he tried to make sense out of his reaction to Leigh's deafness.

The best he could come up with was the passions Leigh fired in him were strong and encompassing. Just the way his passion for his music had always been. Different, yet almost equal in intensity. Maybe his ego was larger than he thought. And the idea of finding a woman who was damned near perfect, only to find out she would never know the passion of his work, had been too much for him.

He didn't know, but he was coming precariously close to hating himself when the cordless phone by him rang. He quickly reached for it, thankful for a distraction, anything to block the images of Leigh that drifted in and out of his mind at will.

"Yes?" he said as he pressed the phone to his ear.

"Ah, so it's the old Sam again," he heard Ted say over the line. "You're not out swimming or sunning or wandering around the island."

"I'm taking it easy," he murmured as he settled in the chair and rested his head on the back. He stared up at the sky where seabirds drifted in lazy circles on an errant breeze, and he wished he could forget the look on Leigh's face when she realized he knew she was deaf. "I hope you're calling with good news. I need some."

"Define good news."

That I was wrong about Leigh being deaf, that it was all an illusion, an aberration, a horrible cosmic joke. He closed his eyes tightly and rubbed his left temple with the tips of his fingers. "You calling to say, 'Sam, this is all over. The weirdo is behind bars, and you can come back to the real world.' That would be good news."

"Then I don't have good news."

His hand dropped to his thigh. "What's happening, Ted?"

"Another letter."

"And?"

"It's the same as the last one, a lot of ranting and raving, talking about being with you for eternity, and she says she knows you're hiding, but she's going to find you, and you'll die together."

"What's Lopez doing about it?"

"Checking out everything and everyone who could have had even passing personal contact with you over the past three months and could have had access to the theater the night of the concert."

"That'll take him forever."

"It might, but it looks as if the security system in the Malibu house will be in in a week or so. And meanwhile, you're well out of this, and even if you're bored to tears down there, you're safe."

Sam closed his eyes, and wondered just how "safe" he was. He felt as if he'd been hit with a battering ram this morning and the emotions hadn't ebbed or mellowed. They'd only intensified.

"Oh, before I forget," Ted said, "I found out what you wanted me to about that artist, Leigh Buchanan."

Sam felt his whole being tense at the mere mention of her name. "What?"

"I talked to the owner of the Gray Gallery and he's very high on her work. He's got some new pieces that he calls 'very remarkable,' and he'll part with them for a very stiff price."

"Did he tell you anything about the artist?"

"He sold her first work about three years ago. She's had two shows since then, one two and a half years ago, and one about a year later. He's working on another show for her, but for now, he's hanging her pieces individually. He says that she's gifted, very special."

That jarred Sam and he sat forward, his hand gripping the telephone receiver so tight that it tingled. That's exactly what he'd thought at the first. Leigh was special.

"Do you want me to look into purchasing some of her work as an investment?" Ted asked.

"Maybe. I'll let you know when I get back."

"All right. You can take it down there for another week, can't you?"

A week, then he'd leave here and go back to his real life. He looked out at the ocean far below the house and realized this place was all an aberration, a time out of time. It had nothing to do with his real life. He wasn't Boone Patton down here, just Sam to a woman who had touched him in the most basic way.

God, he felt fragmented and confused.

"Sam? Are you still there?" Ted asked.

"Yeah, I'm still here," he muttered. "I'm not going anywhere."

"All right, I'll be in touch as soon as we know anything," Ted said, and hung up.

Sam slowly replaced the phone. For so much of his life he'd known clearly what he was going to do, where he was going and what he wanted out of his life, but now, down here, the lines had blurred and shifted. Still, he knew for certain that Leigh *was* special. And with that thought came another, clearly and surely. He wanted to spend what time he had down here with her. No Boone Patton, no music, just him and Leigh.

Then he remembered the look on her face as he was leaving, that closed, protected look that had killed the life he'd seen in her eyes until that moment. His stomach sank. He'd spend time with her *if* she even wanted to have anything to do with him. That thought brought him to his feet and he went inside to shower and change before he headed back to Leigh's.

By the time Johngood came in the afternoon, Leigh felt as if her nerves were raw. She had tried to work again, but nothing came, and Johngood frowned at her as he walked into the studio.

"What's wrong?" he asked, his floral shirt as bright as the sun that was beginning to dip toward the west.

She dropped her brush in the container and turned her back on the canvas that seemed to be taunting her with its emptiness. "Did you have a profitable day?" she asked, avoiding his question completely.

He smiled at her as he came into the studio and stopped by her easel to face her. "Very profitable." He glanced at the canvas, then back at her. "Better than yours, I see."

She shrugged and rubbed her arms. "Some days it just doesn't work. Today's one of them."

He held out two envelopes. "Maybe these will make you feel better."

She took the mail from him and walked into the great room before she glanced at the return addresses, both from New York, one from her parents, one from Satch. "I doubt it," she said, tossing them on the couch.

She turned and Johngood was close behind her, stooping to pick up the clip that she'd thrown earlier. He looked at it, then held it out to her. "You dropped this."

After she took it and pushed it in the pocket of her shorts, she looked at him. "Thanks for bringing my mail."

"Do you have any mail for me to take back?"

"No." She glanced outside at a gentle sky and at potted ferns on the deck rippling from a soft breeze. And she knew that she needed to lose herself, to feel the breeze on her skin and pretend that she could hear the sounds of the ocean and the cry of the seabirds.

Looking back at Johngood, she said, "I'm going jogging. If you're gone before I get back, will you be here tomorrow?"

"Bright and early, and the rail should be finished then. Is there anything else you'll be needing me to do around here?"

She almost said no, but stopped when she knew what she needed him to do, and she made herself say it. "I've been thinking that I'd like to have some way of knowing when someone comes to the door. Do you think you could figure out something for me?"

He nodded. "That's a good idea. Let me think about it, and we can work it out tomorrow."

"Good," Leigh said, knowing that she never wanted to be surprised by someone in her house again. "I'll see you later," she said as she headed for the door.

She stepped outside and crossed the gravel to head for the stairs and the beach. At the bottom of the steps, she took off her sandals and hesitated. Her usual route for jogging went past Sam's place, but to change the route would mean she wouldn't be back before dark. Then she remembered the way Sam had looked at her and how quickly he left, and she knew it wouldn't make any difference to him if she went past his house or not. He wouldn't make any contact.

Skimming her hair back off her face and securing it with the clip from her pocket, she set out.

Sam stepped out on the deck, his mind racing with what he was going to say to Leigh, and as if his thoughts had conjured up a vision, he saw her on the beach. With the sun low in the sky, her shadow stretched behind her on the sand as she glided along at an easy pace. Sam felt mesmerized by the sight. And strangely, he felt that instant physical awareness, yet it was overshadowed by something that he barely understood. He wished he could protect her, that he had it in his power to make her world perfect again, then he realized that she was nearly out of sight.

Quickly he headed down to the beach, but by the time he stepped onto the warm sand, Leigh was nowhere to be seen. Then he realized she'd be back. She had to retrace her steps to get to her house. Sam moved to the bluffs, sank down on the sand and leaned against the rough face of the rock to wait for Leigh.

Leigh stopped on the beach when she was well past Sam's place and stared out at the water. Digging at the warm sand with her toes, she hugged her arms around herself and thought of the moment she'd turned and seen Sam behind her in the house. No matter how hard she tried, her game wouldn't work for her. She never forgot that she was alone, that she couldn't hear the noises around her, and she had no energy to keep going.

And for the first time since she'd come here, she felt as if she was just as vulnerable as she'd been in New York.

No, that wasn't right. Sam would be gone soon, and she'd keep her distance from anyone who came to that house. She'd learned her lesson about letting anyone too close, and she wouldn't forget it.

With a sigh, she turned and started back at a slow jog. As she rounded the extended bluff that delineated the beginning of the beach under Sam's house, she glanced cautiously toward the top and his house. She could see a few lights on, but she couldn't see anyone moving around. Looking away, she kept going, picking up her pace. Then she looked ahead and thought she saw blurred movement on the beach in the dusky shadows of the bluffs.

She stopped dead when she saw Sam materialize from the shadows. No, she wanted to rage, this wasn't fair. She couldn't take any more of what had happened this morning. The tears were long gone, but the pain was still so fresh that she felt as if she could press her hand to her middle and literally feel it behind her breastbone.

But Sam was there, coming toward her, his features gentled by twilight, and he was erasing the distance between them, slowly and surely. She saw the evening breeze ruffle his long hair, his tank top pale against his tan, and his jeans defining his narrow hips.

Every nerve in her body felt raw, and she held her breath as he got within three feet of her and stopped. He hooked his thumbs in the pockets of his jeans and just looked at her.

Finally, when she thought she would scream from the waiting, she saw him say, "Hi. I need to talk to you."

Leigh had to swallow to ease the tightness in her throat before she could speak. "What about?"

"I need to explain about what happened at your house."

"Explain what?" she asked, not wanting to have him put into words what she already knew.

He shifted from foot to foot, as uneasy with this as Leigh, but he didn't back down. He looked right at her. "First, I'm sorry for just walking into your home that way. But the door was open, and when I called for you and you didn't answer, I—"

She didn't want or need this, and all she could think of was putting as much distance between herself and Sam and his pity as she could. "I understand," she murmured and tried to walk around Sam, but he took a single step that put him directly in front of her again. She had to look at him.

"Let me finish," she saw him say.

She closed her eyes for a fleeting moment, then looked back at Sam. "You don't need to do this."

"Yes, I do. What I most regret is the way I acted."

Her throat tightened, but she managed to say, "You didn't do anything wrong. Most people are . . . uncomfortable with a disability."

"It wasn't that. I was just . . . surprised. I never . . . so I didn't . . . you should . . . and I didn't know."

The light was failing and it made it harder and harder for Leigh to see what Sam was saying. She was losing words, scrambling what he was saying. Putting up both hands, she shook her head. "Please, forget it."

"That's just it. I can't."

She hated having to stare at him so hard to see what he was saying, and the urge to run was suffocating her. "Please, I—"

He was talking and she couldn't make it out, and she felt fire in her cheeks. "I—I didn't understand all of that."

Sam moved a bit closer, bringing the mingled scents that seemed uniquely his own, and Leigh braced herself, literally holding her breath as she made herself focus on his lips. "It's the light, isn't it?" he asked.

She nodded without speaking.

Suddenly rain was falling, touching her shoulders and arms, and Leigh looked up, realizing that clouds had come in as the sun left. One of the island's crazy rainstorms was here. She looked back at Sam, saw him say, "Rain," and look surprised.

Suddenly the scattering of soft drops was gone, and the heavens opened. Rain came in a torrent that blocked out any remnants of light. The showers that Leigh had experienced on the island up to now had been gentle misting. This torrential downpour was something she'd never seen here. Sam was saying something she couldn't understand, then he reached out to take her by the hand and pull her with him toward the stairs in the bluff.

He motioned upward with his thumb, rain flattening his hair and soaking his clothes to mold them to his body. It wasn't fair that even in the middle of the storm, Sam Patton was disturbing her, and when he moved aside to let her go first, she went past him, making sure they didn't touch. Grabbing the rough wooden railing, she started upward.

At the top, she turned, saw Sam right behind her, and before she could move, he had her by the hand again. With his fingers laced in hers, he started out and she found herself running through the rain with him, the sea grass whipping around her bare ankles, rain streaming down her face. And for a tiny space in time, she felt the way she had when she was a child, playing in a sudden shower at the family summer house in Maine, tasting the rain on her lips as she lifted her face to the sky, feeling free and invincible.

Then they were at Sam's house, dashing up the stairs onto a wraparound veranda, and he let her go. And the feeling was gone. She was far from invincible now. He swiped at his face, then reached for the knob and pushed the door open. With a sweep of one hand, he motioned her inside.

Leigh stepped into dim coolness, then lights flashed on, flooding a huge central room in front of her, and she stood on the softness of an area rug. There was some noise that she could feel the vibrations of in the air and she glanced at a massive entertainment unit on the far wall, saw red lights on a stereo system, and knew that it had to be turned awfully loud for her to feel it in the air.

She looked down at the white rug and saw the water dripping off her to puddle around her feet, which were stained by the sea grass. "Oh, no," she murmured, then turned to go back out onto the porch and almost ran into Sam.

She pointed to the rug. "I'm making an awful mess," she said.

He looked down at her feet, then at his own, which were as green as hers. "We both are," he said as he looked up. Motioning to his right, he told her, "The bedroom's in there. There's a robe on the back of the bathroom door and plenty of towels. Get out of those wet clothes, and I'll put them in the dryer for you."

When she'd left the house to jog, she didn't think she'd ever see Sam again. Now she was here in his home, and he was acting as if everything was all right. Water trickled off her hair, down her back and shoulders and between her breasts, and she was suddenly cold.

"You need to dry off," Sam was saying.

Leigh nodded. "I won't be very long," she said and hurried toward the open bedroom door.

She went into the bedroom, a wide space with a wall of glass and French doors that opened onto a deck on the ocean side. But she didn't look at the glass streaked with rain. All she was aware of was the bed, a massive four-poster, fashioned out of bleached wood, and with linen that looked as if it had been churned up by a tornado. Pillows were pushed against the headboard, sheets were spilling onto the floor and clothes had been discarded on a chair to one side.

Leigh looked away from it quickly, saw the open door to the bathroom and hurried in. She was stopped by the sight of herself in the mirrors that covered every surface that wasn't lined with ceramic tile. She looked like a drowned rat. No makeup, and the clip was gone again, this time—she bet—for good. And her hair was free, dripping rain, yet retaining that maddening propensity to form a riot of ringlets around her face and shoulders. Her clothes were no more a cover than wet paper would have been.

She closed the door, stripped off her clothes and took a white terry-cloth robe off the peg on the door and slipped it on. After toweling her hair, she wrapped the towel around her head turban-style, then looked down at her feet. Green feet. She grimaced, then crossed to the sunken tub, stepped down in it, turned on the water and sitting on the side of the tub, she held her feet under the water.

With the help of soap and a washcloth, she managed to finally get the grass stains off her feet. After drying, she crossed to pick up her wet clothes, then headed out to the main room.

She stopped in the door when she saw Sam on his hands and knees rubbing at the rug by the door with a sponge. He was wearing only brief white shorts, and she could see his back, the way the muscles rippled as he scrubbed at the nap of the rug. His feet had been cleansed of the grass stains, and whatever he'd been playing on the stereo was either off or turned down to a reasonable level.

She went farther into the room. "Is it coming out?" she asked.

He turned and looked up at her. "No problem." With one last swipe with the sponge, he sat back on his heels as she came to stand over him. "See, no permanent damage."

The spots were gone, and only circles of dampness were left. "I haven't run through grass for years. I forgot about the way it stains."

Sam stood and Leigh found herself looking at his bare chest, uncomfortably aware of the fact that she had nothing on under the robe. Then she thought about his reaction to her deafness. And with an oddly sinking feeling, she knew that she didn't have to worry about what she wore. The passion was gone. Awkwardly she held out her shorts and halter top. "You've got a dryer?"

"Sure do." He took the damp clothes, then asked her, "Have you eaten dinner?"

She shook her head. "No, but . . . ?"

"Neither have I. I've got all the makings for spaghetti. Why don't I whip up some food while your clothes dry?"

He looked past her at the windows. "If this rain keeps up, I can drive you home afterward."

He was being nice, probably feeling guilty about the way he'd acted earlier, and she knew it. It made her feel sad, but she couldn't change anything. Not any more than she could change the weather that had driven her into his house. And she really *was* hungry for the first time in a long while. "I don't want you to go to any trouble."

"I've got to eat, and I'd like the company." He smiled at her, giving him an unfair advantage in the persuasion department. "How about it?"

She hesitated, then nodded. "I think you've got a captive audience."

He crossed to cupboards by the stereo system and when he finally turned, he had two glasses in his hand. "Sit down, relax and I'll get going on dinner," he said as he came back to where she stood. He offered her a glass of white wine. "It won't take me very long."

She took the goblet, feeling the coolness of the glass. "You've rescued me again," she murmured.

He studied her from under thick lashes. "That's a habit I can live with," he said, and with a gentle touch of his finger on her chin, he turned and headed for the kitchen.

Leigh stared after him, uncertain if it was wishful thinking or a trick of the light, but she could have sworn that just before he'd turned away, she'd seen a flicker of desire in his eyes.

She closed her eyes for a moment. "Don't fool yourself," she told herself. She opened her eyes and stared at the rain beating against the windows, then took a drink of her wine.

Chapter 8

The woman had found Boone's Malibu house easily enough the day before, but there had been security men all over. After watching for several hours from a distance, she'd left, needing time to figure out how to get inside and get to him.

Now she was back, the sun was beginning to set, and she sat in her car down the road, partially hidden by a clump of scrubby oaks. She watched the main gate as workmen left, an electric contractor's truck drove off, and finally, everything was still. Nothing moved.

That's when she got out of her car, found a broken spot in a wire and wood rail fence and headed for the house that sat on a high knoll. She moved in a daze, over the property, getting into the house through a window left open to clear the house of the odor of fresh paint, and the next thing she knew, she was in Boone's bedroom.

She moved around the large room that was just beginning to be touched by the shadows of evening and felt a burning rage. Boone wasn't here; no one had lived here for a long time. And she felt lost. She didn't know what to do, where to go.

She looked around the room and began to move, touching, feeling, then she opened the walk-in closet door and stepped into the large area. Clothes were here, some hung up, some still in boxes. And she reached out, touched leather and silk, denim and suede. Boone's clothes. Things that had touched his body.

She saw a black leather aviator jacket, reached for it, tugging it off the hanger and pulled it to her. She buried her face in the fur collar, inhaling the scent that clung to it, then slipped it on. She pulled it tightly around her and went into the bedroom.

She crossed to the stripped bed and fell back on it, staring at the ceiling. Then a horrible, sickening thought came to her. Had Boone lain here with a woman? Had he held her and made love to her? She sat upright, pushing herself off the bed as if she'd been burned. She felt sick, her stomach spasming.

God, it hurt. She felt as if she were going to explode. Ripping the jacket off, she threw it on the floor, then saw a screwdriver someone had dropped there and reached for it. With a primal scream, she lunged forward, ripping and destroying everything offensive in the room.

Finally exhausted, she collapsed in the middle of the feathers of split pillows, the slashed linen, the destroyed clothes and the gutted mattress. And as the shadows gathered, she began to rock back and forth.

Whoever was hiding Boone would make a mistake. One mistake and she'd find him. With that sure knowledge, she stood, stepped over the debris and went into the connecting bathroom. She hit the mirror with a wrench that had been used to work on the plumbing, and she shattered it.

She took the wilted rosebud out of her pocket and tucked it behind a piece of the mirror. Then she took out the tube of lipstick and began to draw it over the shattered surface.

Sam looked across the coffee table in the living room where he'd laid out their dinner and saw Leigh, sitting cross-legged, finishing the last of her spaghetti. She'd eaten everything, including the French rolls and the fruit slices. As she sat back against the seat of the couch with a sigh and pushed her wildly curling hair back from her face, Sam waited for her to look at him, then smiled.

"You were hungry."

She nodded. "And you're a terrific cook. Where did you learn to make such good food?"

"I'm from a large family, and when you're one of seven, you learn to do a lot of things."

"Seven children?"

"All boys. My father said he should have gone for nine, then he'd have a baseball team." Sam pushed his plate back. "You said you were an only child, didn't you?"

"Yes. My parents wanted more children, but they couldn't." She studied him for a minute. "You know, you never told me why you're down here?"

"I thought we'd settled that I was taking a break."

"What from?"

"My life," he said, that life very distant from him at this point in time.

"What kind of life is that?"

He watched her, that inquisitive look in her dark blue eyes, and he knew now was his chance to tell her who he really was. Maybe if he told her, she'd understand more clearly why he'd reacted the way he had to her deafness. "It's complicated," he said.

She watched him intently, and he found he liked the way her eyes trailed to his lips, then to his eyes, then back to his lips. "Everyone's life is complicated," she said.

He spoke without thinking, without measuring his words or their impact on Leigh. "I bet yours is."

He watched her mouth tighten and the way her eyes narrowed, as if she didn't want to look directly at the complications in her life. "I—I don't think about it."

"Leigh? On the beach earlier, I said we needed to talk. I meant it."

"Isn't that what we're doing?"

"Technically, yes. But it's not what I had in mind."

She looked away from him, fiddling with her plate, stacking her silverware on it. And Sam waited until she finally looked back at him to say, "I don't know anything about you, not really, and I want to."

She looked guarded. "What do you want to know?"

How could he ask her the most important things? The words weren't there. There was no way he could come right out and ask her about her deafness. He shook his head and pushed his plate farther back, then pressed his fingertip to the edge of the table. "I don't know."

She got to her feet and bent down to pick up her plate and empty wineglass, as if she was going to take them out to the kitchen, but she didn't. She stood very still for a long moment, her eyes meeting Sam's, then slowly she put the dishes back on the table. "Why don't you just ask me what you're thinking," she said as she hugged her arms around her breasts. "Then I can go home."

He sat there and looked up at her, wishing he knew the words to form the questions, words that wouldn't hurt her, and words that would take that shuttered look out of her eyes. She was protecting herself by taking the offensive, yet he knew the pain was there. Just as it had been this morning when he'd walked away from her. And he'd been a damn fool.

"Sit down," he said.

She hesitated, then sank down on the couch. She sat on the edge of the cushions and kept her arms around herself.

"I owe you an apology," Sam said.

She sat very still. "Why?"

"This morning, I acted like a heel."

The strain on her face deepened as he spoke. "You acted like all the others."

Damn it, he didn't want to be like "all the others." "I'm sorry."

"I'm getting used to it." She exhaled. "For the past two years, I've had a lot of practice."

"That's how long you've been without hearing?"

"Two years and three months. I got very sick, and I ran a high fever. I was unconscious for days, and when I finally knew what was going on around me, I couldn't hear."

He pressed hard against the edge of the table, and his eyes never left her face. "You don't have to—"

"That's what you were wondering, wasn't it? That and the big question—will I ever hear again?" Her tongue touched her lips, and her eyes seemed overly bright, but her voice stayed strangely calm. "And the answer to that is no, even though my parents have made it their mission in life to find a cure." She shrugged, a fluttery, uncertain motion. "There isn't one, but they don't want to believe that."

She stood abruptly, crossed to the windows to stare out at the rainy night and spoke with her back to him. "There's nothing anyone can do." Then she turned to look at him. "It's not as bad as it might seem. Oh, it screwed up my life in a lot of ways, but I'm a painter. I can't imagine a life without being able to see, but I can paint and do what I love without having to be able to hear."

"I think I understand," he said to fill the silence when she stopped talking.

"I doubt it," she said, "Most people don't."

"And that's why you're here?"

"Basically." She came back to the table and dropped on the floor on down on her knees, then sat back on her heels. She studied Sam intently and said, "You know, you still haven't told me what you're doing down here."

Sam hesitated, but if Leigh could be this honest with him, he owed it to her to tell her the truth. And he doubted that she'd swoon or scream or rip off his shirt, although it wouldn't be too terrible if she looked just a bit impressed.

Leigh watched Sam, and she could see the uncertainty in his eyes. Then he nodded. "All right. I'm a musician."

Johngood had been right. Life was a joke, but this time the joke was beyond cruel. A man whose life was music was the first man in a long time who made her feel alive, who made her think of things she'd thought she'd never want again in this life. No wonder he'd looked at her with pity when he found out she was deaf. It must seem to him that it would be like death to have his world of sound taken away.

"A musician," she said, looking down at her hands that were worrying the tie to her robe...his robe. And she wished she had her own clothes, that the rain had stopped and she could go home. She looked back at Sam and knew there was no escape just yet. "What sort of musician?" she asked. He got to his feet, then came around the low table and dropped to his haunches by Leigh. And she hated it. She didn't want him this close...ever. But she had no-where to go.

"Before you got sick, did you listen to much music?" Sam asked.

She touched her tongue to her lips. "Of course."

"What kind of music?"

She forced herself to stop twisting the robe tie. "Rock, easy listening, classical. A bit of everything."

"Any country music?"

"Like Kenny Rogers or Johnny Cash?"

"Exactly."

"Sure, a bit here and there." Then it dawned on her what he was getting at and her heart sank even more. "You're a singer, aren't you?"

"A country singer, although I've been told that I tend to do crossover music."

"Sam Patton." She said his name, hoping she would remember hearing it before, but there was nothing, just a deepening grief for something that had never had a chance to grow before it was gone.

"Sam to my friends," he said. "But on stage I use my middle name, Boone."

Boone Patton was no more familiar to her than Sam Patton had been. "I'm sorry, I never..."

"...paid any attention to who sang that sort of music," he finished with a rueful smile.

She felt heat rise in her face again. "I wasn't going to say that."

"It's okay. People either love country music, or they wonder what all the fuss is about. Over the years, I've gotten used to it."

"Years? How long have you been doing this?"

"I've been involved with music all my life. But I've been performing professionally for about ten years."

Leigh looked at Sam, and as the shock of what he was saying began to wear off, she found herself wishing she'd known about him before she lost her hearing, and that she had a memory of hearing him sing. But she didn't even know how he sounded talking.

He stood and looked down at her. "Would you like a bit of brandy?"

She nodded, and as Sam crossed to the bar, she stood and went to the couch. Sinking down in the loose cushions, she watched Sam splash rich amber liquid in the bottom of two snifters, then he came back to her and offered her a glass. As she cupped her hands around the bulbous container, she sat back and watched Sam sit by her.

He swirled the brandy around and around, then he took a sip. "What do you sound like?" she asked.

He cast her a sideways look. "My voice is deep and kind of rough—not what you'd call trained. I've never taken lessons. I just sing and it seems to work. Music's been there for me."

Leigh looked down into her snifter, watching the overhead lights shimmering in the amber liquid. "It's gone for me. All I can experience of music is the vibrations in the air, the way it was when we first came into the house."

She jumped slightly when Sam cupped her chin and gently urged her to look at him. "What did you just say?"

"You had the stereo so loud that I could feel the vibrations in the air when I stepped into the house."

His fingertips almost burned where they touched her. "How?"

"I don't know. I just do. The air vibrates, the way a hardwood floor does when someone's walking on it. It's all around." She shrugged away from his touch, trying to be casual, but certain her voice must be tight. "Maybe it's compensation. Johngood says that every life has its compensations."

Sam put his brandy snifter on the table, then stood, and when she looked up at him, she saw him ask, "Did you dance before all this happened?"

"Yes, but—"

He strode across to the stereo and almost immediately she could feel the loudness all around, and she scrambled to her feet. When Sam turned back to her, she asked, "What are you doing?"

He came back to her and held out his hand. "Dance with me, Leigh."

She held to the snifter, horrified that he could even think she could do what a normal person could. "No."

His hand dropped, but he took another step toward her. "But you can feel the beat. That's all dancing is, moving to the beat."

"I said I can feel vibrations, but they're blurred. They sort of run together." She shook her head, an annoying burning behind her eyes. "It's not like you think, and I can't dance."

"If you don't try—"

"No." She bit her bottom lip. "It wouldn't work."

He studied her intently. "Can you hear songs in your mind, songs you heard before?"

"I—I guess so."

"Good," he said, then turned and crossed back to the stereo. He opened a set of doors to the right of the unit and inside were special racks that held cassette tapes. He glanced back at Leigh, and motioned her to come to him.

Her impulse was to walk to the door and leave, but she had no idea where her clothes were, and leaving dressed in his robe and walking home through the rain seemed irrational. But maybe not any more irrational than his thinking she could dance.

She stood, put her glass on the table by Sam's, then crossed to the stereo and saw Sam say, "All right. Go through these and find one with a song you remember, something that you can hear in your mind."

"I can't do this. You—"

"I think you can do it. Just find a familiar song."

She turned from Sam and focused on the myriad of tapes, a collection of every type of music there was, from classical to golden oldies. As she skimmed over the titles, she was stopped by gold letters on a red background: *Boone Patton/ Echoes of Roses*.

She hated the unsteadiness in her hand when she reached for it and took it out of its slot. The plastic was cool under her fingers, and as she turned it over, she saw the front of the package. Boone Patton—Sam in a white hat pulled low to partially shadow his face, and a leather jacket trimmed with rhinestones down the front worn over a collarless white shirt. His dark, unreadable eyes were downcast, staring at a single red rose he held.

Even though she hadn't heard much country music, she had a general idea that the music dealt with sadness and broken hearts. Looking at Sam's picture, she felt him project a singular aloneness that touched her. Maybe because she'd felt that way ever since she'd entered a world of silence.

Quickly, she turned the case over and read the list of songs on the album, including the piece, "Echoes of Roses." But she didn't recognize one of them. Slipping the tape case back in its place, she quickly scanned the other titles, then saw a "golden oldies" tape and pulled it out of its slot. Reading the titles, she found a song that she remembered hearing on the radio when she was younger. "This one. 'You Send Me.'"

"Ah, Sam Cooke, my namesake," Sam said as he took the case and slipped the tape out. He took the tape in the machine out, then pushed the other one into the tape deck. He pressed a button, then another, adjusted the bass button, and suddenly she felt the music in the air again. Then she turned and Sam held out his hand to her. "I put on the end of the last song so we can get ready."

Cautiously, she moved closer and as she rested her left hand on his shoulder, Sam took her right hand and brought it to the hollow of his throat. She could feel his pulse under the sleek heat of his skin, the solid beating of his heart against her fingertips.

Then she looked up and felt a vibration against her fingers when Sam's lips moved. "I'll sing the words to the song, emphasizing the beat behind the words and you can feel it in my throat. Read my lips, and match those words with the music in your memory."

"I'm not sure…" she began, feeling overwhelmed by his nearness and the fear that she would make a total fool of herself. As she tried to draw her hand back, Sam quickly covered her hand with his and kept it pressed to his throat.

"Just remember the tune in your mind and follow my lead," he said slowly. "You can do it. And if you can't, it's just me here. No one else ever has to know." He hesitated, then smiled, a gentle curving of his lips. "Trust me."

She didn't even trust herself, but she simply nodded, expecting him to lay his hands lightly on her hips. But he didn't. Instead, he gently framed her face with his hands, keeping her chin tipped so she could easily see his mouth. She stared at his lips, trying to forget how thin the terry-cloth robe was and the fact that she could feel his heartbeat just as clearly as she could feel her own.

"All right," he was saying, mingling the vibration of his words with his pulse. "That's the end of that song and 'You Send Me' is going to start…right…now." And as she saw his lips forming the first words, it was almost as if she could hear the music in her mind.

Then Sam started to move in a simple pattern, and amazingly, she was moving with him. It was as if music was all around her and Sam, and they were a part of it. And it stunned her. She'd thought it was lost to her, but with this man, it wasn't. His hands framed her face as his body drew her along to the beat under her hand and in her mind.

Then his hand slipped to her shoulders and down, finally resting at her waist, and he eased her closer to him, her breasts brushing against his bare chest, her hips against his, and the oneness she felt with the music was shifting to the man who held her.

Concentrate, she told herself, staring at his mouth, but instead of reading his lips, she began to focus on the curve of his mouth, the suggestive fullness of his bottom lip. She felt the beat of his voice under her fingers, but music wasn't on her mind.

The memory of the kiss on the beach seemed to taunt her with its remembered taste and the way it had brought seductive fires to life in her. Without thinking, she touched her tongue to her own lips, and she felt her breathing become tight. Oh, God, what was she doing? She looked away from his mouth to his eyes, and she saw his gaze on her parted lips.

There was no pity there, but a fire in the dark depths, a fire that echoed her own in intensity, and she stumbled, missing the beat altogether.

She almost tripped over his feet, and tried to right herself by grabbing Sam by the shoulders. Then she was steady, his hands around her waist an anchor for her. And she was close enough that her breasts tingled from the contact through the terry cloth, her hips swaying against his.

"I'm sorry," she said, quickly and tried to pull away.

But he didn't let her go. And he didn't move back from her. Instead, he drew her closer, holding her hips firmly against his, and she felt definite proof that he was as affected by their closeness as she was. As his gaze slipped to her lips, she held her breath, then slowly, irrevocably, he lowered his head. His warm lips gently trailed across hers, the caress about as substantial as the brush of a feather.

But the contact sent molten fire through her veins, and she gasped, her lips parting instinctively. For a fleeting moment she had the vividly clear thought that this was a kiss like no other kisses she'd ever experienced. And that the danger she'd foreseen when Sam had grabbed her hand in the rain and brought her up here was all a part of it. Vulnerability was overwhelming her, just as her need to give herself up to the sensations that Sam's touch bred in her.

But before she could grasp at sanity, his kiss deepened, his tongue invading her warmth, and without rhyme or reason, she was responding with an abandon that shocked her. Every nerve in her being was alive, almost painfully so, and she wound her arms around his neck, as much to get closer as to keep herself anchored so she wouldn't float away and lose what was happening to her.

She arched against his solid strength, her breasts crushing against his chest, and she felt a hunger in her, a gnawing ache in the bottom of her heart that she could never remember not being there. And this man holding her, the man whose hands were sliding along the line of her hips, drawing her against him, was what she'd been looking for her whole life.

And all that knowledge came from a simple kiss. Simple? No. There was nothing simple about the deepening invasion of his tongue, of the taste of him that filled her senses, of the heat and strength and growing demands of his lips against hers. She felt as if she were in danger of disappearing, of melting into him, of losing herself and becoming a person she hadn't known existed until this moment in time.

Then his hands moved on her, coming to her shoulders, his fingertips tucking under the lapels of terry, and she felt his touch on her bare skin. With one motion, the soft terry parted and fell off her shoulders, and Sam's hands found her breasts, cupping the fullness. The contact stunned her, almost as much as her reaction to that touch.

She felt a moan building in her throat, and as his thumbs began to massage and tease her nipples, she arched her head back. His lips found her exposed throat, tasting her skin as effectively as his hands were drawing fire to life in her. And she knew that she was close to being well and truly lost in the world of sensations that this man was producing with his touch and with his kiss.

When his mouth trailed down her throat to the hollow there, then moved lower, she wanted to throw all caution to the winds, to give in to the feelings and joy. But a germ of sanity persisted. She couldn't let herself care in the way she knew she would if she let herself go, or she wouldn't walk away whole. And that terrified her. It terrified her more than anything she'd been through. And she'd been right. What she'd felt with Satch wasn't the glimmer of a candle next to the inferno that Sam could produce in her.

She faced the fact that there was nothing here for her, and choked by grief for what she'd never know, she pushed free. Awkwardly she turned away, unable to look in his eyes or at his lips. She didn't want to see what she knew must be in his gaze or see anything he would say.

She stared at the windows and with uncooperative fingers, tugged the robe back to cover her. Then she caught the lapels together at her throat, balling the soft material in her hand. Her breathing was ragged and painful, her skin strangely flushed yet cold at the same time, and she could feel a throbbing every place Sam had touched her.

She looked at the windows and saw her own reflection, the crazy riot of curls, the paleness of her face and the way she was holding the robe shut at her throat. Then she realized the rain had finally stopped. She felt the vibrations of footsteps on the floor as he came up behind her. And she turned, afraid he was going to touch her again.

Sam was two feet from her, staring at her, his face tinged with paleness and sheened with moisture. His nostrils flared with each rapid breath he took.

"This is crazy," he said, and for an insane moment in the midst of an insane situation, she thought she could hear his voice, deep, rough and breathless. But that was as much in her imagination as the idea that she could be around him and not want him to touch her, hold her and kiss her. "I didn't plan this. Not the dancing, or..."

She held the lapels of his robe, and she knew how lonely she'd been in the past six months. That explained the wanton way she'd clung to him, the way she'd let him touch her, and the way she'd exposed her throat for his kiss. And she just hadn't realized it until Sam had come into her world. "I—I have to go." She licked her lips and his taste was still there to taunt her.

He ran both hands roughly over his face, then his hands dropped to his sides, and he looked at her with dark, intense eyes. "I can just imagine what you're thinking."

She desperately hoped he couldn't, not when she was thinking how foolish she was, and how simple it would be to let herself fall in love with a man she barely knew.

Love? Stunned by that unbidden thought, she felt light-headed. Love? No, not with Sam, not with any man who could destroy her with a glance, and a man who lived in a world of attention and crowds and sounds. A man whose passion in life was music. Not love, anything but love.

"You're thinking that I'm in the entertainment business, that I have more women than I know what to do with, and that going to bed with a woman is as simple as taking my next breath and just as inconsequential."

His words brought images to her mind that almost took her breath away—to be with Sam, to be held by him, to have him make love to her. And she knew a sudden jealousy of the women he'd been with, all the women he'd wanted and had. And her emotions shifted dramatically to a basic anger that she would never be one of those women.

"It's not that way." Sam kept talking. "To tell you the truth, I haven't been with a woman for a long time... by choice." A fire burned deep in his eyes. "And I didn't bring you up here to seduce you, although I can't honestly say that the idea of making love with you didn't cross my mind."

She felt fragmented, as if the only thing that held her together was her death grip on the terry cloth at her throat. "Please..."

He took a single step toward her, an action as threatening to her control as any physical contact would be. "Leigh, what I'm trying to say is, I waited for you on the beach to explain things to you, not to ply you with food, wine and music. And now I have to explain something else, a decision I came to before I went down to find you."

"What decision?" she said around the tightness in her throat.

"That I'm only here for a short time, and to be blunt, I hate being alone. It eats me alive. What I really wanted to say to you was, I'd like to spend time with you. Maybe go swimming or..." He smiled, a sudden, brilliant expression of pure humor. "Jogging."

Breathing that had been hard before became impossible for Leigh. She closed her eyes to get her balance. He hated being alone, he'd said, and she knew that meant that his life was people, crowds, fans, audiences. Bitterness rose in the back of her throat, and as she opened her eyes, she wasn't surprised to see Sam just staring at her . . . waiting.

Yes, this man was made to be in the spotlight. And she wondered why she hadn't known that from the start. He certainly wouldn't move through life unnoticed. Yes, she bet that he liked that, too, that he wasn't any shrinking violet. And she wondered why he had come here. He certainly hadn't come for the solitude.

She forced herself to break her death grip on the robe and quickly pushed her hands into the patch pockets. "Why are you really here?" she asked.

"I told you, I was coming to see you, and—"

"No, I mean *here,* on the island. You don't want to be here. You don't even particularly like it. There aren't any audiences, any crowds. Yet you're here."

He didn't touch her, but he came another half step closer. "I told you, I had to get away, to take a break. My manager had this house and offered it to me."

"A break from what?"

"My life," he said bluntly.

"Burnout?"

"In a way. Maybe that's why I liked it when you didn't know who I was. You just saw me as Sam Patton, a neighbor. And I won't be Boone Patton until I go back to my life in Los Angeles."

"And you'll be leaving soon, won't you?"

"Yes. Maybe in a week."

Away from here, he'd be Boone Patton and she knew it would hurt like hell when Sam Patton was gone. Tonight had shown her just how vulnerable she could be. And she knew that real pain was more than just a possibility. "I have to get back to my house."

For a minute, she thought he was going to touch her again, but he didn't. Abruptly he turned from her and strode across the room to disappear into the kitchen. Slowly, she looked around the room. She wouldn't come back here again, and she would never dance again. This was all over. Just one night.

Chapter 9

Sam came back into the living room with Leigh's clothes in his hands, the heat of the dryer still in the fabric. And when he saw Leigh right where he left her, looking delicate and isolated in his ridiculously oversize robe, he had to force himself not to stare, not to cross to her and kiss her again.

She'd put up a wall, an invisible barrier that hadn't been there when they'd danced. But now it was in place and it couldn't have been more formidable if it had been built of bricks. And he didn't know how to get past it now.

That he even wanted to try was something new for him. Hell, it was new to him to want to be with a woman on every imaginable level. He wanted to make love to Leigh, yet he wanted to talk to her, to find out about her, to know what she thought, what she wanted, what she dreamed of.

He shook his head as he crossed and handed her the clothes. It shook him when her hands brushed his, their coolness against the heat of his own skin. He looked down at her, into the deep blue pools of her eyes, and he saw a truth that shook him even more. She hadn't just built barriers, she was shutting him out as effectively as if she had left this house ten minutes ago.

"Do you want to go swimming tomorrow morning?" he asked, not about to give up.

She paled at his question and he knew the answer before she spoke. "I have work to do."

He knew his expression was tightening. "Then how about tomorrow evening?"

She shook her head. "I can't. I—"

"I know you'll be working."

She nibbled on her bottom lip. "I'm sorry."

"What's going on, Leigh?"

Without answering, she ducked her head and went past him to head for the bedroom.

"What in the hell is going on with you?" he yelled after her, hearing the echo of his question bounce off the walls as frustration built in him. Then she disappeared into the bedroom, and he closed his eyes. A moment later, he heard the door to the bathroom close.

With a violent oath, Sam spun around and sank down on the couch. Balling his hand into a fist, he hit the padded arm with such force that it jarred his whole body. Then he dropped his head against the couch back and stared at the ceiling fan that turned slowly overhead.

He didn't understand. He'd felt Leigh respond to him, felt her move closer, press herself to him, felt her open her mouth to him. It wasn't like the first time when she hadn't moved. This time she'd answered kiss for kiss, caress for caress. Her breasts had swelled in his hands, the nipples peaking, and he'd heard her moan. Then she'd stopped dead and put up that damned wall emotionally.

Besides an incredible knot of frustration in him, he felt confused. He'd started to feel connected to her, to want her in a deep, complete way, and she'd pulled back. She'd looked at him with pain, with overly bright eyes and lips swollen from their kisses. It couldn't be her deafness. He hadn't even thought about it since they'd started dancing.

He didn't understand.

The phone rang, startling him, and as he reached for it, he saw Leigh come back into the room. She was wearing her shorts and halter top again, and her hair was tumbling around her shoulders. She was even more beautiful than before, and her eyes even more remote.

He pointed to the phone as it rang for a fourth time. "A call," he said. "I'll just be a minute, then I'll drive you home."

She stopped partway between the couch and the bedroom door, her hands clasped in front of her, her eyes wide. "You don't have to. The rain's stopped. I can walk."

"I don't mind," he said quickly and picked up the receiver. "Hello?"

"Mr. Patton?"

He frowned at the strange voice, but never took his eyes off Leigh. "Who is this?"

"Detective Lopez."

That shocked him. "What is it?"

"Mr. Bigelow was going to call you, but I thought I'd better."

Sam sat up straight, thankful Leigh was looking toward the windows and the startlingly clear night outside. He kept watching her while he spoke to Lopez. "What's going on?"

"She's found your house in Malibu."

That whole world had ceased to exist for him when he was here with Leigh, and the reality hit him right between the eyes. He sat forward, closing his eyes. "What in the hell do you mean, she 'found' the Malibu place?" he demanded.

"She was there, and there's been an incident."

The image of the guard she'd stabbed came to Sam with sickening force, and all he could think of was Ted being at the house making sure the security system was being installed properly.

"Detective Lopez, speak English to me. What happened?"

"A workman went back to the house about an hour ago to get some tools he left behind, and he must have just missed the intruder by minutes." The man spoke calmly, and Sam wondered if anything ever rattled this man.

"What happened?"

"There was damage to your bedroom. The bedding and clothes were torn to shreds."

"How could she find the house?"

"We don't have a clue, but she did."

"Any messages," he asked, his jaw clenched.

"On the mirror, a rose and a lipstick scrawl that she'd find you."

"Damn it," he bit out, his mind reeling. "What now?"

"We're going over everything for prints and clues. I'm sure there'll be something. She's crazy. There has to come a point when she isn't careful. We'll get her."

"When?" he asked. "After she's killed someone?"

"We hope that doesn't happen, Mr. Patton. But that's why you're down there."

"Exiled to never-never land," he muttered as he opened his eyes and stared at the floor. "Is there anything else?" he asked.

"Just be careful. God knows what else she knows. If she found your house, she's smart."

"I'll build up the walls of the fort," Sam said, then hung up.

As he sank back, he glanced at Leigh. Her back was to the view and she was staring at him. He'd spoken in a low voice, but what difference did that make? He could see by the look on her face that she'd read his lips.

"Let me explain," he said as he stood.

She was silent while he crossed to her, but her eyes never left his face.

"You said you were here to rest."

"And I am," he said. "But there's another reason. I've got a fan who's out of control. She's tried to get to me, and I don't want to meet her." He could tell she wasn't buying an overzealous fan, so he admitted, "She stabbed a security guard during a show I was doing on the Fourth of July. Everyone seemed to think it was best for me to disappear."

Leigh stared at him. "Stabbed? You mean she...she tried to...?" She felt sick and couldn't even finish her question.

"*Tried* is the operative word," he said. "She didn't kill him. Almost doesn't count."

Doesn't count? She swallowed bile in her throat, shocked at the intensity of her reaction. Sam could have been killed. And that thought almost took away her ability to breathe. "She...she wanted to kill you, didn't she?"

"She thinks she loves me," he said, speaking quickly. "She's obsessed. That happens in this business. She doesn't even know me, but she's convinced that we should be together forever." He smiled, the expression tight and never touching his eyes. "Hopefully, I'll never meet her, and meanwhile the police are taking care of it, and I'm down here to stay out of the way."

"What if they can't take care of it?" she asked.

He sobered. "They will."

She looked away from Sam, turning to the windows, but instead of the night outside, she saw her own reflection again. And even in that distorted image, she could see fear in her face. Fear for a man she never should have kissed, never should have come this close to caring about. And she knew it was time to leave forever.

She jumped when Sam touched her shoulder, then she turned, moving away from his outstretched hand. "I have to go. It's late."

"Leigh, we need—"

She closed her eyes, the most childish thing she'd done since she'd lost her hearing, but she didn't want to "listen" to his words and she didn't have the strength to run and keep running. She didn't want him to tell her anything else, to explain, or to ask her to be with him again. God, she didn't know how to cope with this. Everything she'd run from in New York seemed to be crashing around her head, and it scared her to death.

She stood very still, forcing herself to breathe, and nothing happened. Sam didn't touch her, he didn't try to get her attention in any way, but she knew he was still there. She hadn't felt him leave. Cautiously, she opened her eyes.

Yes, he was there, in the same spot, waiting, watching her.

"Is that your way of covering your ears?" he asked, his face expressionless.

She wished she could laugh, make a joke out of it, but she didn't have it in her to do that. She just stood there, afraid to move in case she crumbled, and afraid to speak in case she cried. Damn this man, he was making everything crazy again, making her have to deal with things that she'd turned her back on. And he was making her so scared, but not for herself. The idea that someone wanted to kill him almost choked her.

She blinked rapidly, then amazingly, Sam didn't try to talk to her anymore, he didn't ask any more questions and he didn't touch her. Instead, he simply said, "You're tired. I'll take you home."

When he turned to head for the door, she made herself follow him, stepping after him out into the balmy midnight filled with stars, a huge moon and the fragrance of flowers. But she felt cold. Hurrying after Sam, she bypassed puddles on the gravel and went along the side of the house to the carport. The Jeep was there. She walked to the passenger side and got in while he slipped behind the wheel.

The trip to her house was short, not more than a few miles by road, and Leigh didn't look at Sam once. She stared out at the night, trying to keep her mind shut down until she could figure out what was happening in her world. When Sam drove through the stone pillars and up the driveway to her house, he stopped in the parking area, and she scrambled out.

Without looking back, she hurried up the steps and she thought she'd made her escape, but as she reached the door, she felt the vibrations on the porch behind her. He was following her.

She turned and Sam was one step below her, bringing him to her eye level. With the light from the full moon, she could see him clearly, the colorless silver of the moon defining the planes and angles of his face. The image set her nerves on edge. "Thanks for the drive home," she said.

Sam looked at her intently, then asked, "Are you all right?"

"Fine," she said quickly. "Just . . . just tired."

He hesitated, then reached out and brushed his knuckles across her cheek, heat against cold, and it made her tremble. "Yes, you're tired," he said, then drew back. "I'll see you on the beach in the morning to jog. Stress reduction."

He didn't wait for an answer before he turned and walked toward the Jeep. And Leigh didn't move until he'd driven off and the red of the taillights faded from sight. When the unbroken night settled around her, she felt such isolation that it stunned her. The solitude she'd valued so much wasn't her friend anymore. But she wasn't going to be on the beach in the morning.

Johngood was barely out of the purple taxi the next morning when Leigh saw him from the door and called out to him. He looked up, his magenta shirt and lime green shorts painful to her eye. He raised his hand in greeting, then he turned and took a box out of the taxi before he crossed to the porch where Leigh stood.

He stopped at the bottom of the steps and looked up at her, his eyes narrowing, his head cocked. "You look like you've been run over by a truck," he said bluntly.

She pushed at her loose curls, tucking them behind her ears, and shrugged. "I had a rough night." That was an understatement, but the truth.

"Not feeling well?" he asked.

"I'm fine," she lied and looked at the box. "What have you got?"

"Things to do what you asked."

"What...?"

"Some way for you to know if someone is here."

Although she figured it was too late for warnings, she nodded. "Oh, good."

"I've got it all figured out, and—" he grinned at her "—it's ingenious."

"I'm sure it is," she said as he came up the stairs carrying the box. She reached to hold the door open for him, and he went past, put the box down just inside the door and turned to her. "And why aren't you out running on the beach this fine morning?"

She certainly wasn't going to tell him that she had been fighting the urge since before dawn. "I was lazy this morning. I decided to sleep in."

"It didn't do you much good," he said bluntly.

She looked away from Johngood and hunkered down by his box. She took out a package of light bulbs and held them up to him. "Red lights?"

"All part of my plan."

She put the bulbs back, then stood. "Do whatever you need to do. Just make sure no one can come in here without me knowing about it."

"That's the plan," he said, then glanced at the couch. "You didn't read your letters, did you?"

"No, but I will later." She didn't look at the envelopes still resting where Johngood had left them.

"People send letters to tell you something, and they might be important."

"All right, all right. I'll read them. Just let me know when you're done."

"Sure will," he said, then waited for her to cross to the couch before he went back outside.

Leigh reached for the letters, stared at them for a long moment, then tore open the one from her parents. She skimmed over her mother's precise script on pale blue paper, catching a phrase here and there, then stopping when she got to "...a nice man, although I wonder about someone called Johngood." She smiled at that, then kept reading. "I hate the way you shut yourself off from all of us. I saw Satch yesterday, and he was asking about you. I don't understand why it didn't work out between the two of you. He loved you and could have helped you cope..."

Leigh sank back in the cushions and closed her eyes. Cope. How could Satch help cope when he couldn't bear to have anything or anyone less than perfect with him. And as far as love went . . .

The thought came to her with startling clarity. There hadn't been love. There'd been compatibility and the same mutual love—art. But never a real, intense love between them.

If she hadn't lost her hearing, if she hadn't become less than perfect, would she have married Satch, stayed in New York and never realized she didn't love him? Would she never have met Sam, danced to "You Send Me," or known the havoc that one man's touch could cause in her?

She stopped those thoughts as quickly as they had come and opened her eyes. She'd avoided thinking directly about Sam for a few hours, and she wasn't about to start now. Skimming over the last of the letter, she finally folded the paper and dropped it on the cushion over Satch's unopened letter. That one she wouldn't open. She didn't want to read about showings, or ideas for work that he wanted from her and she didn't want to be asked to come back to New York to help with her next show.

At the same moment she felt the vibrations of someone walking toward the couch, she inhaled an unmistakable mixture of fresh air and male scents that were unique. Even as she turned, she knew Sam was there.

In cutoff jeans, a blue tank top and his hair windblown, he stood near the end of the couch, his eyes narrowed on her. And it was all she could manage to get to her feet. "Wh—what are you doing in here?"

"The gentleman outside told me to come on in." He pushed the tips of his fingers in his pockets. "I thought we were going jogging?"

She had been right. It was way too late for any alarm system to let her know when someone was coming. And right now, with her mouth going dry just at the sight of Sam, she felt as if she'd been blindsided. "I wasn't planning to go this morning."

He came closer. "Breaking routine? That's not like you."

"Like me?" she echoed, uneasy with the familiarity those words conjured up. How did he know what was or wasn't like her? "I just decided not to jog today."

"How about a swim?"

She shook her head immediately. She wasn't about to be around Sam in his skimpy swimsuit. "I have to work."

Johngood came up behind Sam, and Leigh glanced at him as he said, "I'll be needing to work in your studio for a while." He glanced at Sam, then back to Leigh. "Go for a walk, and I'll be done in an hour."

Leigh felt trapped, but she wasn't going to be forced into an impossible situation. "I'll just sit on the deck and get some sun. Let me know when you're finished."

Johngood nodded, then turned and went back to the front door. When she dared look at Sam, he said, "Can I sit on the deck with you for a few minutes? I need a rest before I start the long walk back to my place." She caught a gleam of teasing in his eyes. "Poor cardiovascular conditioning, I guess."

She didn't know what was harder to deal with, Sam with fire in his eyes, or this Sam who knew she wanted him gone but wasn't going to make it easier for her. And he seemed to be enjoying her discomfort. "If you want to."

She turned and headed out onto the deck, not looking at Sam as she sat on one of the canvas chairs. Settling back, she stared out at the ocean, then caught movement to her left side. The next thing she knew, Sam was there holding one of the chairs that he proceeded to put on the deck right in front of her. He sat down facing her, his knees not more than six inches from hers. If she moved at all, her feet would tangle with his.

"What are you doing?" she asked, sitting straighter, pulling her feet back under her chair.

"I want to have a conversation, and I'm making it easier on both of us."

At least he wasn't talking with exaggerated care. "What did you want to talk about?"

"You."

"I thought we covered all of that last night," she said, clasping her hands in her lap.

He sat forward, effectively taking away a good deal of her space buffer. "I still don't know a whole lot, and I want to know all there is to know about you."

She swallowed, trying to ease the tightness in her throat. "There isn't anything else."

"I know you're an artist, a very good one, and that you're from New York and you live here alone. You were sick and you can't hear."

Discomfort rose in her as the bare bones of her life were laid out in front of her. "That's about it."

"What about your personal life? Have you been married?"

"No, have you?"

"Not so far," he said without hesitating. "Engaged?"

"Yes."

"What happened?"

She almost said, none of your business, but she knew if she did, she'd have to get up and walk away. And she had nowhere to go that he wouldn't follow. She blinked, trying to focus when his image was beginning to float in front of her. "Why are you doing this?"

He didn't move, his eyes intense and sharp. "Leigh, I told you. I want to know about you, not just the bare facts. And I'm wondering how any man could let you go."

"Maybe that man thought he was getting a normal life, an uncomplicated life, and he found out there was nothing but complications."

"Your hearing loss?"

She nodded, hating talking about this with Sam. "That and other things. He's really a decent man, but he just didn't bargain on having to adjust to that. And I couldn't ask him to."

"I shouldn't be making you relive what happened. It must be pretty painful."

It was painful, but in that moment she knew it wasn't pain from a lost love, or sad memories, but pain that came from fearing Sam would pity her, that that look would come back in his eyes. She didn't want that ever again. "That's all right," she said. "It's the past, and it's over. I just don't understand why you want to know all of this?"

"Because I'm here, you're here, and I just don't understand how your fiancé could have let you walk away like that."

She stared down at her hands. "He didn't let me. I just did it." She looked back at Sam. "Is there anything else you wanted to know?"

"Is that why you're hiding out down here?"

She felt her breath catch in her chest. "Hiding out?"

"Isn't that what you're doing? Just the way I am?"

"No, it's not like that at all."

"What is it like?" he persisted.

She stared at him, then words came out that she hadn't planned on saying to anyone, ever. "I'm taking control of my life, managing it so it's what I want it to be."

"Taking control from whom?"

"Everyone who means well, but doesn't understand. My parents and my friends. I told you they aren't comfortable with . . . what I am."

He stared at her intently. "Are you?"

"Am I what?" she asked with exasperation.

"Comfortable with what you are?"

He hit her with words as effectively as he would have with a fist to her middle. "I am what I am," she muttered tightly.

His eyes narrowed. "And just what are you?"

"I'm me, whatever that means, and I have to get on with my life, and that means being here, and not in New York. It means working at what I love and doing exactly what I want to do when I want to do it."

"What did you have to do in New York that you hated?"

He never let up. "I hated being in a place where there seemed to be the whole world around me, and I couldn't relate to anyone. I hated being dragged from specialist to specialist in the ever-present hope that one of those doctors could make me perfect again. And I hated people finding out I'd been sick, then speaking with exaggerated slowness when they talked to me, or yelling when they spoke, as if that would make a bit of difference to me."

She bit her lip hard, shocked at what she was saying, but the words wouldn't stop. "And I hate seeing that look in people's eyes. I hate it."

"What look?"

"The look you had in your eyes when you figured everything out."

He leaned forward, his elbows on his knees, his hands within inches of her legs. "Did it ever occur to you that shock makes people react in ways they never would normally?"

"Shock and pity," she said.

"And how do you know what people feel?" he asked.

She stood, bumping her knees against his, and she stumbled backward, righting herself by grabbing the back of the chair. "And I hate smug people who ask a million stupid questions and who intrude in a place where there's peace and safety."

She bit back any more words as Sam stood slowly. "A place where you're hiding out," he finally said.

"No," she said, her fingers clenching on the back of the chair. "I told you I'm not hiding out. I'm just getting control of my life."

He shook his head. "Hey, I'm not judging you on it. You do what you have to do. I'm a prime example of that."

"Then what do you want from me?"

His eyes narrowed and he studied her for a long moment before he spoke. "That's simple. I just want to spend time together while I'm here, while we're both exiles from the real world."

And then what? she wanted to ask. If I let down my guard and these feelings get stronger, and you walk away, what then? The idea of such vulnerability made her feel queasy. She shook her head. "No, I can't."

"You won't."

She closed her eyes for a moment and steadied herself before looking back at Sam to repeat, "I said, I can't."

"What are you afraid of?" he asked.

His question stunned her for a moment, then she knew it was time to walk away. "This...this conversation is over, and I need to get to work." And she would have gone back into the house, but he reached out and touched her shoulder.

His action effectively riveted her to the spot and she looked up at him and saw him say, "Leigh, you've got a million reasons for being here, for living the way you want to, but give me one reason why we can't spend some time with each other.''

She tried to speak, to tell him a lie, any lie it took to get him to leave her alone. But she couldn't say a thing when he touched her other shoulder and looked right at her.

"I know you can't hear," he said, his hold on her light but compelling. "And I hate that because I hate what you're missing. But one thing you don't have to miss is right now, this moment. You're here and I'm here, and that's all that matters. Now. Here. The present is all anyone has. The past is gone, and the future isn't real. There isn't any reason for you to be lonely here and me to be lonely at my place."

"I'm alone, not lonely," she said, not trusting anything she felt when Sam was so near. "I don't need anyone." She shut off the instant knowledge in her that she could need him with a desperation that could be staggering if she let it develop. "You... you need people around you. I don't. That's why you're an entertainer, why you live your life at the center of the stage."

That brought a hint of a smile to his lips, a rueful uplifting at the corners of his mouth. "You know, I really do love what I do. I like crowds and the energy they have. I like people, and if anyone had told me a week ago that I'd be happy with just one person with me on this island, I would have thought they were crazy."

The smile began to fade, replaced by a peculiar intensity in the lines and planes of his face. "But here I am, and I don't want anyone sharing my time but you. Not at this moment in time."

She stared at his lips, and knew what he'd said earlier was right on the mark. She was afraid, and she felt raw fear surge through her that had everything to do with her vulnerability to this one man. "Living for the moment?" she asked in what she knew was an unsteady voice.

"It's all we have, this moment."

But what would all the moments be like when he was gone?

She stared up at Sam, and before she fully understood what he was going to do, she saw him repeat, "This moment," and he kissed her. When his lips touched hers, there was no gradual building, no flickering flame that flared inside her. Just an instant, all-consuming white-hot passion that seared Leigh, a fire that threatened to consume her.

There was no place for her to hide, no lie large enough to deny what Sam's caress did to her. And she knew she was lost. Fear and desire mingled as completely as her heat melded with Sam's, and every place Sam touched her, she felt an ironlike bond being forged, a bond as terrifying in its implications as all the emotions she felt struggling inside her.

Chapter 10

Before Leigh could gather enough strength of will to free herself, Sam pulled back. And when she opened her eyes, his dark gaze burned into hers. His hands on her were as unsteady as her own heartbeat. "You're lonely and scared," he said, the heat of his breath brushing her face. "And if you ever want someone to jog with or swim with or dance with . . . or do anything else with, I'll be at the house."

His gaze dropped to her lips, and she braced herself for another kiss. But that didn't happen. Sam broke the contact and took all the heat in her world with him as he strode past her to leave.

Leigh didn't turn to watch him go. She didn't have to. She could feel the deck vibrate with each step he took toward the house. Then she couldn't feel anything but the throbbing in her lips and her heart hammering against her ribs.

He'd been so right. She was scared to death. More scared than he'd ever guess. The idea that she could come even this close to loving a man like Sam Patton terrified her. And she wasn't about to let that happen. Scrubbing her lips with the back of her hand, she saw movement on the beach far below.

She moved closer to the railing, gripping the warm wood with both hands, unable to take her eyes off Sam as he walked slowly away. He never stopped and he never looked back. And by the time he disappeared out of sight, Leigh could feel the roughness of the railing biting into her hands and a pain centering behind her breastbone.

The woman had driven past Boone's Malibu place before coming to the office, saw police cars parked on the narrow road, and fluttering yellow "crime scene" ribbons strung from one pillar to the other.

She shouldn't have gone there again, but she didn't know what else to do. It was as if he'd fallen off the face of the earth. She'd checked any credit card purchases, but none had been recorded on Boone's business cards. She knew they were keeping him from her, and she just had to figure out where they'd forced him to go.

Then as if she had conjured up her own form of magic, she knew what to do. She flipped on the computer, opened up Boone's files and went into a subfile on planned publicity. The screen came up, and the words "Charity Concert" leaped out at her. The date was in two days. She knew everything about Boone, and she knew he would never pass on a charity event. In an old interview, he'd said that he'd known poor times, hard times, and he wouldn't ever stop helping others who were in need.

And he never lied.

Not him, but everyone around him would lie. Especially Ted Bigelow. She sat back in the chair and stared at the glowing monitor. Ted Bigelow. Why hadn't she thought about this before? Why had she let her hatred of the man blind her? He was her ticket to Boone.

She flipped open her address file, found the number and punched out Ted Bigelow's office number. And in less than a minute, she was being put through to the man. Quickly, she explained about the charity event and told him that she was checking to find out if there was any extra PR he wanted done for it.

"You'd better cancel on that," Bigelow said abruptly.

"But there have been print ads and television spots. The money's been spent, and it wouldn't look good to have Mr. Patton pull out at the last minute." Her voice sounded professional and unemotional in her own ears, and she felt pleased that she could speak so rationally to this man. "Press releases were sent out just before the Fourth. It might backfire if Mr. Patton doesn't appear. After all, he's adopted this charity and put a lot of time into it."

"I know, I know, but it's not possible, not right now."

Her heart began to sink. "All right, whatever you say. We'll start damage control, let it leak that he's cancelling for 'personal reasons'?"

Bigelow was silent for a long moment, then seemed to be talking to himself as much as her. "Maybe I could talk to the police, see what they think, get their opinion."

"Excuse me?" she said.

"Don't do anything just yet. Let me check some things out and get back to you."

"When will you know for sure?" she pressed, unexpected tears burning her eyes as she saw a chance that this might work.

"Twenty-four hours. I'll get back to you as soon as we figure out what can be done."

"If it can be worked out, can Mr. Patton be here in time for the show?"

"Yeah, I can arrange for a jet charter. That shouldn't be a problem. Let me check things out and get back to you." He hung up and the line buzzed in her ear.

Slowly she put the receiver in place and rubbed her eyes, then sank back. Twenty-four hours. She didn't know if she could endure that much of a wait. Then she sat up straight. What had Bigelow said—he could arrange a jet charter?

She reached for the phone again and called the Burbank Airport. If he would use a charter to get Boone back, chances were a charter was used to make him disappear. And there had to have been a flight plan filed.

Sam broke into a jog as he rounded the rocks that defined the cove and didn't stop even when he got to the stairs that led up to Ted's house. He kept going, farther down the beach, out of his cove into the next, until his legs refused to go any farther.

He sank down to the sand on his knees, pressing his hands flat on the gritty, warm beach and bowed his head as he gasped for air. He'd done that all wrong. He'd thought just showing up, acting as if nothing had happened, would make everything okay.

He closed his eyes, but he couldn't shut out his last sight of Leigh. Deep blue eyes wide and filled with a fear that tore at his gut, but a fear that he couldn't begin to understand. Her lips parted and inviting. He felt the force between them, the fire that came without bidding, and it shook him. God, he wanted nothing more than to discover all the mysteries of Leigh Buchanan. Instead, he was here, alone.

He sank back on the sand, and sitting down, he looked up to the vastness of the ocean in the distance. He'd heard about people looking at nature and being struck by how finite man was in this world. But when he looked at it right now, he understood how vulnerable he was all because of one woman. A new experience for him. A totally new experience.

Lying back, he stretched out on the gritty warmth and rested his forearm over his eyes. His "fan" had consigned him to this place by her threats, and now that he was here, one woman seemed to be his salvation. He laughed out loud, hearing the sound echoing off the vaulted cliffs behind him. All it took was one woman to destroy his life, and one woman to rebuild it again.

Sometime during the day, Leigh lost count of her reasons for staying away from Sam. They bombarded her from all sides, sensible, self-preserving reasons, and for a brief while she felt safe behind them.

While Johngood explained the light he'd hooked up to a doorbell he'd installed, she tried to focus on what he was saying.

"The light goes every time someone rings the doorbell I put in outside. Watch," he said, and went outside, reaching to his left. Suddenly the light over the door flashed red, on and off, then on again. Then Johngood drew back his hand and the light went off. He smiled at Leigh. "How's that?"

"That's great, but what if I'm not standing here looking at the light?"

"I figured that out. There's a light in the studio, in the kitchen and in your bedroom." He looked pleased as punch with himself. "Pretty good, eh?"

"Yes, pretty good."

He picked up his tools and put them in the box, then stood and looked at Leigh. "Will you be going jogging or swimming with Mr. Patton later on?"

The question took Leigh aback. "Why would you think that?"

"He mentioned that he came to take you for a jog. I thought you must have decided to do it later."

"He did . . . I mean, he thought we were, but we're not."

"That's a shame. I thought you'd be having some company for a change."

She tried to smile, but knew her expression was tight. "I have you for company."

"Oh, I'm first rate, just ask your mother, but you need a bit more than an old man who can make red lights flash." He grinned at her. "A lot more."

She felt her face flame and shook her head. "Johngood, you're way off the mark. I'm perfectly fine with the way things are around here."

"All alone?"

"By myself. That's why I'm down here. And it's the way I want it. I'm happy living like this. You should understand if anyone does, that I'm here to live the sort of life I want to live."

"And why would I be understanding that?" he asked.

"You said you were here by choice, that you wouldn't ever go back to the States and your old life."

"Ah, I did say that, didn't I?"

"Yes, you did."

He studied her for a long moment. "And I meant it, but I'm old. I've lived my life, and it's been a full life."

Johngood had never talked much about his past before, just that he had come here to live out the rest of his days. "Did you do everything you wanted to do before you came here?" she asked.

"I think so. I saw places that most people never see. I did strange and wonderful things, and survived. I even found the love of my life."

She knew he lived alone in a small house near the general store. "What happened to the love of your life?"

"Ah, I walked away from her. I needed to travel. Wanderlust, I guess." He shook his head ruefully. "My one regret, if I have any, is that I left and never told her she was the love of my life."

"Didn't you ever go back?"

"I thought about it once, but I heard she was happily married to an insurance salesman, had six children and got pleasantly plump." He smiled wistfully. "But for a little while, Lola was mine."

"You never fell in love again?"

"Oh, sure," he said breezily. "But never anything like Lola. That happens once in a lifetime." He shrugged philosophically. "Maybe it was for the best. Maybe I would have found out that Lola wasn't what I thought she was. Maybe the anticipation and mystery was the best part." He tapped his head with his forefinger and winked at Leigh. "And I have great memories of a beautiful woman. I can take out those memories when it gets lonely or the nights are too long."

His words said so teasingly hit Leigh hard. Johngood had more than she'd ever have. She really had nothing of Sam, no memories except of dancing, being held by him, kissed by him. And despite all the reasons she'd come up with to stay as far away from Sam as she could, a reason to go to him obliterated all of them. This moment, right now, was all she had. And it was all she'd ever have with Sam. She knew right then that the memories of being with him would be worth any pain that came along with them after he was gone.

Johngood scooped up his box and held it as he looked back at her. "Are you all right? You look a bit pale."

She waved his question aside with a sweep of her hand. "Fine, I'm fine."

"I don't think I can do any work tomorrow. There are two incoming flights and Gertrude at the store needs some help. How about the next day? I can start chopping out the sea grass that's started to spread onto the driveway."

"Sure, all right."

"And I'll check on you tomorrow."

"You don't need to—"

He held up a hand. "Ah, you're forgetting that I'm paid to do it."

Her mother and her interfering seemed light-years away from the present, part of another life, and one she wouldn't think about right now. "All right, check on me. I wouldn't want you to lose any money."

"Exactly the way I feel." He smiled at her. "See you tomorrow." And he left, closing the door behind him.

Leigh looked at the door, then turned and hurried back through the house to change into her swimsuit. For the first time in what seemed an eternity, she was absolutely certain about what she was going to do.

Sam sat on the couch in the house watching the sun swing lower in the sky. His guitar rested on his thighs, and his fingers idly picked at the strings in a tuneless string of sounds. Then his hands stilled.

Silence surrounded him. A soundless world. No, that wasn't right. There were sounds everywhere, from the soft sigh of the breeze rustling the leaves of plants on the deck, to the distant ebb and flow of the ocean. Impulsively, he pressed his hands over his ears, shutting out as much sound as he could. Total, absolute silence. Nothing. A world without any noise.

It was beyond him to think about a world like this and enduring it forever and ever. Yet Leigh did. She awoke to silence and went to sleep in silence. Almost as bad as his waking up without her, or going to sleep without her. The thought left him with an emptiness that made his chest ache.

He stood abruptly, his guitar sliding down to land softly on the floor at his feet. Then he stepped over it and crossed to the stereo. With music bouncing off the walls, he wandered through the house, then went out on the deck and stared at the ocean as the setting sun began to smear it with reds and purples.

Sam had always gone straight ahead with his life. He'd never had time to sit and be reflective. He'd moved, going forward, taking his lumps and never stopping until he got where he wanted to go. He'd made his career happen, and he'd kept on top by knowing what he could do and doing it. But right now, he wasn't at all sure where he was going. All he knew for certain was that Leigh was all tangled up in his thoughts, in his dreams and in his life, even though she wouldn't spend any time with him.

He grabbed the safety railing and leaned forward, his shoulders hunching. Damn it all. What had happened to him? Where had he lost control over his own life? Ever since the Fourth of July concert, he'd felt control slipping away at a frightening speed. Maybe that was why he hated the idea of being isolated here so much. Then he'd met Leigh and his control seemed to slip even more, but in a totally different way.

He closed his eyes, inhaled the sweetness of the air all around him, and concentrated on steadying himself. He wasn't going to let any single person do this to him. Not a crazed fan, and not a woman who had made it very clear that she didn't want any closeness from him. He'd call Ted and tell him to make other plans, to work out a secure place near the city.

He opened his eyes, and just as he was about to head back in the house to get the telephone and call Ted, he saw Leigh on the beach. Her long legs were bare, the flimsy lace cover-up doing little to hide the hot pink of her swimsuit. It was as if he'd conjured her up, he and his overworked emotions. But the excitement of just seeing her, or the way her image made him light-headed and giddy, wasn't an illusion.

Then reality sank in. She was jogging, obviously going for a swim later, but she wasn't coming to his house. She was passing by. And his euphoria was gone as quickly as it came. He was about to turn away when he saw her stop. She looked up at the house, and he could have sworn he felt her eyes on him. Then she raised her hands to cup them at her mouth, and he heard a single word, "Swim?"

This couldn't be what he thought it was. He patted his chest, then pointed at her and made swimming motions with his hands.

Even from the distance, he saw her nod yes. He waved at her, and when she waved back, he went into the house. In a single moment everything had changed. The sense of impending doom was gone, and he felt like a teenager on a first date. He stripped, put on his trunks, grabbed a couple of towels, then ran through the house and went outside. He made himself walk to the stairs in the bluffs and not run, then he climbed down. And when he got to the bottom, he saw Leigh, the sun behind her turning her windblown curls to spun gold, and exposing the curves of her body as if the lace cover-up wasn't even there.

This was really happening. He released a breath he hadn't been aware of holding as she started toward him. She stopped in front of him, her gaze flicking over his attire, then she said in a low voice, "Do you want to go swimming?"

"Are you sure about this?" he asked, not daring to believe she was going to stay and not run from him.

"Yes, I'm sure. You were right. All we have is right now. Tomorrow you'll be Boone Patton and I'll be here working. But today, this afternoon . . ." She shrugged, a fluttery, unsteady motion that touched his heart with its vulnerability. "I'm here, and the ocean's here."

He was startled at how her words touched him, and the way his whole body was responding to her presence. "I'm glad you're here," he admitted.

Leigh stared at Sam, shocked by her own forwardness, and shocked by the truth of every word she said to this man. Now that she was here, now that she had put everything on the line, she didn't know what to do next.

Thankfully, Sam took the decision away from her. He reached for her hand, closed his fingers around it, then led the way toward the water. He let her go to spread his towels out on the sand, turning to her as she took the cover-up off. "No racing, okay?"

She smiled, knowing the expression was unsteady, but one of genuine happiness just being with this man. "No racing," she said, dropping the cover-up on the towels.

"Good," he said, flicking her chin with the tip of his finger. "Let's go swimming."

Then he had her by the hand again, and Leigh held tightly as they ran toward the water. She splashed through the surf with Sam until it was waist deep, then let go of him to dive into the low waves. She stroked away from shore, taking her time, feeling the water around her and sensing Sam to her right. As she took a breath, she looked under her arm and saw him not more than three feet away.

The sun glinted off his water-darkened hair, and his strong arms stroked easily through the calm water. She looked away, closing her eyes, her motions automatic. She felt a touch on her arm, and she stopped to tread water and turn. Sam was right there treading water, one hand skimming the clinging hair off his face. And he stroked closer to her as he spoke: "Anyplace special that you want to head for?"

She hadn't even thought where she was swimming to, just that she was with Sam. And when she looked around, she realized there wasn't any "place" to swim to out here. "I think this is it," she admitted.

He smiled at her, and the expression lit up his eyes. "Then we're here." He reached out and brushed a strand of clinging hair off her cheek. "It's nice, don't you think?"

"It's perfect," she said, totally aware of his fingers trailing along the line of her cheek.

"Absolutely."

With him touching her, she found it difficult to breathe, and she almost forgot to keep her hands moving to stay afloat. For a second, she slipped downward, bobbed back up, and Sam was still smiling. "Tired?"

"A bit," she said.

His fingertips came to rest under her chin. The pressure was light, but riveting, and made her have to keep looking at him. "Want to go back?"

For a split second she wondered if she was making the worst mistake of her life, if she was crazy to think she could take what he offered and make it a memory in her heart for the long days and nights ahead when she would be alone.

She looked into his dark eyes and knew when they went back, this wouldn't end. It wouldn't be a swim, then her going home and Sam going to his house. And a part of her knew that what could happen might shatter her, it might devastate her, yet she knew that whatever the cost, she wasn't going to turn back now.

And when Sam left the island to go back to being Boone Patton, she'd remember. Deep in the nights she'd remember, and that would be her comfort. "Yes, let's go back," she said.

She saw his lips form the word "Wonderful," before he dived to his left and started toward shore.

Leigh followed him, the pace easy, and when they reached the beach, she was barely breathing hard. She walked side by side with Sam out of the water, but they didn't touch. When they got to the towels, she spread her oversize towel out by his, and lay down on it. Aware of Sam to her right, she reached for the other towel, rubbed her hair, trying to dry it as much as possible, and she reached for the brush she'd brought with her, trying to pull it through the tangle of curls.

She chanced a look at Sam half sitting, half lying by her, his used towel discarded on the sand by him. His hair was mussed from his efforts to dry it, and he was leaning back, supporting himself on his elbows. He was watching her intently from under water-spiked lashes. She hesitated, brushing her hair. "Is . . . something wrong?"

He shook his head, not blinking. "No, not at all. I was just wondering why it's so fascinating to watch a woman brush her hair."

She felt heat in her cheeks, and took one last lick at her hair, then dropped the brush to one side. "I don't know why I'm bothering. It's a mess."

Sam didn't move but kept watching her. "It's beautiful."

It wasn't right that with a look and a few words, he could scramble her thinking. "It's a lot of work," she said quickly. "I was thinking of cutting it."

Sam moved then, sitting up, and turning toward her. "Don't do that."

"Pardon me?"

He was closer and reached out to lift an errant ringlet off her shoulder. "Don't cut it." He slowly curled the strand of hair around and around his finger. "It suits you long."

"How…how do you know that?" she asked. "We only met a few days ago."

He shrugged. "True, but it's been long enough for me to find out that you're creative, strong willed, a terrific swimmer, an avid jogger, bright, a bit protective of your privacy and…a very beautiful woman with hair that looks like spun gold."

She didn't know what to say or why she was just sitting here looking at Sam and wanting nothing more than to be closer to him.

As if he'd read her mind, he did come closer and his hand slipped under her damp hair, cupping the nape of her neck. He drew her toward him, and she didn't fight it. It felt inevitable to go to Sam, and in a very real way, the right thing to do.

His fingers tangled in her hair, and she pressed her cheek to his bare chest, to the intoxicating mixture of heat and water-cooled skin, and the hammering of his heart was so close that it felt as if it was echoing her own. In that moment she felt centered, completely focused, and tears of relief and wonder burned her eyes.

She didn't know how long they sat like that, just holding each other before Sam drew back. But he didn't let her go. His hands cupped her face with gentle strength, and even though the light was beginning to fail, she saw him say, "Do you want to leave now, or will you stay with me?"

When he spoke, she felt his chest vibration against her breasts, and her words came unbidden: "I'll stay for now, for this moment."

"For this moment," she saw him say just before his mouth found hers. Her lips parted instinctively, welcoming his pressure, then his invasion in her mouth. His tongue teased hers, flicking in and out, and she strained against him, trying to get even closer. If she could, she would have willed herself to melt into him, to become one with him in the most fundamental and breathtaking way possible. A life that had been flat and just endurable for her for so long became three-dimensional in an explosion of sensations that made her tremble.

She felt everything in that instant, every place he touched her, every spot their bodies met, and the intensity of the experience made her gasp involuntarily.

Sam drew back, his eyes skimming over her face lifted to him, over skin so translucent that it almost glowed, the wild halo of ringlets darkened to a deep bronze, and lips that were made for kissing. Then her eyes fluttered open, and the deep blueness was glazed by the same passion that was filling him.

He pulled her closer, drawing her to her knees as he got to his, and he felt her body fitting with such a neat precision into the angles of his that it was as if they had been purposely made to be like this by some higher force. She pressed her lips to his chest, and as her tongue swirled over his skin, her hands spread on his back.

Then she dropped her head back and looked up. Right then he knew she saw the needing and wanting in his own eyes. It felt as if he was being branded by it.

His hand slipped over her shoulders, trailing down her back, then stopped when he felt the clasp of her bikini top. He hesitated, wanting nothing more than to see all of her, to explore her and discover all the mysteries of Leigh Buchanan. And it was essential to him that she want him as much as he wanted her. He'd never felt a need for a woman that possessed his body, mind and soul all at the same time.

She stared at him with wide blue eyes, her lips softly parted, and her delicate nostrils flaring with each rapid breath she took. His world centered on her, and the need to taste her, to feel her beneath his hands, to possess her and see her face flushed with passion. Yet he moved his hands lower, framing her waist, drawing her hips more tightly against him, and when his mouth found hers again, he felt a happiness he couldn't begin to define when she responded to each kiss, each caress. He was lost.

In wonder, he drew back, his fingers touching her, slowly brushing her hair back off her shoulders, then tucking the unruly curls behind her ears. Unsteadily, he traced the curve of her ears, coming to rest on a spot just below her lobe where he could feel her pulse beating erratically.

"Can you see what I'm saying?" he asked.

"Yes."

"You're so beautiful," he said and the words seemed a shallow version of what he felt. He couldn't even begin to put his feelings into words.

Leigh felt his hips against hers, and the vague rocking that he initiated sent an overload of sensations through her. Her need for him was fierce and dazzling, blotting out anything she'd ever felt before in her life. The thin material of their damp bathing suits was almost like wearing nothing, but not quite, and she didn't want any barriers between them. She could feel that Sam wanted her every bit as much as she wanted him, and his eyes were dark pools, flaring with passion, yet she could see a certain sense of wonder there, the same wonder that was filling her.

She'd never been this brazen, this willing to give everything she had, and she felt dizzy with the heat and strength of the man holding her. Awkwardly she tried to undo the fastener of her bikini top, but she only fumbled, her fingers refusing to obey the simple command to unsnap the top. Then Sam's hand was over hers, and she stared at him, his eyes never leaving hers, as he deftly flicked the fastener undone.

Without looking down, he slipped the string straps off her shoulders, then down her arms until the small piece of damp material was free from her skin. And he flicked it back over his shoulder.

Leigh was shocked that she didn't feel embarrassment at her own nakedness, but as Sam drew back and looked at her, she felt giddy, and she swayed toward him again. With unsteady hands, she reached out, touching his chest, feeling the light sprinkling of damp hair, the heat, the ripple of muscles and the hammering of his heart under her palms.

Then he was easing her back onto the towels, supporting himself on one elbow to look down at her, and he touched her, his hand cupping the weight of her breast. She gasped at the contact and closed her eyes to try to absorb sensation that threatened to explode deep in her being. His thumbs teased her nipples to hard buds, and her breasts throbbed and swelled under his touch.

Her eyes fluttered open, meeting the burning gaze of his, and he leaned over her, his mouth finding what his hands had just discovered. She cried out from the intensity of sensations that zinged through her whole body, before centering in her most feminine parts. For an instant she couldn't move. She couldn't think. As his tongue swirled around her nipple, and his hand skimmed over her stomach to the top of her bikini pants, she arched upward, toward his touch.

In less than a heartbeat, her panties were gone, and as she felt his hand go lower, her legs opened willingly, and he touched her. And she pressed against the contact. "Oh, yes," she managed as he pressed then drew back, only to press again. "Yes, yes," she moaned.

When his hand stilled on her, she raised her hips, wanting that rhythm again, but when it didn't come, she opened her eyes. His face was so close to hers that she could see the flaring of gold in his irises. "Tell me what you want," he said, the heat of his breath against her lips.

She moved, reaching for his swimming trunks, tugging at the waistband. "You," she said, "Just you."

Chapter 11

Sam was motionless for what seemed an eternity, then he moved away from Leigh, rolling to his right, and she turned to watch him, to reach out to touch his back as he slipped off his trunks. Then he came back to her, and for a fleeting moment, she saw him. Anything she might have fantasized about in her wildest imaginings couldn't come close to the reality of the man. His evident need for her literally took her breath away and she closed her eyes for an instant to try to ease her reaction, to control the way her body tightened.

But as soon as he touched her again, and she opened her eyes, she knew how foolish she was. She didn't want control. She wanted to give up, to give in and take whatever she could. His fingers touched her lips, tracing the unsteadiness there, then dropped to the line of her jaw. "Do you want to go up to the house?" he asked.

All she wanted was Sam. "No," she said.

"Here?"

"Yes, here and now."

"Here and now," he echoed. "This moment."

"Yes," she breathed and circled her arms around his neck to pull him back down to her. He smiled, an expression unsteady with intensity, and he was kissing her again. His hands roamed over her body, building fires and needs with the swiftness of a bolt of lightning.

And the words "this moment" echoed over and over again in her mind as Sam kissed and tasted her, as his fingers explored her, as she strained toward that touch. And when he found the aching throb in her, she held her breath. Then his fingers moved, the rhythm strong and sure, and she felt a stunning concentration of such pure ecstasy that she was sure she wouldn't survive.

His hand stilled, and just when she was ready to cry out from frustration, Sam was over her. Supporting himself with his hands on the towel at either side of her head, she felt his weight barely brush the length of her body. And that wasn't what Leigh wanted. She wanted complete, intimate contact, and as she took in a shuddering breath, she wrapped her arms around his neck and tried to pull him down to her.

She ached with the need to feel his weight on her, to feel him deep inside her, to feel him fill her and know what it felt like to be one with him. And she lifted her hips, parting her legs, all caution gone as if it had never been.

He was still for a long moment, his eyes locked with hers, then he took her invitation. She felt him touch her with silky heat, test her and as she lifted her hips even higher, she felt him enter her. Slowly, sweetly, he filled her, and as he began to move, to thrust and move inside her, a deep, radiating ecstasy shimmered through her.

And with each deep connection, the ecstasy grew, until it flashed through her, exploding every nerve in her body.

For a moment she couldn't endure it, and she pushed against Sam's shoulders, crying out, "No, please," and he stopped, motionless over her, but not leaving her.

"Leigh?" she saw him say, and she could feel the vibration of his voice through her whole body. His face was flushed and damp with perspiration. His jaw was clenched, but he didn't move. "Do you want to stop?"

"Oh, Lord," she moaned. "No, please." She had thought she'd die if he kept moving, but she knew she would surely die if he stopped now.

And he started to move again, slowly, the thrusts deeper each time, and the intensity inside her only grew. She dug her fingers into his shoulders, wrapped her legs around his hips, almost afraid now that he would stop. But he didn't. And as she fell further and further into a blinding explosion of sensations, she never closed her eyes. She never took her gaze off Sam's face, and he never stopped looking at her.

He thrust deeper and deeper, harder and harder, until the world consisted only of Sam and what he made her feel. She was jolted by a surge of pure rapture, that amazingly grew and grew until it possessed her. And when she thought she couldn't take the intensity of the pleasure, it moved to a higher level. She saw him gasp her name and felt him shudder, the world exploded into shimmering, melting pleasure that took her beyond anything she'd ever known in her life.

When the intensity began to shift and mellow, and the spasms of fulfillment subsided, Sam felt as if he was returning to the world again from a place that there was no way to describe except for one word—Leigh. And she was wrapped around him, her arms around his neck, her legs around his hips, and gently, with regret, he left her body.

Settling beside her, he felt the gentle breeze off the ocean skimming over his damp skin, yet there was no chill.

He put his arm around, and drew her to him, the image of her flushed with pleasure, her eyes heavy with fulfillment engraved in his mind. And he experienced such a sense of completeness that he could barely absorb it. When she snuggled contentedly into his side, he felt his breath catch, then her hand rested high on his chest, the tips of her fingers against the hollow of his throat.

He stared up at the night sky, stars dusting the darkness, and he wondered if he'd ever felt as much at peace in his life. Lazily, his hand played with Leigh's hair, the curls tickling his skin. It was as if there had been no women before her, yet he knew that was a lie. But it didn't stop the feeling of newness or the sense of uniqueness that he experienced.

When Leigh shifted and rested her thigh across his, he didn't dare move. He could feel the instant response in him, that nudging of desire that just moments ago he thought had been quenched thoroughly and completely. Then he closed his eyes, and wondered what was going on. He'd never fitted the norm in his family, getting married, having children, settling down. He'd never found one person who even made him think in those directions.

Now, in this place away from the real world, the idea had begun to grow in him. All because of Leigh. He stroked her hair, letting his fingers tangle in the unruly curls, and he whispered, "Maybe this is the way love starts."

Leigh edged up on one elbow to look down at him. "What did you say?" she asked, and even her voice played havoc with his nerves.

He stared at her, all shadows and softness in the night, and he couldn't say the words again. Instead, he said, "Do you want to go up to the house?"

He could see her straining to make out what he was saying, but she obviously understood. "I don't know. I love it down here, all shut off from the world."

"And what if Johngood comes looking for you?" he teased, needing humor to break whatever hold she was weaving around him.

She chuckled at that. "He's been married several times, so I hardly think he'd be shocked. But I would be." She moved away from him, reaching for her clothes and her cover-up.

Sam stood, taking one look at his wet trunks and reached for the towel on the sand. He quickly wrapped it around him sarong-style, then picked up the rest of his things. When he turned, he found Leigh with a towel wrapped around her, her clothes and the other towel in her arms.

He got close enough to her so she could see his lips and knew he had to ask her something. "Do you want me to take you back to *your* house?"

She hesitated for just a fraction of a second, then shook her head. "No, not just yet."

With a wonderful sense of relief that she wasn't going to leave him for now, he reached for her. He circled her shoulders with his free arm and led the way to the stairs to take Leigh up to his home.

Leigh knew she was drifting toward wakefulness, but she hesitated, staying in that twilight zone of softness between sleep and waking. She could feel sunlight on her eyelids, and she had a sense of being in a strange place, but being completely safe as long as she stayed asleep.

When she opened her eyes, she knew she was going to have to face something she wasn't sure she could deal with. So she let herself drift, staying in that gentleness. Gradually, she became aware of heat along her back, strong legs bent to match hers, and an arm lying heavily around her waist. And she remembered. Sam. The beach. Loving him.

She felt her breath catch at that thought. But she couldn't deny it. She loved him. She probably had from the first, but to admit it was earth-shattering. She'd loved him and stayed with him. She'd come up to the house with him, turned to him in this room and went to him with a sense of rightness that should have only come after years of intimacy.

The touching, the kissing, the exploring had gone on for what seemed an eternity before Sam took her again. And that time it had been as intense and shattering as the first, leaving her weak and sated. She'd fallen asleep in Sam's arms, allowing herself the luxury of staying until morning...until now.

She felt him stir, his breath ruffle her hair, his hand move at her waist to cup the fullness of her hip, and she rolled over to face him. The sight of him close to her, his eyes still heavy with sleep, a slight smile touching his lips made her heart leap in her chest. Yes, she loved him and she'd have memories that would last a lifetime.

"Morning," he said, his finger tangling with her hair.

She touched his jaw and felt the prickling of a beard under her fingertips. She loved him, and she had no idea what to say or what to do. Part of her never wanted to leave this bed, but the sane part told her that it was time to go.

But before she could do or say anything, Sam moved, rolling away from her, and she saw him reach for the phone on the nightstand. He pulled the receiver to his ear and sank back in the pillow and put his other arm around Leigh. He mouthed the words "a phone call" to her, then spoke into the receiver as he pulled Leigh against his chest.

His chin rested against the top of her head, and she felt the vibrations against her cheek as he spoke into the phone. She closed her eyes, letting herself experience the sensations of nearness to Sam, storing up the feelings of his heat against her. She spread her hand on his stomach, reveling in the softness of hair against her palm, the way his muscles rippled, the gentle way he massaged her upper arm and buried his fingers in her hair.

Contentment was a new sensation to her, and she found that she liked it. But there was something just beyond it, the same thing she'd known was there when she was waking. There was a goodbye sooner or later, and the contentment would dissolve as if it had never been. But for now she clutched at it.

Sam shifted, stretching to his right, and settled back, his arm closing around Leigh again. Leigh moved back a bit to look up at him. Finding him staring at the ceiling, his jaw working with tension, she lifted herself on her elbow to look down at him. Tucking her hair behind her ear, she pressed her hand to his chest against the reassuring beat of his heart. "What's wrong?" she asked.

It took him a moment to look at her, then his dark eyes met hers. "That was Ted, my manager. I've got a problem."

She tensed. "That woman?"

"Partly."

He pushed up, breaking the contact with Leigh to lean back against the headboard. And she sat up, tugging the sheet with her to sit cross-legged on the bed facing Sam. With sleep-tousled hair and the shadow of a beard, he looked endearingly vulnerable, until she saw the expression in his eyes. "Is it that bad?" she asked.

"Bad?" He shook his head, then combed his fingers through his hair, spiking it around his face. "No, at least I don't think it's all bad."

She frowned at him. "What are you talking about?"

She saw him exhale before he spoke again. "Ted says that someone's been inquiring about the flight plans filed with the charter service where he got the jet that flew me down here. He's uncomfortable about it, and he wanted me to know."

"He thinks it's that woman?"

"Could be. Or it could be some ambitious reporter." He smiled, a wry, crooked smile. "They're pretty inventive when it comes to getting a line on a story."

"That's why he called?"

"Partly. The other thing is something I forgot about. I promised to be at a show that benefits a charity I've worked with over the years. Ted thought at first I should forgo it, but now he's not so sure."

She began to feel a chill that came from the inside out. "What sort of show?"

"A gala event where all the proceeds go to the charity, and the performers donate their talents. And it's really worthwhile. It raises a lot of money for the charity."

"Which charity is it?"

He named a group that helped abused children, one that Leigh had heard about before. "That's a good cause."

"A very good cause."

She had to ask the next question. "When is the show?"

"Tonight."

She could barely utter the word. "Where?"

"Los Angeles."

"Oh," she said, knowing it must be a flat word, and she looked away from him to the sheet she was clutching in her hands. "I see."

What she really saw was, this was it, the end. It was over. And she knew without a doubt that the memories would never be enough. She couldn't look at Sam, not yet, so she scrambled out of the bed. She felt the sheet slip off of her, and she hurried toward the bathroom and protection. But before she could get to the door, Sam was behind her, his hand on her shoulder, stopping her dead.

She stared at the bathroom door, not daring to turn to Sam. But she had no choice as he gently pulled her around until she had to look at him. The urge to cover herself was overwhelming, almost as intense as her need to get into the bathroom and close the door. But she didn't. She looked at Sam, and the impact of his image before her was so intense that she had to hug her arms around herself to stop a spontaneous trembling that began deep in her soul.

Naked, with no embarrassment, he stood in front of her and frowned at her. "What's going on?" he demanded.

"I thought that was clear. You're leaving." She bit her lip hard. "The moment's gone, isn't it?"

"It doesn't have to be," he said.

She hugged herself so tightly that her fingers dug into her upper arms. "But it is. That was the deal. We took the moment, then you'd go off and be Boone Patton in the rest of the world."

"And I will. Tonight in Los Angeles." He didn't come closer, but she was finding it harder and harder to breathe. "Leigh, I want you to come with me."

She stared at him, stunned. "What?"

"I want you to come with me to Los Angeles. We'll fly out on the plane Ted's chartered and go to the charity show."

She held out both hands in front of her, and began to back up. "No...no..." she breathed, shaking her head. "Don't do this. Please, don't do this."

He came closer to her, but didn't touch her. "Let me explain. The plane will be at the airport on the island in an hour, ready to go back. We can make the flight—"

She closed her eyes and hugged her arms around herself again. She couldn't see him say those things. She couldn't, not when they conjured up flashes of the nightmare she hadn't had for six months, scenes that seared through her mind—people staring at her, pitying her, confusing her and scaring her.

She didn't move, just trying to breathe. Finally she opened her eyes, and Sam wasn't there. For one beat of her heart, she thought he'd left, that he was gone, and she would never see him again. Then he was back, coming around from behind her. He slipped on a pair of cutoff shorts and held out his robe to her.

"I got this while you were shutting me out. Put it on. It'll make it easier to talk sense."

She grabbed at the soft terry, fumbling with it until she had it around her, and she tied the belt at her waist. Then she looked up at Sam, who stood right in front of her.

"Don't ever do that to me again," he said.

"What?"

"Don't ever shut me out like that." His face looked strained and tight. "I hate it. I feel as if I'm all alone, even though you're here."

So do I, she wanted to say, and it's just beginning. You aren't even gone and I've never felt more alone. "I—I don't want to talk about this. You're going, and I—"

"You're coming with me. I'm not ready to just walk away, to say 'it's been fun' and fly off into the sunset."

She felt her eyes burn, and Sam's image was beginning to swim in front of her. "But that's exactly what you're going to do. This . . . this was for now, for here. That's it."

"No," he said, his face darkening with impatience. "That's not it." He reached out as if he would touch her, and she moved quickly, crossing the room to find her clothes. She was getting out of here now. But before she could gather up her bikini and cover-up, Sam had her by her upper arm and was pulling her around to face him.

She tried to jerk out of his hold, but he only tightened his grip. "Let me go," she said.

"No."

She looked into his face, at the determination there, and she managed, "I have to go."

"Why can't you fly out with me, go to the show, then I'll fly back here with you."

"You don't have to come back here. Your manager might be right about that woman. She could be coming here right now."

Sam was choked by frustration and the fear that Leigh was going to walk out of his life and he'd never be with her again. He didn't understand what was happening between the two of them, but one thing was crystal clear...he didn't want to leave her. And now she was saying things that Ted had said minutes ago.

"If it's her inquiring about the flights, you can't go back there. I'll set up security at the Hollywood Oasis, one of the bungalows. You can be there until the ranch is completely secure, or until Lopez finds the woman." Now Leigh was telling him the same thing, and he couldn't deny it.

"I probably can't come back here to stay, but I can fly back with you. And you can see my world, see what I do and see that it's not so terrifying out there."

He thought his words would be comforting, hopefully persuasive. He didn't expect her to pale and her eyes to widen. "You don't understand," she whispered in an unsteady voice.

No, he didn't. But he'd be damned if he left this room before he did understand. "Explain it to me."

He thought she was going to turn and run, bolt for the door, but she didn't. She was very still, then she crossed and sat on the side of the bed. When she looked up at him, her eyes were overly bright. "I told you, I came here to be in control of my life."

He went across to her, dropping to his haunches in front of her. "Yes, you did."

"I never told you how out of control my life was before I came here. I never told you about waking to a world that held no sounds, not even whispers. Or about how when that happens, you lose your sense of balance sometimes. That's why Johngood is putting in the higher railing on the stairs at my house."

She worried the tie on her robe, and she looked down at her hands, her voice becoming flat, as if she was reciting something that held no reality for her.

"I tried to adjust, to be hopeful about getting better. But every specialist said the same thing—irreversibly hearing-impaired. And I finally accepted that. I tried to keep going, to fit in, to live the way I had, but I couldn't."

He wanted to touch her, to hold her hand, to let her know he was there and she wasn't alone, but he was afraid to make any contact. He didn't want to stop her words, which were giving him the first real glimpse into what she'd gone through.

"I tried. I really did. Satch—the man I was engaged to—he tried. But he couldn't accept it, not really. And my parents tried. Everyone tried, but it didn't work. I learned to lip-read. Some can't do it, but I could. And I thought..." She licked her lips nervously. "I had a showing at Satch's gallery, and it was the first time I was really going out into the world and I thought it could work."

She took a shaky breath and kept talking, the words coming faster and her voice growing less steady.

"We got to the gallery. Satch gave me a necklace, and the people started to arrive. And it went well at first." She twisted the robe tie until it was coiled tightly around her finger. "Then I got confused, and I didn't see what people were saying, and I was dizzy, and I—I had to leave. I just walked out, and everyone was looking at me. I never did it again."

He touched her chin, lifting her face until she was looking at him. "Didn't the guests understand?"

Her eyes looked glazed, as if she didn't even know he was still there. "They didn't know how...how sick I'd been."

"You didn't tell them you couldn't hear?"

Her gaze sharpened and dots of high color touched her cheeks. "God, no. I couldn't." She moved her head to avoid his touch, and he drew his hand back.

"The way you didn't tell me? So I had to find out for myself?"

"You don't understand. If people know you're...not well, they look at you differently. They pity you, and they make concessions for you. You aren't the same person to them anymore."

"You're not being fair," he said.

"What?"

"You're not playing fair when you don't tell them and give them a chance to do the right thing."

"I don't worry about fair. I worry about survival. That's why I'm here. I had nightmares about that showing. They were awful. I couldn't sleep, and I couldn't work. And I knew I had to make a clean break and be someplace where I was safe, where I'd never be in that position again."

Sam was stunned that he could almost feel her pain, her need to be protected, and strangely, he wanted to be the one to protect her.

"You see why I can't come back with you? I left that all behind. I don't fit in in places like that because..." She let her voice trail off.

"Because you're deaf," he finished for her.

As soon as he said the words, he wished he hadn't. She stood, almost knocking him over. And she was partway to the door before he stopped her by hurrying to stand directly in her path and block her exit. "Please, let me go."

"I can't," he said with so much honesty that it hurt. "I know how you feel. But come with me to Los Angeles, give me a chance to show you how good it can be. The people I work with are good people, decent people. They wouldn't do anything to hurt you."

She shook her head sharply, her curls dancing around her face from the action. "No, no, that's just it. They'll look at me like I'm handicapped."

"Then they don't have to know. You can be with me, stay by the stage, see the show, then we'll fly right back out." He saw her hesitate and pressed his advantage. "I promise you, you won't be alone. I won't leave you except when I'm onstage."

"I don't fit in that world," she said, but there wasn't as much conviction behind the words.

"And we'll come back here. If there's any danger for me to return, I'll fly you back, make sure you get here, then I'll leave. I won't push for any more." He tried to smile, but his expression felt as tight as his chest was becoming. "I promise you that." He went closer, so close that he could hear her ragged breathing, but he didn't touch her. "I just want a bit more time with you."

Leigh wanted to close her eyes, to block out everything, but she didn't. She kept looking at Sam, and she knew he was telling her the truth. What made it worse, she knew she wanted more time, too. She shouldn't. She should be running out of the house right now, but something stopped her. She *did* trust him. She would never have come here yesterday if she didn't. And she loved him. And all he was asking of her was one more day.

She was crushing the clothes in her hands. "Just there and back?" she asked.

He nodded. "We'll leave in about an hour, be there for a rehearsal, then the show, and we can fly right out after the show's finished. We can be back here by tomorrow morning at the latest." He came a step closer and touched her cheek with the back of his knuckles. "Come with me?"

His touch feathered across her cheek, and she dropped her clothes to the floor as she reached up to take his hand. Drawing it to her breasts, she nodded. "For one more day."

"Thank you," Sam said simply, then he pulled her to him.

It was too easy to lean against him, to let his essence surround her, but she didn't move away. She let him hold her, let him press his lips to her hair, then she stepped back to look up at him. "I—I have to go back home to get some clothes, and I need to leave a note for Johngood. He's expecting me to be there today."

"All right." He glanced at the bedside clock, then back to Leigh, his hands resting on her shoulders. "We both need to shower and change." A teasing smile touched his lips. "One shower is faster than two."

"But . . . my clothes are at my house," she said, heat beginning to flow through her from the look in his eyes.

"I'll give you my robe. You can wear it home—" his hands moved until his thumbs rested on either side of her throat "—and get dressed there."

She tried to smile, to tease the way he was, but her heart was beating too fast. "I guess one shower . . ."

Her voice trailed off as his hands dropped to the belt of her robe and began to undo it. She stood very still, breathing almost impossible, as he pushed the terry cloth off her shoulders and let it slip to the floor around her feet.

"Now…" Sam said as he unzipped his shorts and neatly stepped out of them, "the shower." And he reached for Leigh, sweeping her up into his arms and headed for the bathroom. She wrapped her arms around his neck and looked up at him as he smiled and winked. "Water conservation."

"But we don't have a water shortage down here," she said as they stepped into the bathroom, and Sam set her on her feet by the shower stall.

"You never know," Sam said as he reached into the large stall and turned on the water. "And we have a tight time schedule." With a pat on her bottom, he urged her through the open door. "Let's get on with this."

Leigh went ahead of him, and as steam and warmth began to fill the air, Sam came in with her and closed the door. He stepped under the water. It plastered his hair around his head and shoulders, sheeting over his body and he reached out to grab her by the hand.

Then Leigh was under the water with him, warmth and comfort all around, and his hands cupped her breasts. As he lowered his head to find her lips with his, as the water rained all around them, she was hit by how right this all felt. And how it wouldn't be after tomorrow. Tears came, silent scalding tears that mingled with the shower stream, and as Sam's hands began to roam over her, cupping her hips, pulling her tightly against him, and his lips tasted that spot beneath her ear, she let the tears fall. Tears for what could never be.

Chapter 12

Half an hour later, Sam and Leigh were at her house and she was in the bedroom hurriedly dressing in jeans, a tank top and leather sandals. She packed an overnight bag with a white, off-the-shoulder sundress, toiletries, makeup and low heels, then pulled her hair back off her face with a fabric band. Laying Sam's robe across the foot of her bed, she picked up her bag and headed for the door.

As she came out of her bedroom, she saw Sam at the windows looking outside. The sun of the day clearly defined the man, the line of his jaw, the way his hair fell to his shoulders, vaguely curling from the dampness that lingered from the shower, and the way his shoulders strained against the fine material of the loose white shirt he wore with fresh jeans and scuffed running shoes.

As she remembered the time she'd spent with Sam, the tears and their coming together with the water all around, and that feeling that the center of the universe was right here and now, she looked away.

She was startled when the red light over the front door began to flash, and she turned to Sam. "Someone's at the door."

He turned, his eyes meeting hers for one intense moment of awareness, then he glanced at the door and saw the light. He headed for the door and pulled it open.

Leigh trailed after him and saw Johngood in a lemon yellow shirt staring at Sam, his mouth agape. Then he grinned. "So you're visiting?"

Sam was speaking to him, but Leigh couldn't see what he was saying until he turned toward her. "And she wanted to leave you a note, but now she can explain for herself."

Johngood stepped in and came to Leigh, eyeing the case in her hand. "So you're going off for a bit?"

"Just for today, and I'll be back tomorrow morning at the latest."

"What about your call?"

"We can do it tomorrow." She hesitated, then added, "And we don't need to mention this little trip when we make the call, do we?"

"Of course not." His smile deepened. "I've been telling you that you needed to get out a bit. L.A. is a bit, indeed."

Sam came up behind Johngood. "Time to go, Leigh. We can just make it to the airport if we leave now."

Johngood held up one hand. "Go. I'll close up."

"All right," Leigh said as Sam reached around Johngood to take her bag. "I'll be home tomorrow."

During the flight to Los Angeles, Leigh sat opposite Sam, managed to eat a light lunch, and sipped some white wine. While the constant throb of the jet engines seemed to be all around, she watched Sam, letting him talk, fascinated by his childhood in Connecticut, his family and his life. And she wondered what his brothers looked like, how they acted, what his parents were like.

A large family was as foreign to her as the idea of getting on a stage and performing in front of thousands of people.

"I don't know how you can do that," she said to Sam, enjoying the way his eyes sparkled and the pleasure in his face when he spoke about his music.

"I was scared to death the first time I had to perform in front of an audience, but once I got on stage and the music started, it felt right." He sat back, his drink resting on his thigh. "It's a rush after a while, feeling the energy of the audience, knowing you're really controlling them with your talent." He shook his head. "I sound like an egomaniac, don't I?"

He sounded like a man who loved what he did, and that saddened Leigh. How she wished she could share it, feel it and hear it. And that thought dampened all the good feelings that had been growing while Sam told her about his life. "No, you sound as if it's the most important thing in the world to you."

His eyes narrowed. "Yes, I always thought it was." He glanced at a digital clock by the cabin door that constantly adjusted for the time changes as they flew west, then back to Leigh. "Just another hour or so until we land."

She covered a yawn with her hand, then sat forward and set her drink on the table between them. "This show, what do you have to do exactly?"

"Just two songs, and say a few words about the charity, and we're out of there. We might have to show at a small gathering afterward for a few minutes, then we can head back to the island."

It sounded simple enough, but Leigh wondered if that was wishful thinking. She just hoped that this hadn't been a horrible mistake coming here with him. If she hadn't been so greedy for that extra bit of time with Sam, she would have stayed on the island where she was safe.

One of the crew came into the cabin and crossed to talk to Sam. She saw the man saying something about their arrival, that it was covered, and security was already in place.

Leigh looked away from the two men, rested her head back on the seat support and closed her eyes. She felt a strange lethargy, probably a bit from the wine and probably from not getting a lot of sleep the night before. She thought about that, letting the memory push aside her growing misgivings, and with a sigh, she felt herself slipping into a light sleep.

At first she welcomed it, a way to relax and forget for a few minutes, then everything went wrong. The nightmare was back, but changed and distorted, more horrible than the original. The gallery was gone, replaced by a theater packed with yelling, screaming people, and she was in the middle of them, being pushed and shoved. A spotlight cut a circle out of darkness on the stage, and Sam was there, but not the man she knew.

He was dressed the way he had been on the tape cover, sequins and color and studied sexuality. And when he saw her, he shook his head, his eyes in deep shadows from the stark light above.

He was singing, she knew he was, but when the crowds began to sway together, she couldn't move. There was no vibration, no sense of sound around her, and the more fluidly the crowd moved in unison, the more stiff she became.

Then she realized people were looking at her, not at Sam, and they were yelling at her, shaking their hands in anger. "Don't you hear the music?" they screamed at her. "Don't you hear him singing?"

She wanted to scream back at them, to make them stop, to make them go away. But she couldn't move. She couldn't utter a word. And they came closer and closer, then Sam was there right in front of her. He was looking at her, and now she could see his eyes.

The pity in the brown depths made her sick. She felt her stomach spasm, and the world began to spin horribly. And even before she saw him speak, she knew what he was going to say.

"She's deaf. She can't hear."

And in a horrible twist that could only come in a nightmare, she heard every word he said, and they burned into her soul.

"No!" she screamed, wanting to shut him up, to shut his words out of her mind and heart. "No, no, stop!"

With wrenching speed, she was awake, sitting straight up in her chair, and when she opened her eyes, she saw Sam quickly getting up and coming around the table to her. The next moment she was on her feet, being pulled into his arms, and her cheek was pressed against the vibrations of his heart.

She balled her hands into fists on Sam's chest and felt choked with tears, but none would come. Her eyes ached and burned, and yet she couldn't cry. She was beyond that release.

Then Sam was holding her back, and she was looking into his face, at concern and worry. "A nightmare?" she saw him ask.

She pressed her fingertips to her mouth and nodded.

His hands shifted to cup her face, his thumbs moving slowly, seductively on her cheeks. "The same one you told me about?"

"Sort of," she said, as one of the crew came up behind Sam.

She moved back to drop down in her seat as the men talked, then Sam took his seat opposite her. "Buckle up," he said, "they're getting ready to land."

She fumbled with her seat belt, finally pushed the buckle together and sat back, gripping the arms of the chair tightly. She felt the engine power change, the nose tilt down, and she waited for that moment when the tires made contact with the earth.

When she looked back at Sam, he asked, "Are you all right?"

She didn't know if she'd recognize the state of being "all right" anymore. It seemed as if it had been forever that she was adjusting, coping, making do, except for her time with Sam. And now she had to start all over again. "I'm not a good flyer. This is the first time I've flown in a little plane."

Sam shifted, leaning forward against the restraint of the seat belt and managed to cover her hand with his just as the tires bounced on the runway. "This is one of the best small jets made. Ted only uses the best." His fingers closed over hers. "And we're down in one piece."

She closed her eyes for a moment, then let go of the chair arm to lace her fingers with Sam's. "What now?"

Sam unsnapped his belt and moved to the edge of his seat, still holding her hand. "Ted said there would be a security escort waiting for us, and we'd go directly to the auditorium." He glanced at the digital clock. "It's five now. The show's at seven. I can get in a quick rehearsal with the backup band before it's time to start."

Leigh saw the door being opened from the outside, then a man stepped in. He was large and imposing, dressed all in black—a black suit, black turtleneck shirt under it and black cowboy boots. Even his hair was black, a true black that almost reflected back blue highlights. It was skimmed back in a ponytail from a face that had a faintly exotic look, with high cheekbones, a strong jaw and startling pale blue eyes.

His head almost touched the roof of the cabin, and when he came toward Sam, Leigh felt the weight of his steps making the plane tremble. "Mr. Patton?"

Sam let go of Leigh and stood to hold his hand out to the large man. "Yes, and you're the security?"

"Yes, sir. I'm Quint," he said as he shook hands with Sam. "Bigelow wants you to go right to the auditorium." As he let Sam's hand go, he cast a slanting glance at Leigh, then back to Sam. "He said you were alone."

"Well, I'm not. Miss Buchanan gets the same protection I do."

"Yes, sir," Quint said, and inclined his head to Leigh in acknowledgment, then looked back at Sam. "Sorry to say it leaked out that you were coming in, and there's half the world out there waiting to see you."

Sam didn't look terribly concerned by the news. "All right, what do we do?"

"Here's the plan. We've got you covered. All you need to do is go down the stairs, straight ahead to the gate, and the limo's right there. We'll run interference and cover your back. You two just get in the limo as quickly as you can. Let me worry about the rest."

Sam reached for Leigh's hand and asked Quint, "When do we go?"

"Just a minute," he said, then crossed to the door and looked out. The pale eyes turned back on Sam. "Right now. Let's do it."

Sam looked down at Leigh. "Did you get all of that?"

"To... to the gate and into the limousine."

"Right. Don't stop, and stay with me." He kissed her quickly, his lips warm on her cold cheek. "Trust me—it'll all be over before you know it," he said. With his free hand, he reached for a white Stetson that had been lying on a nearby chair.

He put it on, pulling it low in front, then looked at Leigh and nodded to the door. "Ready?"

She nodded and went with Sam. They followed Quint out the door onto portable stairs and into bright sun. Leigh didn't mean to, but she stopped dead after taking a single step.

They had about fifty feet from the bottom of the steps to the gate where a white stretch limousine was parked. But that fifty-foot stretch of pavement was lined by a surging crowd, mostly women and girls, barely contained by airport personnel who were linking hands to form a human barrier.

Leigh could tell the crowd was yelling, and the air vibrated with what she could see them saying, "Boone, Boone, Boone," over and over again. Some held up signs ranging from "I love you, Boone!" to "You can sing to me anytime!" Her first instinct was to go back inside the plane and hide, but before she had a chance to act, Sam was urging her along with him, down the metal stairs.

As they got to the bottom, more men dressed like Quint appeared, stepping to the front and the side of them, forming a human wedge to get past the people who surged closer and closer. Leigh felt as if she had been propelled into a whole new nightmare, where hands were reaching out, the air was getting close and she was hurtling toward some unimaginable horror.

Then they were at the gate with the limo less than five feet away, and a uniformed man was pulling the door open. Airport officials were trying to keep people away from it, and Leigh felt someone pushing her in the small of her back, keeping her going toward the car as she hesitated.

She was at the gate, going through, and for a brief instant, she saw a single woman standing back from the crush, leaning against the fence, probably the only one there who wasn't in a frenzy to get closer to Sam. Dark and tiny in a red tailored suit, the woman simply stared at Sam, a smile on her lips. Sanity in a sea of insanity, Leigh thought, then the woman looked at her, and the smile was gone as if it had never been. And in that instant Leigh felt such hatred that she was stunned.

But before she could assimilate it, she was being propelled into the limo. She half fell onto the leather seats, and as she righted herself, Sam was beside her, the door was being shut, and for a brief time, she thought the world had returned to just the two of them. Then she noticed a third person in the luxury car.

As the limo started to drive off, she looked at a slender man in a dark blue suit sitting in the facing seat, his deeply tanned face set in a frown. "Mr. Patton," she saw him say looking at Sam. "Welcome back to Los Angeles."

Sam touched Leigh's hand when he saw Detective Lopez was in the limousine, looking as cool and controlled as the last time they met. He sensed Leigh looking at him, but he spoke to the slender man. "Detective. Do I get a personal escort?"

"I thought I'd ride along and see how you people live." He glanced around the limousine's plush leather interior. "Not bad. Not bad at all. It sure beats the hell out of a squad car."

Sam felt Leigh lace her fingers with his and hold on tightly. And when he glanced at her, she was looking at him questioningly. "Leigh, this is Detective Lopez. He's been working on my case."

He looked at Lopez. "This is Leigh Buchanan. She's going to be with me while I'm here. I already told my security people that she gets the same protection I do. Maybe you could tell your people who she is and to keep an eye on her.''

Lopez nodded. ''I'll make sure there's a man put on her. Now, have you decided what you're going to do after the show?''

''I'm heading back to the island.''

''Ted told you about the inquiries into your flight plan?''

Sam felt Leigh's hold on him tighten. ''Yes, he did.''

The detective sat back in the leather seat as the car drove silently out of the airport and onto the congested street. ''We don't know who made the inquiry, so I don't want you to take any chances. Going back to the island isn't a good idea.''

''I figured as much. Ted said he was setting up a bungalow at the Oasis, and I'll come back tomorrow and go there until they get the Malibu place secured.''

''Good idea. Bigelow's on top of things. He's hired an excellent private security firm, and we'll give you as much coverage tonight as we can...to both of you.'' Lopez looked at Leigh, then back at Sam. ''I think it's important to keep your relationship with the lady quiet.''

''What are you talking about?''

''Jealousy, irrational hate.''

Sam hadn't even considered the fact that Leigh herself would be in danger other than in his fallout. ''You don't think this psycho would...?''

''What do you think?'' Lopez countered.

When Sam looked at Leigh, she was staring at Lopez, her eyes unblinking. Why hadn't he thought of this? God, he'd been so wrapped up in having her with him, of reassuring her, that it never crossed his mind that his ''fan'' would direct any of her psychotic behavior at Leigh.

Selfish bastard, he thought to himself and sat back in the seat, never letting go of Leigh.

"Detective Lopez, just how close are you to finding this lunatic?"

The man shrugged, his face impassive. "Closer than we were when you left, but not close enough to tell you this is going to be over soon."

Sam took off his hat, tossed it across to land on the seat next to the policeman and murmured, "Great."

He spotted the built-in bar, and turned to ask Leigh if she wanted a drink. But he never got the words out. Her eyes were closed, and he felt, even though she was letting him hold her hand, she was effectively shutting him and his world out of her life.

He looked back at Lopez. "Do you want a drink?"

The man nodded, "I could use a club soda."

Sam motioned to the bar with his free hand. "Good. Help yourself and while you're doing it, pour me some Scotch."

The euphoria the woman had felt when she'd found out Boone was on Serenity Island was nothing to match the feelings she experienced when she was contacted by Bigelow's office to tell her he'd be coming back. Or the rage she'd felt when he'd stepped off the plane with that woman.

She stared at the limousine, its gleaming white disappearing into the surging crowd as it headed for the exit from the airport. Rage made her head spin, and flarings of red rimmed her vision. She fought for control, to hide her feelings until it was time to put her plan into action. She closed her eyes, trying to concentrate on Boone when he'd stepped off the plane—tanned, lean, sexy and here.

But she couldn't keep that image in place. The woman edged it out, the woman he'd been holding by the hand when they stepped out of the plane, the woman he'd stayed so close to, protectively, his hand on her back urging her forward.

That should have been her. It would have been, if there hadn't been lies and denial. Reddish-blond hair, tanned, slender. She'd watched him intently. Then the woman had looked right at her as she came through the gate, and hatred had filled her. She was probably the woman he'd had at his house in Malibu, the one who'd shared his bed.

Screams cut through her inside her head, but she kept her mouth clamped shut. Then she slowly opened her eyes and took deep, even breaths.

This would soon be over—all the pain, all the agony. Boone would be hers. This woman just made things a bit more complicated. When she got Boone to meet her, he'd bring the woman. First the woman would die, then she'd make Boone understand that she loved him so much that she would die with him.

Leigh eased her hand out of Sam's, and stayed in her self-imposed exile for a long while, getting herself under control. When she finally opened her eyes, she saw Sam talking to the policeman. She'd told Sam that when he left the island he'd be Boone Patton, and he was, with the cowboy boots, the white hat, the crowd of screaming fans.

Yet the man she'd let herself fall in love with was still there, and it was all she could do not to reach out and touch him, just to make contact and reassure herself that he was real. But she settled for second best, the safest thing, just watching, taking in little things, like the way he sat with one booted foot on the opposite knee and a glass resting on the faded denim of his jeans. Or the way he tensed and relaxed the muscles in his forearms.

Remember, she told herself, just remember.

As the limousine began to slow, she looked to her right out the tinted window and saw a four-story building with distinctive columns. The broad sidewalk out in front was lined with bright orange barricades and uniformed police that kept a surging crowd back from the entrance. A huge marquee that arched over the entrance announced the charity show. Boone Patton got top billing.

When Sam touched her hand, she was startled, but when she turned and he kept a hold on her hand, she didn't draw back.

"They're here for everyone in the show, not just me," he said, his hold on her tightening just for an instant. "Besides, for security, we'll drive to the back, and we'll be in the building before they know what's going on."

The limousine swung to the right before the main entry and headed down a side drive marked "deliveries." It sloped downward to below ground level, and Sam didn't let go of Leigh until the limousine stopped and Quint was there opening the door beside Leigh. He reached in, took her by the hand and she saw him say, "Stay with my men," then he helped her out. Two men were with her on either side, propelling her toward double metal doors that were propped open.

She was separated from Sam completely, the men with her walking quickly, their hands on her arms light but compelling. Everything happened in a blur until they were inside the coolness of the building. Then Sam was beside her again, his arm slipped around her shoulders, and she went with him up a ramp, into a wide hallway that smelled of stale cigarette smoke. It was empty except for uniformed security officers spotted along it, and a scattering of civilians who wore blue badges on their collars.

They went up a shallow flight of stairs, and into a half-circle place that was probably forty feet across and laced and cross-laced with cables on the floor and heavy wiring overhead. The men with Quint never left their places to the side and in front of Leigh and Sam. And when everyone stopped, one of the men produced a badge and snapped it on Leigh's top. Heavy curtains hung on the flat wall, and Leigh could feel a lot of vibrations in the floor. Yet no one around them was actually moving.

Sam nudged her to get her attention and when she looked at him, he said, "There's plenty of security all around. And no one can get back here without a badge. I need to do a quick run-through with the backup band. We've worked together before, so it won't take long. Then in an hour I've got the show to do."

He looked beyond Leigh, and she turned in that direction to see the curtains part, and for a brief moment she saw the source of the vibrations—dancers in gold lamé costumes were going through a routine on a huge stage. Then she saw the man who had parted the curtains, a heavyset man in shirt sleeves, gray hair pulled back in a ponytail and sporting a blue badge clipped to his collar. She saw him spot Sam and head directly for him.

She tensed, before she turned to Sam and saw him smile and say, "Hello, there." And the knots eased when he glanced down at her and said, "My manager, Ted Bigelow."

Leigh looked at the man as he came to stand in front of them, his face flushed but showing definite relief. "Thank God you're in one piece. They tell me Quint's the best in the business, so I've hired him for the duration. I take it he met you at the airport?"

Sam kept his arm around her shoulders, and she could feel him speaking. But she kept looking at Bigelow. The man nodded and slapped Sam on the shoulder, and she had an idea it was a substitute for a hug. Leigh liked the man.

He obviously cared about Sam the person, not just Boone Patton the client.

Then she realized Ted was looking at her. "I'm Ted Bigelow, and you're . . . ?"

"Leigh Buchanan," she said.

She saw him frown, then his face cleared and he smiled. "You're the artist Sam was talking about. Where in the hell did he find you?"

She knew Sam was speaking, but she didn't dare look away from Bigelow, who was smiling at her again. "So you live in the Swan house? A great place."

He was being nice, making small talk, but she could see the tension in his face. "I like it," she said.

Ted was looking at Sam again. "You're staying at the Oasis when you're done here?"

"After I take Leigh back to the island."

Ted's expression grew even more tense. "You're kidding? Didn't Lopez tell you that it isn't a good idea to go back to the island?"

"I'm just going to fly there with Leigh and come right back."

Ted glanced at Leigh, then at Sam. "Damn it, Sam, I've been sweating bullets about you getting here safely, and paying a small fortune to get the Oasis secure for you."

Sam touched Ted on the shoulder with his free hand, and Leigh saw him say, "And I appreciate it, but I've made my plans. I'll be back here tomorrow and you can lock me up in the Oasis."

Right then a petite woman in a white pant suit and with chestnut hair caught in a chignon came up to Sam and touched his cheek with a tiny hand. "Thank God you got here in one piece. I was furious about the leak of your arrival."

Sam motioned to Leigh with a nod of his head. "Laura, I brought a guest, Leigh Buchanan. She's here to see the show."

Laura frowned at Sam. "Is this such a good idea, what with all the things that are going on?"

"I just explained it all to Ted. He'll explain it to you."

The woman shrugged, but Leigh could see that she wasn't pleased. When she looked at Leigh, her expression eased just a bit. "I'm Laura Bigelow, and I'm sorry for being rude, but we've been really worried about this man."

"I understand," Leigh said, and liked her for caring. Sam was right. He was surrounded by good people, people who genuinely cared about him. No wonder he didn't want to be sent off by himself.

Quint came up to the group and leaned close to Sam, said something Leigh couldn't catch and stood back.

Sam looked at Leigh. "I've got to rehearse. Quint says you can stand by the front curtains while I run through my number. You can see the stage from there." He motioned past Leigh and she looked in the direction to a parting in the heavy draperies near a whitewashed wall.

His hand tightened on her shoulder, and she looked back at him. "You'll be fine. Quint will take care of everything. He's going to put a man on."

Laura touched Leigh's arm, her hand cool and light on her skin, and Leigh saw her say, "I'll stay with her. You go ahead and work."

Ted motioned for Sam to go to the stage. "It's time. They need to get it done, then set up for the opening number."

Leigh looked from Ted to Laura to Sam and welcomed the idea of being with just one person. Sam looked at her, and she said, "I'll stand over there with Laura. It's okay."

Sam hesitated, then shocked Leigh by giving her a quick kiss before letting her go and walking toward the stage with

Quint and two of his men right with him. When Sam went through the curtains, Quint's men stayed back by the heavy fabric, looking out onto the stage.

Leigh turned to Laura, who motioned her over to the side by the curtains, and one of Quint's men went with them. He stood about five feet from the two women and leaned against the side wall. Leigh looked out onto the stage, saw Sam in the middle talking to the band, an acoustic guitar in his hand. He nodded, turned away from the band and moved close to a standing microphone. In the next moment Leigh felt the vibrations of sound in the air, and she saw Sam start to play his guitar and sing.

She watched him, the way he leaned toward the microphone, his lips almost touching it, the pleasure in his face as he closed his eyes when he held a note. She could almost feel him caressing each word he sang. "I dreamed of forever, you and me, and now it's gone. Echoes of roses in my heart. All that's there, for time unending, echoes of roses."

With his white hat low over his eyes, and an easy smile on his face, he was in his element. Even when he stumbled over part of the song, stopped and laughed with the band at his mistake, he looked as if he fitted here. He was a natural. A performer born to it. And even though she'd thought she'd accepted that, the idea constricted her throat.

As he held up his hand to the band behind him, then said, "Once more with feeling," and started over, she felt a touch on her arm and turned to Laura.

"I'm sorry, did you say something?" she asked quickly, so preoccupied with Sam that she had forgotten about Laura being there.

"That's a beautiful song, isn't it?" Laura asked her.

Leigh swallowed hard, fighting the urge to turn away from the woman's question and just watch Sam. "Oh, yes," she agreed, watching the woman carefully. "The words... they're beautiful."

Laura spoke quickly, and she had a nervous habit of lifting her hand to her mouth every so often. It made it hard for Leigh, and she missed some words. She tried harder to follow what she was saying, catching enough to figure out what she was going on.

"... horrible the way human beings can be. I know, I stunned and... really frightening. Ted's been at his wits' end, working with that detective, but they can't... really awful."

Leigh nodded. "It's terrible. Sam's so...so gentle, I can't believe anyone could want to hurt him."

"...totally crazy...Sam, I mean, my God, the man's not someone anyone would hate. He's so kind... and charity... doesn't take a penny... so..."

Leigh felt dizzy from concentrating so hard, and she almost forgot to breathe as she worked at deciphering what Laura was saying.

Then Laura was looking at her. "Did he tell you that?"

She nodded, praying that was the right thing to do, and it must have been because Laura said, "I thought so. He seemed so protective... and I just knew it."

Leigh felt hot, as if the air in the building was being diminished more and more with each passing moment. And the old feelings of confusion and disorientation were so close to the surface that she knew they wouldn't stop. She wanted to tell Laura to go away, to let her watch Sam, to let her have peace.

She touched her tongue to her lips, not sure how to stop this, but before she could do anything, she saw Laura gasp, her eyes grow wide with raw fear, then the woman dived onto the floor. The world went into slow motion for Leigh. She was turning, trying to see Sam, trying to figure out what happened, and she saw the bodyguards rushing the stage. At the same moment, her bodyguard who had been leaning against the wall was literally hurling himself at Leigh.

Terror filled her as she was pushed to the floor, the air rushing out of her lungs, then her bodyguard was scrambling to his feet, his gun drawn.

Chapter 13

Sam heard a cracking explosion just as he started the last verse of "Roses," swiftly followed by a blazing rain of light. A gunshot! Sam spun around, his one thought to get to Leigh, to stop whatever madness had begun, but before he could move, he saw Quint.

The big man was rushing at him from the sidelines, then executed a flying tackle, sending Sam crashing to the floor. His guitar flew to one side, the microphone toppled away from him, and the next thing Sam knew, he was facedown on the floor with incredible weight on his back.

Then the weight was gone, Sam twisted to his left, and saw Quint scrambling to his feet, more of his men with him, and all of them had their guns drawn. Sam looked at the floor all around him, at blackened shards of glass everywhere, and he understood. He twisted and looked overhead at one of the huge stage lights dangling precariously from a cable, its face shattered and smoke trickling out, and up toward the ceiling.

A light, a damned light. He almost laughed with relief. And everyone, including himself, thought someone had been shooting. Nerves did strange things to people.

"The light," he said to Quint, but the man was already looking up and pushing his gun back in the shoulder holster he wore under his jacket.

The big man exhaled harshly and shook his head as he called out, "It's all right. The light exploded." He held out a hand to Sam to help him up. "Sorry for knocking you down," he said as he levered Sam to his feet. "But I thought all hell was breaking loose."

Sam felt the grit of glass under his boots and brushed at his jeans. "No problem," he said, trying to look around Quint to find Leigh. "Miss Buchanan, is she . . . ?"

He heard Quint saying, "She's fine. Randy's with her," as he spotted Leigh. Quint's man was beside her, and Laura had her by her arm. Then Leigh turned and looked at him over the people who were rushing around to clean up the stage. And what he saw in her expression shook him to the core. Her dark blue eyes were filled with pure fear. He ignored the guitar one of the stagehands was bringing over to him along with his hat, and he hurried across to Leigh.

Leigh knew she'd been thrown into the nightmare and she wasn't even asleep. Everything had dissolved into madness. She had been pulled to her feet, and turned around to face the angry bodyguard.

"My God," he'd said to her, and she'd known he was screaming. "What's wrong with you, lady? Why didn't you hit the floor when I told you to? That could have been a shot! You could have been killed!"

And Laura, her eyes wide in her pale face, had said, "This isn't a joke, Leigh. I thought you understood that there's some crazy person out there. God, you act as if it's a game. What's wrong with you? That sound could have woken the dead, and you just stood there.''

That's when Leigh had turned, needing to break free of the madness, to get away from people staring at her and yelling at her. Then she saw Sam looking at her, and the next thing she knew he was striding across the stage toward her.

She watched him coming closer, saying, "Hey, it was just a light." Then he was right in front of her, his hands resting on her shoulders, looking right at her. "I've had it happen before, and I should have known what it was. But with everything that's going on, everyone just overreacted."

Everyone but me, Leigh thought, and she knew how wrong she had been to come here. She saw Laura talking to Ted, and she caught the words "I don't know what's wrong with her..." She saw the bodyguard talking to Quint. "...have a long talk with her. Explain that what I say..."

She closed her eyes for a moment, then opened them to Sam. Even he felt sorry for her. She could see it in his eyes. And she'd had enough.

Without a word, Leigh turned from Sam and began to make her way through the crowd backstage. Sam hurried after her and went past, getting in front of her and blocking her path. "Where are you going?" he asked.

She looked at him and pressed an unsteady hand to her chest. "Home. To the island."

He looked past her at Ted who was by the curtains with Laura and Quint. "Ted?" he called, and when the man looked at him, he had to yell to be heard over the growing noise. "Where can I get some privacy for a few minutes?"

Ted said something to Quint, and both men came over to where Sam stood with Leigh. "Quint can show you. Take a few minutes while they clean up, then you can—"

"I don't need more rehearsal," he said, cutting him off. "I'll be ready for the show."

He looked at Quint. "Where can we get some privacy?"

"Follow me," Quint said, motioning for Sam and Leigh to go with him across the backstage area.

Sam reached for Leigh's arm, and even though she flinched at the contact, he didn't let go. He drew her along with him as he followed Quint into a side hall and to a door marked "Manager."

Quint held up a hand to Sam, then opened the door and disappeared inside. A moment later he came back and nodded. "Go ahead. It's clear."

Sam took Leigh into the room, a sterile-looking office with beige carpeting, pale paneled walls and only a few pieces of furniture—a massive cherrywood desk with a leather swivel chair behind it. A series of file cabinets were lined up under a window at the back, and off-white drapes were closed.

As soon as they were in the room, Leigh moved out of his hold. Quint closed the door behind him, and Sam looked at Leigh. All of his instincts told him to hold her and never let go, but when he started to reach out to her, she moved back even farther, her hips pressed against the desk.

"Don't," she whispered, holding up her hands as if to ward him off. "Please, don't. I just want to go back to the island . . . now."

Leigh saw Sam through a shimmering haze, and all she knew for sure was that she had to get out of here. She had to go back where she felt safe and where life was sane. This had been a horrible, selfish mistake. She should have let go and not been greedy for this time with Sam.

"Don't do this," Sam told her. "You're all right. I'm fine. Let's just forget about it and get through the next hour or two, then we can both leave."

Leigh knew that she never had and never would love anyone the way she did Sam, and that made it all the more horrible that he could have been shot and she wouldn't have even known. She could still see Laura yelling at her, "What's wrong with you?" and that nightmare overlapped with the one she had had on the jet. Sam speaking. "She's deaf. She can't hear."

"No, I have to leave now," she said.

"We'll go back to the island together in a few hours."

"You don't have to come back. I'll go by myself."

He took a step toward her. "I want to go back with you."

Leigh suddenly didn't want him even this close, and she didn't know what else to do but tell him the truth. "I don't belong here. I should have never come."

"What do you mean? Just because you didn't hear the light explode, you want to run off?"

She wanted to move back even farther, to build a buffer of space to help her think clearly. But the edge of the desk pressed against her hips, and she had nowhere to go. "I can't do this to you."

"Do what?"

She felt her eyes begin to burn, but no tears came. Her eyes were as dry as they had been on the plane after the nightmare. There was just a horrible tightness that seemed to be threading its way through her body and centering in her chest. "Embarrass you like that."

"Embarrass me? What in the hell—"

She cut off his words. "Just think of the headlines. The press would have a field day. It would be horrible."

"You have to be kidding."

"I wish I was. I don't belong here. I—I've never heard you sing. I don't...I don't even know what your voice sounds like. Imagine what some reporter could do with that."

She exhaled, a trembling starting deep inside her, making her vaguely sick. And it didn't help that Sam was just looking at her, not blinking, not moving. She shifted, about to go around him and leave when he finally spoke to her.

"I think I understand," he said.

She didn't know what she expected, or why it felt so horrible to have him so calmly accept her exit. She just wanted to leave, to get something close to sanity back again. "Good. If you could call the airport and tell them—"

"I understand what's going on."

She swallowed hard. "What?"

"It's not because of me, what the publicity could be, or how it would affect me, it's about you, isn't it?"

This was all about him, all the pain, all the anguish came from loving him. "No, it's not about me."

"Sure it is," he said. "It's about you being terrified of people finding out that you can't hear, that you're involved with a man who makes music, and it's about people pitying you."

She felt the blood drain from her face.

"It's about you not being able to admit to yourself that you're deaf. So you put people in a position where they react wrongly when they think you were just standing there like a fool when everyone else was scrambling for cover."

She didn't want to see any of this, and just as she thought of closing her eyes, Sam moved. As if he read her mind, he cupped her chin in strong fingers and said, "And don't close your eyes. Don't shut me out just because you don't want to hear what I'm saying to you." She stared at him. "Until you can look someone in the eye and tell them you're deaf, you're your own worst enemy, and you'll keep hiding out on that island, pretending it's paradise, but it's really your own personal hell. You've never made your peace with what happened. You've never accepted it.''

She jerked away from his touch and felt a pure rage in her. "Damn you, it's others who won't accept it, not me.''

"How can others accept your deafness when you deny it with everything you do?''

Didn't he know that she'd been pummelled with the fact that she'd never hear again every waking hour since it had happened, and that she'd just gone through hell because she'd come here with him, trying to fit in and be normal? "You don't know what you're talking about," she gasped, her throat tight and painful.

"Tell me you're deaf," he said suddenly.

She stared at him. If he was trying to destroy her, he was doing a good job of it. She kept her mouth clamped shut.

"Leigh, tell me you're deaf," he repeated slowly, carefully, his eyes narrowed and his jaw tight.

She felt the tears then, hot, scalding tears that blurred her eyes. "Don't do this to me.''

"You can't say it, can you? You can't even use the word.''

"What do you want from me? Do you want me to tell you that I have nightmares about this sort of thing, that I see myself standing in the middle of crowds, not knowing what's going on, that I have people yelling at me and their mouths move, but I can't even read their lips, that I almost pass out and that I end up screaming? And I can't even hear my screams? Or do you want me to tell you that while someone could have been killing you, I was trying to figure out what Laura Bigelow was saying to me? That I was so scared she'd find out, that anyone would find out, that I couldn't even breathe?''

"No, I want you to say that you're deaf. I want you to say it to me.''

The world froze in that moment, and all she could feel was a scream of rage in her that started at her toes and began to sear its way up through her body. And she knew without a doubt that if she ever let that scream free from her lips, it would kill her. The nightmares, the fear, were all centered there, all fodder for that rending scream.

Terrified, she spun around and grabbed the first thing she saw, a metal water pitcher on the desk with condensation from icy liquid fogging the sides. She picked it up and threw it with all her might, sending it crashing against the wall, and water flew everywhere.

Then she spun on Sam who hadn't moved, who just stared at her. "I didn't hear that!" she said, knowing she was yelling. She reached for a pen and pencil set on the desk and threw that against the other wall. "And I didn't hear that!"

She turned on Sam, screaming at him, "Are you satisfied? I didn't hear any of that, and I didn't hear that light explode and I didn't hear you singing, or you talking to me, or anything! And I never will, not ever! And I can't stay here, I have to go back. I have to go where it doesn't matter, where it doesn't hurt. D-don't you...understand? Don't y-you...?"

Her words stopped on a sob as Sam reached out to her and pulled her to him. And she fought his embrace, pushing with her hands against the thundering of his heart, and tried to free herself. But he simply held her, her strength no match for his. And she knew he wasn't going to let her go.

With nothing left to fight him or the world, she collapsed against his chest and the tears came, not the gentle grieving tears when they had made love in the shower, and the tears she'd cried at the house after he'd found out she couldn't hear and she thought he was gone. But tears for her future, a life without Sam.

She cried until she couldn't cry anymore, then Sam gently eased her back. She looked up at him, and when his lips touched her forehead, she closed her eyes. Then his kiss was on each eyelid, on her cheeks still wet with tears. And it almost broke her heart.

Then he let her go, and she was free. She turned from him, swiping weakly at her eyes, and she saw the dark pattern of dampness from the water on the wall, and the silver pitcher lying on its side on the carpet. Unsteadily, she crossed and picked up the pitcher, then took it back to the desk. Without turning to Sam, she put the pitcher down on the polished top and pressed her hands flat on the desk at either side of the pitcher. She closed her eyes.

She felt empty and drained, as if she'd fought a war and lost and been put into isolation. But she wasn't. She knew Sam was still here, that he was watching her, waiting. And it took all her willpower to be able to turn to him.

All the gentleness in the world had been in his touch a moment ago, but his expression held none of it. He looked tense and wary, his hands balled into fists at his sides.

"Are you deaf, Leigh?" he asked, and she could have sworn she heard his voice, its deep roughness echoing through her being. An illusion, as much as her believing she could come here, then leave without it hurting like hell.

"Oh, God," she breathed, "can't you just leave me alone, just get me a ride back to the airport and let me go back to the island?"

He shook his head, his eyes bleak, almost as if he was sharing the pain she was experiencing. "No, I can't."

"Why?"

Sam couldn't take his eyes off Leigh, off the tearstains on her face, the pain in her eyes, or the way she was wringing her hands. The vulnerability broke his heart, yet he couldn't just walk away. He couldn't turn his back on her. And he knew why he couldn't stop, why he couldn't let her hide and live with this fear. And he was shocked that he hadn't realized why until right now.

He loved Leigh Buchanan.

And he knew he'd never loved another woman like this. He'd always wanted her, but he knew the love had started when he'd been so terrified finding her floating facedown in the ocean. And it had grown with each passing moment. He thought back and knew exactly when that love had become a fact, when a need for her had become a permanent part of his soul. When they'd danced.

"We danced," he said. "And we swam, and we jogged, and we talked, and we made love." Her paleness grew with each word he uttered, but he kept going. "And I can't let you run back to that island and pretend that this never happened."

"It's my life," she whispered, "it's mine."

"And, come hell or high water, I'm in that life."

"I—I told you I didn't want to go jogging or swimming or to spend time with you. But you wouldn't let it go, you kept insisting, and I knew I shouldn't do it, but I did. I didn't mean to."

He braced himself, then put everything he had on the table. "I didn't mean to fall in love with you."

She froze, totally motionless, not even breathing, and her eyes widened in her pale face. "No," she gasped. "You didn't. You can't."

"But I did. I never expected to feel like this about anyone, and I'm trying to make sense out of it." He pushed his hands into his pockets and forced himself not to go any closer to her. "I love you, Leigh, it's that simple. And I want you to be part of my life."

He didn't know what he expected, but it wasn't the fear that began to tighten her face, or the way she held up one hand in front of her as if she was trying to protect herself. "Please, no."

"It's the truth. It just took me a while to realize why I couldn't leave you on the island, why I couldn't just walk away and come back by myself, and I'll be damned if I'll let you leave me now." He knew that with each word he said, he was exposing himself more and more, but he couldn't stop. He'd come this far. He had to go all the way. "And I know you care about me. I know we can build something on this."

Leigh had to swallow as sickness welled up in her throat. Words that would have thrilled her, if she'd met Sam when her world had been whole, horrified her. "Build on it?" she said in an unsteady voice. "You're crazy. I don't fit in here. I can't." She took in a deep, unsteady breath and as she exhaled, a numbness began to come over her, a blessed barrier for all the confusion and the pain.

It was simple, so clear. She knew the truth, even if Sam didn't. And she could say the words without flinching, without feeling anything at all. "Your life is here, in this world, and I can't ever share that with you. The time on the island with you was a . . . a dream, a wonderful dream, but this is reality. And I don't belong here." Thank God the numbness stayed firmly in place, and she could watch the scene as if she was an observer and not experiencing it. "I was fine before you came to the island, and I was in control, and—"

"And what?"

"I was surviving," she said bluntly.

"Is that all you want, to survive?"

She was outside the scene, far away from any pain or hurt. "It's enough," she saw herself say.

Sam came closer, obliterating any buffer of space between them, and she saw him say, "I don't think so," before he touched her shoulder and pulled her to him. His mouth captured hers with a fervor that destroyed the numbness and replaced it with a world of joy and sorrow. And she almost hated him for that, but she couldn't.

Then he was holding her back, and when she opened her eyes, he said, "You tell me, is surviving enough, Leigh?"

Before she could think of what to do or say, Sam turned to speak to someone behind him who must have come into the room, but his body blocked her from seeing what was going on. He looked back at her. "I have to go. I've got to do makeup and costumes." But he didn't let her go. "Do one thing for me? Just stay until I'm done, think about what I said, and if you still want to go, if you can walk away from what we have, I'll personally take you to the airport. I'll put you on the plane, and I'll hope like hell that you'll be happy."

She wanted to close her eyes and deny everything he'd been saying, but his hold on her made that impossible. She could see a muscle working in his jaw. "Just wait. And think." She could feel a trembling in his hold that made her heart catch. "Damn it, I've never begged for anything, and I'm no good at it. But I'm asking you . . . please don't run away."

No, she wasn't going to run away. She was going to wait and have the courage to do this right. She owed Sam that much. She owed herself that much. "I'll wait so you can arrange for me to go to the airport."

The tension in Sam's face etched a deep line between his eyes and bracketed his mouth. And it broke her heart to know the very thing that had been inevitable since she'd first seen him was about to happen. He would be in his world. She would be alone in hers.

And she couldn't bear to keep looking at him. As she turned from him, he let her go, and she pressed her fingertips to the desktop. She closed her eyes, shutting out everything, but she couldn't shut out the worst thing of all. This was over, completely and irrevocably.

That thought was so horrible that Leigh turned, just needing to see Sam, to know that when this was over, she'd remember him clearly, that she'd never forget. But the room was empty.

She went around the desk and sat in the leather high-backed chair. Staring blindly ahead, she realized how much she'd changed. A week ago, she could have said she'd forget about this, that she'd put it behind her and get on with her life. Just the way she had when she'd come to the island. But this time she knew it wouldn't be like that.

When she closed her eyes, the image of Sam came to her so clearly that she felt she could reach out and touch him. No, she'd never forget. And the words Sam had sung before the explosion came to her in a rush. "I dreamed of forever, you and me, and now it's gone. Echoes of roses in my heart. All that's there, for time unending, echoes of roses."

No tears were left in her, just the emptiness. And all she had were echoes, memories that she knew now would never be enough. Never. And she knew how right Sam was. She would never have peace without him. But being with Sam meant putting herself into a world she knew she couldn't survive in. That had been pointed out by the incident with the light.

"Damn it," she muttered, getting to her feet. It had all seemed so simple this morning. Come here with Sam, have a bit more time with him, then go back and get on with her life. But now she knew she couldn't. She couldn't go, and she couldn't stay.

The light explosion had scared the woman almost as much as it had everyone else. And she'd joined in with the nervous laughter of relief when they'd found out it had been an overheated light, not a gunshot. She'd laughed as much as the others, maybe a bit more.

They were all so stupid. Did they think she'd shoot Boone like that? So stupid. He had to understand before he died, and before she died with him. And they would die together, peacefully, forever.

She closed her fingers around the bottle of sleeping pills in the pocket of her red jacket and watched the door where Boone and the blonde had disappeared ten minutes ago. As the music of the opening number on stage filled the air, she never looked away from the door, or the two men guarding it.

Boone finally came out, and Quint, the head of security was right there. They spoke for a moment, then Quint and another man accompanied Boone down the hall to the dressing rooms. One man stayed by the office door, and the others went with Boone, Quint going in the room with him, the other man stationing himself by the door.

She had set everything up, and it looked as if it was going to be easy to carry out. The woman was alone, and Boone was going to be onstage in less than ten minutes. She'd even decided that people had to know, and she knew how to make her feelings public. Ted Bigelow. She hated the man, but he was the one who would tell the world how much she loved Boone, and why they had to die together.

She let go of the pill bottle and adjusted her purse on her shoulder, the small gun in it reassuring her of the control she had. She went up to the guard still by the office door. The man looked at her, at the badge she wore attached to her collar. "Yes?"

"I'm with the firm of Pearson and May." She held up the badge. "I'm Evelyn Ryan, and I'm handling publicity for

Mr. Patton's appearance at this function. I need to get together with Mr. Patton for a print interview after he's through performing. I need you to bring Mr. Patton here when he's done."

He looked at her badge again and pulled a list out of his pocket, scanned it and found her name. Then he looked at her. "The press room's all set up, and I'm sure—"

"No," she said quickly. "Not the press room. We'll be using the conference room at the end of the hall to make sure it's totally private."

"All right. I'll get a clearance from my boss and talk to Mr. Bigelow."

"It's cleared with Mr. Bigelow," she said truthfully. Ted Bigelow had been very cooperative. "What I need from you is to make sure Mr. Patton's in that room as quickly as you can get him there after he's done. It won't take more than twenty minutes of his time."

The man was undecided, then he said, "What about the lady who's here with him?"

"What about her?"

"I've got orders that she's to be with Mr. Patton as soon as he's offstage."

She controlled her anger and tried to smile as if she understood completely. "No problem. Have her escorted to the room now, and she can sit in on the interview." Actually this would be fine. To know the blonde was dead would only add to her ultimate satisfaction. "Just make sure Mr. Patton's there as quickly as possible." Her smile became easy and genuine as she realized how close she was to total happiness. "I'll be waiting."

Chapter 14

Leigh was still sitting in the chair behind the desk when Quint strode into the office. "Mr. Patton just went on-stage, and I've been notified that there's been a change of plans," he said as he came toward her. "I'm to take you to another room. Mr. Patton will meet you there after he's finished performing."

Leigh didn't care where she waited. She knew it wouldn't change anything just to move locations. That thought stopped her, and she stared at Quint, who was waiting patiently for her to get up and go with him. Going to the island wouldn't make her stop loving Sam. Staying hidden away from the world wouldn't change anything. Denying it wouldn't change it. It was an illusion of change, but it wasn't real.

Quint rocked forward on the balls of his feet. "We should go now. My men have the corridor cleared."

She moved by rote, getting up, following Quint to the door, and as soon as she stepped out into the hallway where

the air trembled with the vibrations of sound, two more
men were there. One stood behind her, Quint took one side,
the other man took the other, and when they would have
led her away from the stage and farther down the hall, she
glanced back to the curtains.

They were parted by the security people watching the
stage, and she could see through the opening. For a moment Leigh saw Sam, the spotlight isolating him in darkness all around.

She stopped, staring at him, the light gleaming off the
sequins that lined the lapels of a short blue suede jacket.
His white hat shadowed his eyes, and his hands moved on
the guitar. Leaning close to the floor microphone, she saw
him singing, "Echoes of roses, echoes of roses, for time
unending, just echoes of roses."

And somewhere deep inside, she could almost hear him
singing those words. Maybe her sanity was gone, but for
that instant, she didn't feel deaf. Every other sense in her
body was so alive that she couldn't tell where wishful
thinking ended and reality took over.

And the only thing she knew was real was her love for
Sam. That simple. That complete. That wonderful. Then
she felt Quint touch her in the small of her back, and she
looked at him. "This way," he said, nodding back down
the hall.

Leigh didn't want to go. She wanted to stay right where
she was, where reality finally made sense to her. And scared
her at the same time. To be in his world was terrifying, but
she knew right then that being without Sam forever was
even more terrifying. And she knew she wanted to try. She
had one last glimpse of Sam, before Quint led her off.

They went to a door near the end of the hallway and
Quint opened it and looked inside. Then he stood to one

side, holding the door open. "I'll bring Mr. Patton in here as soon as he gets off the stage."

Leigh stepped into a large, empty room that had no windows and all the light was provided by fluorescent fixtures behind low ceiling panels. A leather couch and chairs were positioned with potted plants to the right in a conversation area, and in the middle of the room was a large, round table with high-back chairs arranged around it. A telephone, several ashtrays and a stack of slick-looking brochures were on the table.

All of a sudden, Leigh knew she wasn't alone. She could sense someone looking at her, and she turned to her left. She saw a woman standing in front of a full bar, a bottle of wine in her hand. Petite, in a red tailored suit and with a rather sharp-featured face framed by feathery black hair, the woman stared at Leigh for a long moment before she put the bottle of wine on the bar and came toward Leigh.

"So you're Boone's newest friend," she said, a smile curving her red lips, but not touching eyes that looked as if they were layered with mascara.

Leigh recognized her from the airport, the woman she'd glimpsed at the gate before getting into the limousine. And the discomfort she'd felt then came back full force. She glanced at the woman's badge—"Evelyn Ryan, Pearson and May Inc."

"I'm Evelyn Ryan," she said, "with the firm who handles Boone's publicity, and I'm in charge of this session."

The word "publicity" made Leigh cringe. To decide that she wanted to be with Sam was one thing, but to have this thrown at her immediately nudged her off balance. She didn't want to share the spotlight with Sam in any way, shape or form. "I'm Leigh Buchanan," she said.

Evelyn eyed Leigh openly, her eyes flicking over the jeans and casual top and the cold smile was gone. "You certainly aren't Boone's type."

The words were so unexpected that Leigh could only stare at the woman, wondering if she'd read them wrong. "Excuse me?"

Evelyn waved a hand dismissively and said, "No matter. This won't take very long."

"What won't?" Leigh asked.

Evelyn rolled her eyes, obviously impatient with the questions. "We're doing an interview for a magazine article when Boone's finished with his performance. I'm here to make sure it goes right."

She really didn't want any part of it, not when she could see the probable headline—"Boone Patton Involved with Deaf Artist." She shook her head. "I don't think I belong in something like this. I'll go and wait someplace else until it's over."

The woman came closer, bringing a scent of heavy perfume with her. "You can't. I wish you could, but you can't. They said you have to be here. But don't worry. You won't have any part in the interview. It's just Boone. You can sit over there and watch." She motioned to the couch and chairs. Leigh was glad to do that, to sit off to the side, watch the interview, then get a chance to be alone with Sam. She had so much she needed to say, to explain. But before she could go to the couch, Evelyn said, "Before you get settled, let me get you a drink. The bar's fully stocked, but I'd recommend the wine. It's wonderful."

"Oh, I don't think—"

"You'd love it. I made sure they had some of Boone's favorite wine. You like that, don't you?"

She had no idea what Sam liked or didn't like. There was so much to learn about him, and she hoped there would be a lifetime to do it. "I'm sorry, I don't know what it is."

For some reason the woman looked vaguely pleased at Leigh's ignorance about Sam's likes and dislikes in wine. "It's a Burgundy, Californian, Napa Valley," she recited, then turned from Leigh abruptly and crossed to the bar. Leigh watched her for a moment, her dislike a solid thing, and she turned to cross to the couch.

Just as Leigh sank down in the supple leather cushions, Evelyn came across to her and held out a goblet. "Drink this and relax."

Leigh took the glass half filled with a rich red liquid. "Thank you."

"You must be exhausted after flying all day."

Leigh did feel tired, but it surprised her that the woman knew about the island. She could have sworn Sam said only he, Ted Bigelow and Detective Lopez knew. Maybe she'd misunderstood. "I am."

Evelyn stood over her, and flicked her hand into the air impatiently. "Then you need this drink."

Leigh took a sip and let the room-temperature liquid rest in her mouth for a moment before she swallowed. It was rich and smooth, but after she swallowed, she tasted a vague bitterness on her tongue that was unpleasant. "It's very good," she said.

Evelyn looked a bit relieved, then asked her another question. "Do you know Boone's favorite color?"

This didn't make any sense. "What?"

Evelyn frowned as she glanced at the door, then back to Leigh. "You'd think they could soundproof a room better than this, wouldn't you? That noise is really annoying." Leigh could tell she was making herself speak louder. "Boone's favorite color—do you know what it is?"

Leigh fingered the cool crystal in her hand and shook her head.

"Red. He loves red. And he likes Rocky Road ice cream, very feminine women and his favorite perfume is 'Dreaming.'" The woman sounded like a blurb from a fan magazine. She glanced at Leigh's wineglass. "Please, drink your wine. It's going to go to waste if you and Boone don't drink it all."

Leigh didn't want any more. The bitterness on her tongue was getting more and more pronounced, but she made a token show of touching the glass to her lips and getting just a tiny bit of the wine in her mouth. She swallowed it quickly, and said, "You're doing this interview?"

Evelyn rolled her eyes as if she couldn't believe the stupidity of Leigh's question. "Heavens, no. There's a magazine reporter coming in for it. In fact, I need to call him, to tell him we changed rooms. Just finish your wine and relax. This will all be over before you know it."

She turned from Leigh and crossed to the table, taking a seat near the bar, facing Leigh. As Leigh watched Evelyn pick up the receiver and push several buttons, she realized the air in the room felt close and overly warm. She took a deep breath to try and clear a vague fuzziness in her head and almost took another drink of the wine. But as she lifted the glass, she saw Evelyn start to speak. The woman said something into the mouthpiece of the phone that didn't make sense.

"Mr. Bigelow," she was saying. "This is Evelyn Ryan."

Ted? Leigh thought she'd said she was calling a reporter. She lowered the wineglass and watched Evelyn close her eyes and say, "I'm leaving this message on your machine to explain everything."

Leigh kept watching and saw Evelyn's expression go from intense to almost beatific as she spoke. "By the time you hear this, it will all be over, but you'll know why it had to be. I love Boone. And it will be gentle, very beautiful. I have a gun, but I won't use it unless I have to. I put sleeping pills in his favorite wine, so we can drift off together. So tell the police that they don't have to do any horrible examinations. Tell them to just leave us alone."

Leigh looked down at the wine still in her glass. God, it was joke, a bad joke. It had to be. Then she looked back at Evelyn and she knew it wasn't a joke. "Boone and I are meant to be together. And I won't let anyone stop us. No one. Certainly not another woman."

The truth hit Leigh with all the impact of a runaway freight train. Evelyn was the one who had been threatening Sam, who had driven him to the island, who was willing to kill Sam to keep him for herself. And she was going to kill Leigh, too.

She looked down at her wine and saw her hand trembling making the red liquid shimmer back the glints of light from the overhead fixtures. How much had she drunk? Surely it wasn't enough to be fatal. One drink, a small sip. Not enough to take away the future she was just beginning to see. And she knew the hard truth of what Sam had told her. A person only has now, this moment.

She looked at a plant to her left, a huge ficus tree set in a brass pot. Then she glanced back to Evelyn who still had her eyes closed and was speaking into the phone. She never took her eyes off the woman, watching her say, "Just tell everyone that we're happy, that Boone and I are together forever." And Leigh extended her arm and tipped the contents of the goblet into the plant pot.

She just drew her hand back when Evelyn put down the phone and opened her eyes. The woman looked right at Leigh, and the smile was gone. She stood and came toward Leigh, glancing down at her empty wineglass.

"Good. You drank it all," she said. "Let me get you some more."

Leigh had to get out of here and stop Sam from coming in. She had to get to the door and run. If Evelyn was at the bar with her back to Leigh, she might have a chance of making it to the door before she could stop her or get to her gun. Leigh had noticed a small leather purse on the table by the phone. That had to be where the gun was. And the purse was ten feet from where Evelyn stood. If Leigh could get to the door, Quint or one of his men would be out there. She just had to get outside and stop Sam from walking into this room.

"Yes, please," she said, handing Evelyn her glass.

As the woman started across to the bar, Leigh stood. For a moment she felt a slight dizziness, then the room steadied, and never looking away from Evelyn by the bar, she slowly started for the door.

But before she could get more than halfway there, Evelyn turned, and Leigh stopped and met her gaze. "Where are you going?" the woman demanded, holding a full glass of the red wine.

Bluff, just bluff, she told herself. "I'm leaving. I really shouldn't be in here. You don't need me. And I have a cab waiting for me. I was supposed to—"

"A cab?" she asked, coming toward Leigh. "Why?"

"I—I was leaving. I'm not staying for the rest of this show. I was supposed to be . . . be at a friend's place. And I called a cab." She pretended to check the wall clock. "He should be at the back entrance any minute now."

Evelyn was no more than three feet from her, extending the wineglass to her. "Forget about it. Have some more wine. You can't leave."

Leigh tried to think. Screaming wouldn't do any good, not if the music was still going. And there was no way she could get to the door without Evelyn's knowing what she was doing. She made herself take the glass the woman was offering her, and glanced past her. The telephone and the purse with the gun was right beside it.

And she knew getting to the gun was her only hope.

"I should really call and cancel the taxi. Then they won't be coming back here looking for me and disturbing the interview."

It took a moment for Evelyn to react, and Leigh was thankful she agreed. "All right. Go ahead. Just make it fast. Boone's going to be here any minute and this interview has to be perfect."

Leigh was mildly surprised that she could walk past the woman without flinching as she inhaled the sickening perfume and the sense of evil the woman emanated. She got to the chair, put her glass of wine on the table, then started to sit down, but her knees buckled and she literally slid down into the seat.

She forced a full breath of air into her lungs. She'd taken sleeping pills after the illness, and almost became dependent on them for sleep. But they'd been mild, just making her a bit relaxed. She never remembered this weakness after taking them. Pressing a hand flat on the cool tabletop within inches of the purse, she glanced up at Evelyn.

Before she knew what was happening, the woman was there, grabbing the purse before Leigh could even form the thought to pick it up. Evelyn clutched it to her chest and said, "Well, hurry up," before she turned and crossed to the bar.

Leigh looked down at the phone, and hysterical laughter almost bubbled out of her. A phone. What could she do with a phone? Then she grasped at one thread of hope. She could speak, and if someone was on the other end, *they* could hear. She looked at the phone, and for a horrifying moment her eyes wouldn't focus, then she could make out a chart to one side of the dial that listed all the offices in the theater.

Security was at the bottom. She reached for the receiver, praying that the phone wouldn't ring before she could pick it up. Then she had the receiver in her hand, lifted it and pressed it to her ear.

She glanced at Evelyn who was pacing back and forth in the area between the table and the door. Quickly, Leigh pushed the buttons for security, counted silently to five, hoping it was long enough for someone to answer, and she kept watching Evelyn pace back and forth.

Please let the music be loud enough to cover what I'm saying, Leigh prayed silently, then she began to speak in a low voice. "This is Leigh Buchanan. I'm in a conference room. Please don't let Sam Patton come in here. Evelyn Ryan is with me and she has a gun. She's going to kill Sam. She gave me sleeping pills. Please don't let Sam come in here." Evelyn glanced at her, making Leigh's breath catch, but the woman kept pacing.

Leigh spoke as quickly as she could, saying the same thing over and over again, not knowing if anyone was listening, if anyone was even there, or if she even got the right number.

She just prayed that someone would hear her. And she never took her eyes off Evelyn. The woman was still moving back and forth, nibbling on her fingernails as she paced, then she stopped and looked at the doors, her back to Leigh.

Leigh picked up her wineglass and carefully put it under the table and tipped it. "Please help me. She's got a gun. She's going to kill Sam," she said in a rush, drawing the glass back. Less than half the wine was left. She put the goblet on the table. "Don't let Sam come in here."

Evelyn turned abruptly and frowned at Leigh. "Aren't you finished yet?" she asked.

"I'm almost done," Leigh called out, then spoke softly into the receiver as Evelyn started to come around the table toward her. "I have to go. I'll try to leave this off the hook. Please don't let Sam come in here."

She put the receiver down, managing to rest the earpiece on the lip just above the disconnect button, and knew she had to make Evelyn think the sleeping pills were working. She started to stand, then sank back down.

Evelyn was there looking down at her, the purse clutched to her chest. Leigh tried to smile. "Silly, isn't it," she said. "But I think the wine's gone to my head."

Evelyn nodded. "Wine can do that. Why don't you just get on the couch and rest. You'll feel much better in a few minutes."

Leigh closed her eyes, then looked at Evelyn who still stood over her. "I'm all right, I just feel a bit woozy. I think I'll just sit here for a few minutes."

"The couch is better," Evelyn was saying.

"I..." Leigh licked her lips and blinked her eyes as if to clear her vision. "No, I—I'll stay here. I just need to put my head down for a minute."

Evelyn looked as if she was going to insist on the couch, but something distracted her. She turned sharply to look in the direction of the door. And Leigh followed her gaze, barely covering a gasp when she saw Sam striding into the room.

No nightmare she'd ever had prepared her for the horror she felt when she saw him walking in and closing the door behind him. She darted a look at Evelyn who was walking toward him, the purse in one hand, the other hand stretched out toward Sam.

Leigh looked back at Sam. His hat was gone, his jacket open, and as he looked at Leigh, he smiled. "Hi, there. They said you were waiting in here for me." Before she could do or say anything, he'd turned to Evelyn, taking her hand in his and she saw him say, "Did you get the interview all set up?" He nodded. "Good. I want to get out of here as soon as possible."

Evelyn was saying something. Sam listened, then shook his head. "No, thanks. I don't want any. I just want to do this interview and get out."

Leigh started to stand, ready to do anything to make this nightmare stop, then the horror increased. Evelyn reached in her purse and she had the gun in her hand and was pointing it at Sam.

Everything became incredibly clear to Leigh. She saw one of the heavy ashtrays on the table, picked up its cool weight, screamed and threw it with all her might in the direction of the woman. She saw Evelyn start to turn, the look of shock in her eyes. Sam lunged to the right, and the ashtray crashed to the table three feet short of its target.

The gun was on Leigh, and she saw Evelyn's eyes, the rage and insanity mingling in one incredible heartbeat, and Leigh knew she was going to die. Then Sam was there, his hand striking out, Evelyn's head snapping to one side, and the gun flew from her hand, sailing across the room. The door burst open, and Quint was there with his men. In a crazy patchwork of comprehension, Leigh saw Quint heading for Evelyn, Evelyn turning to Sam, her arms stretched out to him. Quint grabbed her arms from behind, and jerked her sharply backward.

Sam turned and came around the table toward Leigh, and then he was holding her tightly, burying her face in his chest. Everything was soft and warm and safe. Sam's hand stroked her back, the other one tangled in her hair holding her head to the beat of his heart.

And it felt so right.

Sam moved back from her just a bit but didn't let her go. His hands cupped her face gently. "Are you all right?"

"I'm fine now," she said. "I poured out most of the wine. I just had a taste. I didn't know if anyone would be listening."

"Listening?" he asked.

"To the phone, when I called security."

She saw the disbelief in his eyes. "You called security?"

"I told her I had to call a taxi to cancel it, and I just kept talking."

"God, I love you," he said and touched his lips to hers. As he drew back, she saw the look in his eyes that she knew she'd been waiting for all her life.

"Sam, I want to—"

But before she could tell him what she needed to, his hands dropped to her shoulders, and he looked past her and said, "Detective Lopez. Where have you been?"

Leigh turned, thankful when Sam slipped his arm around her and held her tightly to his side. She circled his waist with her arm and looked at the policeman. He had what looked like a computer printout in his hand and he held it up to Sam.

"Coming to get Evelyn Ryan. We just got background on her. Her real name's Evelyn Rice, and she's been in and out of therapy and hospitals in the Atlanta area the better part of her life. Last year she disappeared just after her boss was murdered, stabbed to death." He looked at the top page of the printout. "Ray O'Neil. Atlanta's been looking for her. And it looks as if I got here about five minutes too late."

Sam's hold on Leigh tightened as the detective was speaking, then Leigh looked toward the door. Quint was talking to some uniformed officers, motioning to the wall near the bar. She glanced over there and saw Evelyn sitting in a chair, a policeman standing on either side, and she was staring straight ahead. Her expression was blank, as if her body was there, but the woman inside wasn't in that room any longer. Leigh doubted she was ever going to come back.

Sam tapped her arm to get her attention and she looked back at him. He glanced toward Detective Lopez. She looked at the policeman. "I'm sorry?"

"I need you to make a statement for my report. As soon as you feel up to it, you'll need to..." He turned away for a moment to look in Quint's direction, still talking and Leigh lost what he was saying to her. When he looked back at her, he said, "Is that all right with you?"

Leigh felt the old fear come rushing back, that loss of control when she couldn't make sense of what was going on. Then she felt Sam holding her, his strength hers, and she glanced up at him. His eyes were dark and intense, and she knew what he was waiting for.

She turned back to Detective Lopez, and she rested the coffee mug on her lap. "I'm sorry, I didn't understand what you said."

"My fault," he said. "The noise around here is pretty bad."

She touched her tongue to her lips, closed her eyes for a fleeting moment before she opened them and said words she'd never been able to say before she met Sam. "It's not the noise. I'm deaf."

Detective Lopez looked at her for a long moment, then simply nodded. "Oh, I didn't know. I take it you read lips?"

"Yes, yes I do," she said and she felt Sam press his lips to her hair. Without looking at him, she covered his hand on her shoulder with hers. "What did you say before?"

"You'll need to get together with Mr. Patton and arrange a time to come down to the station," he said.

She nodded. "Yes, we will."

He glanced at Sam, said, "I'll be in touch," then turned and crossed the room to where Evelyn was being watched.

Leigh looked up at Sam and said, "You were right."

"About what?" he asked.

She yawned unexpectedly, and felt a heaviness in her eyes. "Everything."

He turned her to face him. "Then you believe that I love you?"

A peace that Leigh had never known before flooded over her, and she knew that being in Sam Patton's world would be hard, but it was right. It was the only place she wanted to be. "Yes, I believe you," she whispered. "And I love you. I really... really love you," she said.

With the world milling all around, with the chaos of shouted orders and the sound of the other musical acts still onstage, Sam only heard one thing. Leigh's words. And he knew that his life was with her, with this woman he was holding, with her deep blue eyes, halo of curls and a touch that could lay his soul bare.

He knew the words he wanted to say, but it took all of his courage to say them. "Will you stay with me, Leigh?"

Her hand lifted to touch his face, her fingers trailing along his jawline to touch his lips. "As long as you'll have me," she said.

In a burst of pure joy, he said, "Then we've got a deal that's going to last forever," and he touched his lips to hers, needing to feel that warmth and promise. A world of commitment was in that kiss, an eternity of passion, of caring and loving.

Then Sam drew back and looked at her, and he realized she was awfully pale, her eyes heavy. He'd totally forgotten about the drugged wine she'd taken. "How much of that wine did you drink?" he asked.

She lifted her hand for him to see her thumb and forefinger just half of an inch apart. "A tiny little bit."

Her eyes began to droop. "Leigh, are you sure you're all right?"

"Of course," she mumbled. "I'm wonderful. Everything's wonderful. I love..." Her eyes closed, her head lolled forward and she collapsed against him.

Epilogue

Leigh awoke to soft shadows and a deep sense of real peace.

She shifted in the large bed, reached out for Sam and felt disappointment that he wasn't there. With a sigh of regret, she lay on her back, letting the remnants of sleep slip away from her, and realized how drastically her life had changed in a week's time. And in the past twenty-four hours, it had changed forever.

Since the doctors at the hospital had agreed she would be fine, that she didn't ingest enough of the medication to do real harm, and she could sleep it off, Sam had brought her to his Malibu home.

They had used the small guest house beyond the pool at the back of his house, and even before he'd finished pulling the cool linen over her, she'd been asleep. And she'd slept almost constantly. And when she stirred, Sam had been there with her, holding her until she drifted off again.

For the first time since she'd collapsed, her head felt clear, and she knew she was through with sleep for a while. She pushed herself up in the bed, the T-shirt Sam had lent her cool on her bare skin. Pushing her tangled hair back off her face, she looked around, really seeing the room for the first time since she'd come here.

The guest house was tiny, but lovely, with the sleeping area overlooking the pool with the main house beyond it, a small kitchen and a living area decorated around a low arched adobe fireplace. Pale beige walls were a perfect backdrop to the wooden poster bed, bleached oak furniture and the pale aqua throw rugs scattered across the clay-tile flooring. She knew she could stay here forever and be happy, as long as Sam was with her.

As if her need of him had made him materialize, the door opened and Sam walked in. And the minute she saw him, she knew that loving someone only got stronger and stronger. It almost took her breath away to see him crossing the living area, coming toward her, his hair damp from a shower, his jaw cleanly shaven. He was clad only in a pair of well-worn jeans.

He smiled when he saw her sitting up, an expression that seemed to add to the sunlight in the room. And she smiled back. "Good morning, or good afternoon," she said.

He crossed the room, set the tray on the nightstand, then dropped down on the edge of the bed. "It's afternoon. All the sleeping done?"

"For now." She stretched her arms over her head and laughed. "I feel wonderful."

His smile faltered just a bit. "I need to show you something." Then he reached toward the tray and turned back to her. "These have been on the stands since early this morning."

He laid three newspapers on the bed, front pages face up. And Leigh read them. "Deaf Artist Saves Singer's Life." "Crazed Fan Tries to Kill Singer and Deaf Girlfriend." "Deaf Artist Heroine to Boone Patton." She didn't bother reading the stories that went with the headlines. She just sank back against the headboard and closed her eyes.

Sam touched her, his fingers light on her chin. She opened her eyes to him. "Leigh, this is the worst it's going to get," he said.

"And what about her?"

"Evelyn Rice is catatonic. They don't know what's going to happen to her." He rubbed his thumb in slow circles on her chin. "Hey, we're still here. We're in one piece, and trust me, the stories are great, and there've been calls for television interviews. I've turned them all down, but you're coming out of this as a real heroine."

Newspapers and television. Leigh felt her stomach sink. "Sam, the story's everywhere, isn't it?"

"Just about."

"God, my parents...?"

He drew back, resting his hand on her knee. "They know all about it. I called the gallery in New York, explained things to Satch, and he was very excited about the publicity. He also gave me your parents' phone number, and I called them. They were worried, but I assured them you were just fine, that I was taking good care of you."

She closed her eyes for a moment, then looked back at him. "They aren't coming here, are they?"

"No, they wanted to, but I explained that we won't be here very long."

She didn't understand. "Where are we going?"

"To the island for a rest."

Oh, yes, that was exactly what she wanted, to be there with Sam. "For how long?"

"Long enough for a honeymoon."

She stared at him as his words sank in. She went to him, wrapping her arms around his neck and holding on to him, almost afraid to let go in case this all turned out to be a dream and she woke up. His lips touched the side of her throat, their heat searing against her skin, and she knew she'd never had a dream like this. A dream where she was falling back into the bed with Sam, his lips and touch wreaking havoc with her, bringing a life to her that was brilliant and new and wonderful.

Sam drew back, lifting himself on one elbow to look down at her. "How about a small wedding, very private, just the two of us, maybe Ted and Laura as witnesses?"

"What about your family? Don't you want them there?"

He smiled at that. "They'll be thrilled, but to get them all together would take until Christmas, and I can't wait that long."

"Could we do it on the island?"

"Wonderful idea. Johngood will definitely approve."

"Johngood?"

"I called him. First he said to tell you he found your pearl-and-silver clip on the beach. Then I told him everything, and he asked me if I was going to make an honest woman out of you."

Leigh laughed, but as Sam's hand found its way under the T-shirt, she stopped on a shudder. "And... and what did you tell him?" she managed.

"I said I might be a performer, but I believed in love and marriage and forever after." His hand skimmed over her skin, found her breast, and Sam smiled knowingly when Leigh inhaled sharply at his touch. "And now, the question is, do you believe in the same things?"

She closed her eyes for a fleeting moment when his fingers began to trace circles on her nipple. She looked at him, so close, so dear. "I—I do," she whispered.

"Remember those words," he said, then his hand stilled on her, and his smile faltered. "You know what you're getting into, don't you? I can't marry you and leave you on the island while I go off and tour, doing shows for forty weeks out of the year. And I can't stay on the island forever, no matter how much you'd want it to be that way."

She looked at Sam, and brushed at his hair, feeling the silkiness under her fingers, then she unsteadily traced the line of his jaw. She tried to smile, to ease the emotions in her that were becoming so strong that she could barely breathe—love, need, joy, fear, excitement, uncertainty and wonderment. And they all added up to one thing—she loved Sam, and she could deal with whatever life brought as long as it was with him.

Her hand moved to his chest, and the beat of his heart against her palm gave her the courage to speak the truth. "I can't say that my basic instincts aren't to dig in on the island with you and never let you go. But you were right. I was hiding out. And I don't want to anymore. I want to be with you, and if that means going into a whole new scary world, I'll do it."

"Thank you," he said and shook his head, as if he couldn't believe what was happening. "You know, I was killing myself trying to write a song about a woman with eyes so blue they looked like the color of midnight, a woman who could hold my heart in the palm of her hand. Just now, I realized that the song wouldn't come to me because there's already a song about how I feel about you." He smiled, the expression endearing and so unsteady, and she knew what he was going to say even before the words came.

" 'You Send Me'?" she asked.

"Yes, and I want to make it the lead on my next album. The old songs are coming back, and I want to do that one. Most of all, I want you to be there when I do it onstage for the first time."

She had never experienced such overwhelming love for one person in her whole life. And she had to try twice to say the words that she felt in her heart. "I'll be there because I love you, Sam."

She saw him utter her name, then his lips found hers, and she knew that if they had a hundred years together, she would never grow tired of this man. She would never be satisfied; this hunger for him that lived in her, would know no end. Sam drew back, easing the T-shirt over her head, then tossing it away from the bed. He shifted from her long enough to take off his pants, then he was over her, looking down at her with fire in his eyes.

"I love you, Leigh," he said, and she could feel the vibrations of the words along the entire length of her body.

She wrapped her arms around his neck and smiled from the pure joy he gave her. "I need to tell you something, something really important."

He kissed her quickly and fiercely, then drew back. "What is it?"

"You're the love of my life, and I wanted to make sure you knew that."

She saw him whisper, "I love you," and in that single moment, she could have sworn, she heard it in her heart.

*   *   *   *   *

OFFICIAL RULES • MILLION DOLLAR BIG WIN SWEEPSTAKES
NO PURCHASE OR OBLIGATION NECESSARY TO ENTER

To enter, follow the directions published. If the Big Win Game Card is missing, hand-print your name and address on a 3″ × 5″ card and mail to either: Silhouette Big Win, 3010 Walden Ave., P.O. Box 1867, Buffalo, NY 14269-1867, or Silhouette Big Win, P.O. Box 609, Fort Erie, Ontario L2A 5X3, and we will assign your Sweepstakes numbers (Limit: one entry per envelope). For eligibility, entries must be received no later than March 31, 1994 and be sent via 1st-class mail. No liability is assumed for printing errors or lost, late or misdirected entries.

To determine winners, the sweepstakes numbers on submitted entries will be compared against a list of randomly preselected prizewinning numbers. In the event all prizes are not claimed via the return of prizewinning numbers, random drawings will be held from among all other entries received to award unclaimed prizes.

Prizewinners will be determined no later than May 30, 1994. Selection of winning numbers and random drawings are under the supervision of D.L. Blair, Inc., an independent judging organization whose decisions are final. One prize to a family or organization. No substitution will be made for any prize, except as offered. Taxes and duties on all prizes are the sole responsibility of winners. Winners will be notified by mail. Chances of winning are determined by the number of entries distributed and received.

Sweepstakes open to persons 18 years of age or older, except employees and immediate family members of Torstar Corporation, D.L. Blair, Inc., their affiliates, subsidiaries and all other agencies, entities and persons connected with the use, marketing or conduct of this Sweepstakes. All applicable laws and regulations apply. Sweepstakes offer void wherever prohibited by law. Any litigation within the province of Quebec respecting the conduct and awarding of a prize in this Sweepstakes must be submitted to the Régies des Loteries et Courses du Quebec. In order to win a prize, residents of Canada will be required to correctly answer a time-limited arithmetical skill-testing question. Values of all prizes are in U.S. currency.

Winners of major prizes will be obligated to sign and return an affidavit of eligibility and release of liability within 30 days of notification. In the event of non-compliance within this time period, prize may be awarded to an alternate winner. Any prize or prize notification returned as undeliverable will result in the awarding of the prize to an alternate winner. By acceptance of their prize, winners consent to use of their names, photographs or other likenesses for purposes of advertising, trade and promotion on behalf of Torstar Corporation without further compensation, unless prohibited by law.

This Sweepstakes is presented by Torstar Corporation, its subsidiaries and affiliates in conjunction with book, merchandise and/or product offerings. Prizes are as follows: Grand Prize—$1,000,000 (payable at $33,333.33 a year for 30 years). First through Sixth Prizes may be presented in different creative executions, each with the following approximate values: First Prize—$35,000; Second Prize—$10,000; 2 Third Prizes—$5,000 each; 5 Fourth Prizes—$1,000 each; 10 Fifth Prizes—$250 each; 1,000 Sixth Prizes—$100 each. Prizewinners will have the opportunity of selecting any prize offered for that level. A travel-prize option if offered and selected by winner, must be completed within 12 months of selection and is subject to hotel and flight accommodations availability. Torstar Corporation may present this sweepstakes utilizing names other than Million Dollar Sweepstakes. For a current list of all prize options offered within prize levels and all names the Sweepstakes may utilize, send a self-addressed stamped envelope (WA residents need not affix return postage) to: Million Dollar Sweepstakes Prize Options/Names, P.O. Box 7410, Blair, NE 68009.

For a list of prizewinners (available after July 31, 1994) send a separate, stamped self-addressed envelope to: Million Dollar Sweepstakes Winners, P.O. Box 4728, Blair NE 68009.

BWS792